You're Home

A Windsor Peak Novel

Book 5

Denise Latham

ISBN: 979-8-9888952-7-5

Cover design by Book Designs by Shae.

www.deniselatham.com

Windsor Peak Series

Coming Home

Staying Home

Finding Home

Forever Home

Holiday Home

Dedication

To my mom and dad.

Your unwavering support through my life made it possible for me to be brave enough to start writing. Every book that I finish is a tribute to you both, for the love you show everyone around you, and the lessons you've taught me through my life. I'm so lucky to have you in my corner, and I love you both!

Chapter 1

"Natalie, let's go." The voice coming from behind the door belonged to Liam Dorsey, one of her best friends and the person determined to make her go out. She chose to ignore him, settling into the blanket mound on the soft couch even deeper, and turning the volume up on the television.

"Maybe we should let her stay home." Liam's girlfriend's voice came through, soft enough that Nat had to turn the volume down to hear.

"She's not staying home," Liam responded. He knocked on the door again, louder this time. "Nat, I have a key. I'm going to come in and throw you over my shoulder if necessary."

"Liam!"

"Holly, she needs to get out. Especially tonight."

A softer knock then, and then Holly's voice calling out to her. "Nat, can I please come in?"

Natalie sighed and pushed the blankets aside, unable to resist Holly's sweet plea. She disarmed the alarm and opened the door to reveal her friends, both dressed up for a party, staring at her. Holly wore a black dress and Liam looked dashing in a suit, and Nat was in sweats with her hair in a messy bun. She was the thing wrong in this picture, and she knew it.

"I'm going to stay in," she said. "I'm really tired."

"From what?" Liam challenged her, popping an eyebrow as he asked. This stare, with one brow lifted, was the same one he was prompted to use in every promotional photoshoot they did together. On the movie screen, Liam was intimidating and broody, but he was the total opposite these days. The transition from movie star playboy to small town boyfriend had him constantly wearing a large grin and being far more approachable than he ever had been before. Falling in love had softened her friend, and she was happy for him. Just not happy enough to be convinced by him to do something she didn't want to do.

"Come with us for an hour," Holly begged. "If you don't want to stay, we'll bring you home."

"It's going to be crowded and—"

"I think there's twelve people going, and you know all of them," Liam said, with an eye roll this time. "Patrick and Emma. Jake, Shea, Dan and Kendra. JJ and Zoe. Us. You. Mike. That's it. I don't think you'll be swarmed."

"What he's trying to say," Holly interjected. "Is that everyone there cares about you and wants you to be there. One hour, please. Let's start the new year off together, in a positive way."

Nat felt herself softening, knowing her friends were right. Staring the new year off alone, crying on the couch, was going to set the tone for the next twelve months. She needed to take her therapist's advice and force herself to be in uncomfortable situations as long as she felt safe. And she knew that the group tonight would go out of their way to make her feel protected.

"Fine," she said, sighing as she threw the blanket she had been holding on the couch. "But I'm not promising more than an hour."

"Let me help you get ready," Holly said, pulling her towards the bedroom. "Liam, go open a bottle of champagne."

Nat let herself be pulled along by her friend, plopping into the cozy chair in her bedroom while Holly went into the closet. The sound of hangers moving came from behind the door before she popped back out holding a red dress on a hanger, a pair of heels dangling from her fingers.

"I'm not wearing that," Nat said, even as she pictured herself in the dress. She had been given it by a designer at a fashion show she had attended in Paris the previous spring and had never had a chance to wear it. The fabric was soft and clung to her in all the right places, and the red made her stand out in a crowd. Which she typically loved, but not lately. "I'll wear black, like you. Or pants. That would be better. And definitely not heels."

Holly hung the dress carefully on the outside of the closet before crossing to where Natalie sat. She sat down next to her and Nat could see the concern and sincerity in her friends' eyes as she spoke. "It's okay to be you," she said quietly. "You can be beautiful and attention grabbing. Let yourself do it tonight and see how you feel. If you're miserable, Emma will let you borrow something to change into, or you can come home. But try to be movie star Natalie Cloud tonight and let that version of you start the year fresh."

Nat felt tears prick her eyes and blinked quickly, fighting them off. She had cried enough in the last few months to last her a lifetime, and she could see the advice was given with the best intentions at heart. She needed to reset her mind and energy and try to find herself again. Natalie took a deep breath and nodded. "Okay, you're right."

"Great," Holly exclaimed. "I'll do your hair, but I'm not nearly as good at makeup as you are."

"I won't wear much," she said, even as she reached for her makeup tote. As Holly fussed over her hair, she smoothed moisturizer on and started applying the basics, soothed by the habit of it. Before she knew it, she had a full face of makeup and her hair was half up, with some curls still falling over her face. It was a softer look than what she was used to, but it worked.

The dress slid up over her waist without an issue, since she had probably lost even more weight in the last few months. The fabric still felt silky and soft, reminding her of all the finely made clothes that were in her closets around the world. Even in her closet in Windsor Peak, the expensive items were hidden behind flannel and bulky sweaters, her normal life pushed to the side to make room for the comfort she needed.

As the two women walked out of the bedroom, Liam wolf whistled at them. "Looking fantastic, Nat," he said. "As do you, my lovely."

"You already told me that," Holly laughed.

"Never hurts to repeat it, especially on a night like this. You two ready?" He held out a coat for Holly to slip her arms into and then reached for Natalie's to do the same. "I'm a lucky guy, with the two hottest women on my arm tonight."

"You know we should lecture you on looks being less important than what's inside," Holly said. "But we'll let it slide just for tonight."

***

The drive to the party was short, as Natalie and Liam's frequent co-star and friend lived just a few miles away. Much like Liam's house, where Natalie had recently moved into, the farmhouse was sprawling and indicated the success the actors had found. Patrick had refurbished his while they shot their last movie together, so every part of the large house demonstrated luxury. Liam had only recently bought his, and it was still being partly used as a youth center for the town, holding up any renovations in the house. Natalie and Liam occupied the two caretaker apartments on either side of the house, allowing them both privacy.

It was a far cry from her home in California, but Natalie tried not to think about that. Or the apartment she kept on the Upper East side in New York city, or the home in France. All of it seemed to be a part of a life she wasn't sure she was comfortable in anymore, so the small one-bedroom apartment in her best friend's house was perfect for the time being.

Patrick's driveway was filled with cars, and Nat glanced at Liam as they got out of the car. "I think you may have underestimated the number of people coming tonight," she said drolly.

"I promise, he told me it was a small group," he objected. "I didn't lie to you."

"I know you didn't," she said quickly. She hadn't meant to insinuate that she thought he would do so and added it to her internal list of things that she had done wrong in recent months. "I'm sorry. I didn't mean to make it seem like it was your fault."

"Nat," Liam said quietly, moving closer to her. "It's not a big deal. I'm not upset; you didn't do anything wrong. Just try to relax tonight, okay?"

She nodded quickly, fighting off tears once again, and accepted his arm to walk the icy path to the front door. Holly was clinging to his other arm, laughing as she slipped on the ice. Natalie was either more experienced walking in heels or more adept at the terrain, because she was able to make it to the porch with less fanfare, but her friends squeals had made her laugh at least.

The door opened, revealing a party in full swing in Patrick's open living room and kitchen. Nat spotted their host and his girlfriend, Emma, standing at the bar, both turning to smile as the newcomers walked in. Emma quickly crossed the room to hug the three of them, holding Natalie for an extra second before letting Patrick take his turn.

"Lots of people here," Natalie said to the couple.

"You know everyone, though," Patrick said.

Patrick's brother Jake approached, with his wife Shea and his service dog Rex. The duo greeted everyone before Shea pulled Natalie toward the bar, pointing to an open bottle of champagne. "Can I pour you a glass?"

"Please," Natalie said.

Patrick's oldest brother, Dan, and his wife Kendra joined them at the bar as Shea poured. Kendra held out her empty glass and smiled at her sister-in-law as she filled it. "Thanks," she said.

"Is Zoe doing the cooking?" Natalie asked, looking toward the space where Emma's sister was in complete control of the kitchen appliances. Zoe's husband, JJ, was sitting at the island with a few of his fellow officers, watching his wife with an amused look on his face.

"She's not supposed to be," Kendra said. "We had a deal that we would both take tonight off and let the catering staff run things. But she can't help herself."

Kendra and Zoe had recently opened a new business, expanding on Kendra's local restaurant to make a space where Zoe could really unleash her culinary creativity. She catered, gave cooking lessons, sold ready-to-cook meals, and hosted small events in the small space next to the large restaurant.

"Speaking as an English teacher, it's hard to imagine that some people just can't get enough of work," Shea said. "I'm happy to see my students in the morning, and to send them home at the end of the day. Zoe doesn't seem to ever want to leave the kitchen."

"That's good and bad for us," Dan said. "I don't know how much more I can work out, but I also can't say no to her food."

Natalie looked around the room as the other three talked, smiling at familiar faces. Two of the officers who had been with her the day of the shooting, Jeff and Nick, were sitting with their wives. Danielle and Larissa had sent meals to the house and invited her to social events, which she felt bad declining, but she hadn't been ready to be out of the house. Since their husbands had also witnessed the horrible scene she had been a part of, she knew they sympathized with what she was going through, and she appreciated their kindness. She made a mental note to spend some time with them this evening, once she got fully comfortable.

JJ's siblings were talking by the fire with Piper, the owner of the local bakery. Everyone in the room was friendly and appeared happy to see her, and she had no reason to panic. Yet she felt the tendrils start to curl around her chest, making it feel harder to pull in a breath of air. The conversation flowed around her, no one seeming to be aware of what was happening with her, and she tried to force herself to calm down.

Focus on something small, her brain screamed, repeating the words the therapist had told her over and over again. She forced herself to take a deep breath while focused on a piece of confetti on the bar top. As the air reached her lungs, she forced herself to focus on things she was touching. The cold glass in her hand. The bar where her arm was resting. The feel of her fingers tapping lightly on the wood of the bar. The slight ache of her toes in the shoes.

"Are you okay?"

The words were said quietly into her ear, and she felt the hand of the man saying them rest on her back. It felt warm and secure, and she wanted to lean into it with every fiber of her being. She allowed herself to move slightly closer, so she could feel the warmth of his body through the thin fabric of his dress shirt. She nodded slightly, and his fingers seemed to tighten slightly, nudging her even closer to him.

"I think so," she finally whispered. When she looked up at him, she couldn't help but relax even further. Mike Collins towered over her by a foot, standing well over six feet tall, and was as broad as two men. Everything about him suggested strength and confidence, and she always felt protected when near him.

The downside was, he was also the strongest reminder of what she had gone through. Which meant that just being near him could trigger her worst emotions. She felt a constant struggle between feeling comfort near him and yet wanting to avoid any reminder of what had happened. Her therapist told her it wouldn't work to push the memories far away so she didn't have to deal with them, and keeping Mike at arm's length wasn't avoiding the issue. It was even more difficult because of his persistence in being near her, and her inability to pack up and leave this small town once and for all.

Chapter 2

She took his breath away. Mike had slowly grown used to seeing Natalie in her casual clothes, where he could almost pretend that she was just a normal woman around Windsor Peak. Now, in a red dress that should be illegal, he felt a flush rising from his toes to his ears. His skin felt too tight, and his first instinct was to run away from her. But then he saw the panic in her eyes and felt something inside him shift. Before he knew it, he was at her side, hand on her back, and she almost seemed happy to see him.

Even though she had responded that she was alright, he couldn't help feeling like she was overwhelmed. He didn't blame her; they were in the same house where they had been held at gunpoint a few months ago. They had witnessed their friend JJ being shot and the intruder killed. Mike had rushed to help JJ, leaving Natalie standing alone to face the bloody scene, and he hated that he had done that. He relived the night constantly, wondering why he hadn't pushed her out of the door, or told her to close her eyes, before tending to JJ. Being back in the same space brought him right back to that night, and he knew it did the same to her. This was first time she was back since the shooting, and he remembered his own feelings when he had been back a few days after the incident. It had taken him weeks to get used to being in Patrick's house again, but he had spent those days forcing himself to stand in the same spot and soften the memories with new ones. He slowly stopped looking for gunmen hiding in corners or bodies on the floor and getting comfortable again, and he hoped Natalie could do the same.

Thoughts of Natalie Cloud had helped distract him over the last few weeks, and concern for her as he watched her withdraw into herself and away from her friends. During the incident, he had made a point of keeping her safely tucked behind his body, and he knew he would have died to protect her. They hadn't had the kind of relationship that would foster such sacrifices, mainly because he was too scared to talk to her half the time, but he had faced the gun without a thought. She had been a regular feature in his life since he became friends with Patrick, who co-starred in a movie series with her, but the weekend of the shooting had been the first time they had really gotten to know each other. Until that day, he had been so intimidated by her; he lost his ability to speak in her presence. However, that day he had finally had the chance to get to know her and had shared some fun moments with her. And once he looked past her beauty and fame, he realized she was an incredibly sweet person.

She was also a movie star, and he would never admit it out loud, but he had watched the franchise many times over to see her. In the movies, she was a tough superhero, able to crush the enemy with seemingly little effort. Although he knew from their few workout sessions that she was strong, he had seen what had happened when actual danger had presented itself. Unlike her character, she had reacted the same way most people would, rather than fighting the gunman like she would have on the screen. She had remained calm, though, and impressed him with her composure throughout.

Her finger touched his chin lightly, forcing his eyes to meet hers, and he realized he had been standing there lost in thought for long enough to make it awkward. He cleared his throat and tried to fight yet another blush from rising, glancing around the room. "Want to get something to eat?" he asked, pointing to the kitchen.

"I need to catch my breath a little first," she said. "Would you mind taking a quick walk with me?"

"Of course not," he said, the words coming out way too fast. "Let me grab our coats."

She followed him to point out her jacket, which he helped her into before pulling on his own. He followed her out the front door, which was just a few steps from the closet, so it could have made more sense to her logistically. Or she could be avoiding the kitchen door, which they had last gone through together to find a crazed gunman on the other side.

They strolled down the path, and when he reached out once to make sure she wouldn't slip, she grabbed onto his arm and left her hand there. Although he was wearing a thick, puffy ski jacket, he would swear he could feel the warmth of her small hand against his skin.

"Want to go check on the horses? It will be warm in the stable," he suggested.

She nodded, so they headed in that direction down a shoveled path. He pulled the door open when they arrived, and she slipped through before him, turning the light on while he slid the door shut. She shivered slightly, rubbing her hands on her arms.

"You okay? It's pretty cold out there," he said, like the rocket scientist he clearly was.

"It's cold," she laughed. "But I'll warm up in here."

She started walking down the row of horses, patting them on the nose and accepting nuzzles from a few. He found the stash of sugar cubes and joined her, stopping outside the stall where

Emma's horse, Whiskey, resided. The horse accepted the treat and nudged his shoulder for more, making Natalie laugh.

"This was the last place where I felt peaceful," she said, so softly he had to strain to make out the words.

"When we put the horses back after our ride?"

"Yes," she said with a nod. "We had such a nice morning together, remember?"

"I do." It was seared on his brain, there was no way he would have forgotten. Patrick had asked him to keep her company while everyone else was busy with the local Harvest Festival. JJ, the town Sheriff, had been concerned that a local string of robberies could be exasperated if the thief knew that two rich celebrities were staying in Patrick's house. JJ had asked Nat to keep a low profile until the weekend was over, and Mike had been the logical choice to spend the day with her. He knew that his size was intimidating to most people, and they had all thought he would be able to both entertain her and keep her safe while they were gone for the day. He would have done it again, even knowing the end result.

"We were laughing when we walked to the house," she recollected. "I can't remember why. I just know that I was laughing and thinking about how much I enjoyed your company when you finally relaxed."

"Thanks. I think?"

She laughed again, putting her head against his bicep and squeezing his arm. "It's a compliment."

"I was having the best day of my life," he admitted.

"Really? A workout and a horseback ride is the highlight of your entire life?"

"Well, when you put it like that it sounds ridiculous," he said. "But if you were to say that I was doing that with you, then it makes sense."

She studied him, and he wished he could know what was running through her mind. A thousand emotions seemed to dance through her eyes, before she seemed to shut them all down. "I'm really not that special," she said finally.

"It's not because of the movie star thing," he said, too fast to stop himself. "I mean, yes, that's how I knew who you were at first. And why I freak out when I try and talk to you. But that day, we were able to actually have a conversation, and I didn't act like a total buffoon."

"You aren't," she said. "And you were never."

She walked away, and he could have kicked himself for missing the opportunity to share how he really felt. Why were words so hard when he looked at her? He watched as she made her way down the row of horses, giving each a sugar cube and a pat, before rejoining him.

"I suppose we should get back to the party," she said. "I feel better now, thank you."

"Anytime," he said.

"You can't help but save me," she said suddenly. "That day, and so many times since then. When we tried to go to dinner that night with Patricks' family, you brought me home. The night that I went shopping with Liam and Holly, you dropped whatever you were doing to come be with me so I would feel safe."

"I was only watching football," he said.

"Still, I appreciate it. Very much."

He felt like there was more behind the words, but she was pulling her coat on before he could figure it out. Minutes later, they reentered the house through the front door, and Natalie seemed calmer. She let him take her coat and waited while he hung it up, then they moved into the party.

"There you two are," Emma called over. "We are about to start playing a game. Come sit."

They moved to join their friends, and he tried to ignore the stab of dejection when she went and sat between Emma and Holly. He took a seat next to Patrick, who grinned and passed him a beer. "Hey, bud," he said. "Where have you been?"

"Nat and I just took a walk," he explained. "Went out to see the horses."

"She looks calmer," Patrick responded. "Emma put these games together, I told her that I didn't think we needed them, but I can't say no to her."

Emma was explaining the rules, and he realized he hadn't been paying attention when he watched in confusion as JJ pulled on oven mitts and a Santa hat before trying to unwrap a present. Zoe was next to him, rolling dice frantically on the large dining table, screaming when she got what she had been waiting for and grabbing the mitts and hat from JJ. She started trying to unwrap as Shea began rolling the dice frantically.

"Is this a bad time to admit I have no idea what's happening?" he asked, leaning close to Patrick.

"Whoever unwraps the gift gets to keep what's inside," Patrick explained. "The person next to you is trying to roll doubles to take the gift and start their turn. You have to be wearing the hat and mitts before you start to unwrap."

"But Christmas is over."

"Not to Emma," Patrick said, looking at his girlfriend with affection. "She loves the season and thought it would be fun to incorporate a little extra fun for New Years. Otherwise, we'd just be sitting around waiting for the ball to drop."

"True," Mike agreed, laughing when Shea finally got her doubles and grabbed the items from Zoe.

"I have to admit, knowing who I'll be kissing at midnight is a nice perk of being coupled up," Patrick said. "Years past, I would be trying to escape a party before midnight so that no one would be trying to lay one on me."

Mike nodded, but his thoughts were suddenly consumed with thoughts of what would happen when the clock struck midnight. The only other single people in the room were JJ's siblings and Piper, and the twins had disappeared while he and Nat were walking. They were likely going to a livelier party in town, if he had to guess. That left him, Nat, Colin and Piper as the only single people in a room full of happy couples. And as much as he enjoyed Piper's company, and had enjoyed becoming friends with JJ's brother Colin, he wasn't thinking about kissing either of them.

***

The next few hours passed in a blur of games and laughter, with some playful fighting. Jake had won a gift card to a local spa, which he had tried to pass to Shea before she reminded him that a couple's massage would be romantic. The thought immediately made Mike think of having one with Natalie, and he had to take a long drink of his beer to wipe the thought from his brain.

Nat seemed to be having fun, and had definitely relaxed as the night went on. She laughed along with everyone else and had seemed to be completely engaged in the group activities that Emma had planned. When one game had her perusing all the gifts in front of the people at the table, she had paused for a painfully long time behind him, leaning on his shoulder slightly as she studied his. When she swapped out the wrapped present in her hand for a gift bag in front of him, he felt as though he had won a prize.

After the last turn had been taken, he found himself with a gift certificate to a small restaurant in a nearby town that he had been hoping to try, a new winter hat and hand warmers, and several scratch tickets. Everyone was comparing prizes and making trades when Natalie came and settled next to him, clutching several small gift bags and wearing a smile.

"That was really fun," she said. "I wasn't expecting that at all. Emma did such a good job putting this all together."

"I know, I wish I had known so I could have helped with the gifts. Having three per person for this must have added up," he said. "Not to mention all the other prizes."

"Patrick is fine," she said lightly. "And I thought you might have helped, considering what I got."

"What was it?" He hadn't seen what she opened, probably because he was too conscious of whether she knew how much he enjoyed watching her. The night was a constant battle between wanting to look at her and fearing being caught staring, so he was constantly on edge.

"Training sessions with you," she said. "I had to keep stealing them back from JJ. Doesn't he already work out with you?"

"He does," Mike said, confusion making the words come out slowly. "But so do you. At least, I try. I ask you all the time to work out with me, you don't need to book them."

"Well, maybe I will now. My resolution for next year is to get out more, be braver."

"You're the bravest person I know," he said. He caught her hand when she tried to wave him off and waited until she looked at him before continuing. "You are."

"I'm really not," she said softly. "I have been hiding for months."

"You've been dealing with trauma for months," he corrected her. "And no one blames you for how you've handled it."

"You didn't seem to have the same problem," she said, tears glistening on her lower lashes.

"Everyone deals with things differently, you know that. And I think we have different perceptions of what happened. I blame the guy who broke in here and caused everything that happened. You blame yourself."

She studied him for a long minute, blinking away the tears. "You don't blame me?"

"Of course not," he said, his voice louder than he meant it to be. He quieted his tone after glancing around to see that no one else was paying attention to them. "I have never once, at any time, thought that any part of it was your fault. If anything, I am thankful that you were able to save us. I give you credit for that, not blame."

"But it was my fault he was there."

"No, it wasn't. It was his fault he was there. You didn't make the decisions for him. You did nothing to be responsible for him breaking into Patrick's house, never mind going back further to when he decided to buy a gun and be a criminal in the first place," he said adamantly. "All of the people that he terrorized before he broke in here, do you think any of them blame themselves? The Clarks are tortured that it was their son in danger and not one of them, but even they don't blame themselves. Nothing any of us did or didn't do could have changed what happened."

"If I hadn't come here—"

"No," he said, shaking his head. "You can't do that. You are a good person, and you're free to go anywhere and do anything, and you don't deserve to be held at gunpoint and threatened. There is no circumstance in which that is okay, or your fault."

Around them, their friends started counting down, indicating that it was just about midnight. A new year was starting, and despite the festivities around them, he could only stare at the woman in front of him. She met his eyes, and he saw a litany of emotions pass through them in the ten seconds that were being counted loudly. Her eyes flitted to his lips so quickly he thought he must have imagined it, and it took all his will to keep his eyes from dropping to her mouth.

Then she kissed him.

Chapter 3

Natalie had read enough scripts and been instructed on how a kiss was supposed to affect someone. The words had seemed silly to her, because she had kissed a lot of men over the years, and although it was –usually– pleasant, the descriptions had seemed over exaggerated. Exchanging kisses in front of a camera, with a whole crew watching, was always awkward. It didn't matter who the other person was; it was never something that she looked forward to. Men she had dated were a different story, but none had been like this.

When Mike's lips touched hers, it was as if an electric shock ran through her. She had joked in the past about him being so tall and muscular that she could climb him like a tree, and suddenly, that's all she wanted to do. For that one moment, her entire focus was on the sensation of the kiss. She didn't hear anything else, wasn't aware of their friends around them, or feel the fear that had been clawing at her for weeks. It was simply this kiss, this man who wrapped his arms around her and held on as if he would never let go, and the heat that ran through her entire body.

He pulled back just slightly, looking as stunned as she felt. What had just happened? Dis he kiss her or was she the one who made the move? She couldn't make words, or even rationalize what she should do. Normal Nat would have laughed and made a joke, diminished the butterflies in her belly, but that version of her had vanished. Instead, she was stunned into silence and could only think of how she could repeat the kiss as soon as possible.

"You okay?" he asked, his voice sounding rougher than usual.

His hands were resting on her upper arms, and she stood so close to him that she envied the fabric on her dress where it clung to his shirt. She didn't even remember standing up. The last few moments were dancing around in her head as puzzle pieces that she needed to put together. She nodded slowly, torn between resting her head on his broad chest or stepping away from him.

Liam solved the question for her, approaching with Holly in tow to offer hugs. "Happy New Year," he said into her ear as they hugged.

Holly finished hugging Mike and squeezed Nat tight. "Happy New Year. I'm so glad we are friends."

"Me too," she whispered, feeling that deep in her heart as well. Suddenly she had actual girlfriends who enjoyed spending time with her because of who she was, not what she was, and she appreciated them so much.

Emma and Patrick were next, followed by the rest of the crowd, all laughing and exchanging cheek kisses and hugs. The married couples with young babies at home slipped out shortly after the well wishes, followed by JJ and Zoe, who claimed they needed to get home so he could rest. They had all laughed when JJ winked at them and then feigned a yawn when his wife looked to see what they were responding to.

"We can head home whenever you want," Liam said to Natalie and Holly.

"I wanted to talk to Emma first," Holly responded. "Sorry, Nat."

Natalie shook her head and waved a hand. "It's totally fine. I'm in no hurry."

She watched as the couple walked away and turned to where she felt Mike's eyes on her. He hadn't moved, but she had been pulled a few steps away in the mass celebration that had taken place. He looked completely at ease as he met her gaze, allowing her to study him without flinching. He was physically bigger than any man she had ever encountered, and not classically handsome in the Hollywood way she was used to. Instead, his nose looked as though it had been broken at some point in time and was just slightly crooked. His skin always looked warmly tanned, which was unusual for winter in Vermont, but suited him with his chocolate brown eyes and jet-black hair. He wasn't perfect by any stretch of the imagination, and most of her fellow Hollywood elite would overlook him. But suddenly he was the only thing she could look at.

"I seem to always be asking you if you're okay," he said quietly enough that only she could hear him. "But I have to ask this one last time."

She moved closer to him again, nodding as she walked. "I'm good. I'm just—"

"Me too," he said, saving her when her mouth wouldn't continue the thought. "Want me to bring you home?"

The visions that flew through her mind shocked even her, and she knew that the last thing she could do right now was be alone with him. First, she needed to examine these feelings and figure out what was happening. If she had him take her home, there was no way she would let him leave. But she couldn't think beyond the next five minutes, never mind the upcoming weeks and months, to know what would happen next. There was a good chance she would find herself recovering and going back to her life, leaving him behind. And breaking his heart was not in the cards, not after all he had done for her since the robbery.

"Liam is almost ready to go," she said lightly. "I'll ride with him and Holly. No need for you to go out of your way."

"I wouldn't mind."

Before she could reply, Liam was joining them, holding their coats. Without a word, Mike took hers from his friend's hands and went behind Natalie to help her into it. As she slid her arms into the sleeves, his hands ran down her arms, and she would swear his lips grazed the area just behind her ear. "Good night, Natalie. Happy New Year."

When she turned to respond, he was already moving away from her, toward where Patrick stood at the bar. Liam and Holly were waving to her from the door, encouraging her to hurry to the warming car with them. She settled into the backseat, watching the falling snow cover the steps they had just taken, and wondered if this new year was starting off exactly like that. A pretty layer of beginnings, a new foundation to set herself in. Or was it a coating over the problems that had plagued her, and would continue to, no matter what she did?

***

"Wakey-wakey," Liam's voice rang through the small apartment from outside the door. As usual, she had locked up tight when she got home from the party, even the door that led to the main house that their apartments were wings of. They shared the enormous main kitchen if they wanted to cook beyond the capabilities of their small kitchenettes, but most of the space was being used to house the youth center and its staff. They had all been misplaced when a fire had recently destroyed the building they were normally in, and repairs were underway. Although Nat had met most of the office staff and liked them, knowing they had keys to the house had put her on edge, requiring her to even lock out Liam.

She pulled on a robe as she walked to the door, pulling it open to expose Liam on the other side. "Why are you waking me up so early?"

"Early? It's ten," he said with a laugh. "You should know by now that this small town doesn't operate like Los Angeles. People are up and out already, and we're due for a New Year's Day brunch in an hour."

"You're making me go out again?"

"First of all," he said. "I'm not *making* you do anything. I'm encouraging. Second, Holly said you already agreed to this?"

She groaned, remembering a promise she had made on Christmas Day. She had wanted to leave the festivities at Patrick's house, where it seemed half the town was stopping by to wish the Burrows family a happy holiday, and had sworn she would go today to make up for it. Part of her had hoped that Holly would have forgotten, but she clearly did not.

"It's just at Dan's house, right?"

"Yes," Liam said with a nod. "They are having a bigger one at the Palace, but we all figured you would rather do something small."

Natalie considered what he said, the gentleness that her friends had been treating her with for weeks now. It had to be taking a toll on them all, and she realized that her inability to cope had put them all in a difficult situation.

"We can go to the Palace," she said.

Liam looked surprised, looking over his shoulder before back at her. "You sure? Is this a joke?"

"No," she said with more conviction. "This is a new year, and I'm going to start fresh. Confront my fear."

"If you're positive, I can text them. I'm sure even if Kendra has started cooking, they can move it down to the restaurant."

"We both know that Zoe is doing the cooking, and Dan was planning to pick it up," she said with an eye roll. "We can save him the trip."

***

Close to an hour later, they entered the Palace, where a crowd was waiting for tables and the bar was completely full. It was as if the entire town had descended on the restaurant to celebrate together. Natalie had to swallow hard, and felt better when Holly linked arms with her and Liam stood on her other side, book ending her with support. This was a room filled with people who had cared about her, sent casseroles to the house in the aftermath, and sent cards and letters of support. No one here would hurt her, and she took a fortifying breath before stepping further inside.

Kendra had reserved them a table that was nestled in a corner, where she frequently preferred to seat them. Neighbors were at the closest tables to them, blocking the paths effectively so the ski crowd wouldn't be able to surround the table where the three movie stars would be sitting. It tended to be easier on her than Liam and Patrick, who had women throwing themselves at them constantly. Men tended to be more subtle, not wanting to appear too eager, in her presence. And women tended to look down on her or ignore her entirely, convinced she was someone they wouldn't want to socialize with.

Holly led her to a chair at the end of the table, where Natalie settled in between Holly and Shea. Zoe and Emma were across the table, although Nat suspected that Zoe would end up spending more time in the kitchen than in her seat. JJ had an arm clamped around the back of his wife's chair as if that would prevent her from darting off.

"Happy New Year," Natalie said with a smile as she sat. "Sorry for the change of venue at the last minute."

"Not a problem at all," Shea said kindly. "We were all happy to hear that you felt up to it."

The women settled into a quiet conversation as the men at the opposite end of the table became more animated watching the football game on the large screen tv's around the room. Jake, Patrick, Dan and JJ were all present, and an empty seat indicated they expected at least one more person to come. Logic would suggest it would be Mike, but she couldn't bring herself to ask. Somehow, seeing the chair at the opposite end of the table seemed wrong, but she had no right to move the seating around so that she could sit next to him. Most of the people at the table weren't sitting next to their other half, and it wasn't like she and Mike were in a relationship.

"Don't you think?"

Natalie was jerked back to reality when all the women turned to face her, and she realized she had completely tuned them out. "Sorry, I was off in space. What are you talking about?"

"We were talking about doing some kind of fundraiser for the organization that Jake got Rex from," Shea explained. Her husband had recently received a service dog to help with his service inflicted PTSD, and the dog was calmly lying next to his master when Natalie glanced down. She knew that if Jake started exhibiting signs of anxiety, the dog would jump into action, offering immediate relief and support. It was remarkable to watch, and Natalie had to admit the dog had offered her similar comfort in the past weeks. Something about a dog just forced someone to feel better about their day, she had decided.

"Patrick was trying to decide if it would be better to do something in California, where it can get a lot of attention, or doing it here," Emma said. "I thought that having it here really showcases the effect the dog has on Jake, rather than going to Los Angeles and having it be more about the lights and glitz."

"That's true," Natalie said thoughtfully. "Plus, it can get lost in the shuffle there. So many parties, so little time."

"Liam offered to host it in the event space on his property, since it worked so well for the Holiday ball," Holly said.

"As long as it doesn't disrupt the kids," Natalie responded, thinking of the many students who came to use the youth center after school. It had been full for the week of school vacation, and she had seen the need for it in this community.

"We can plan for a Saturday," Shea said. "And coordinate with the school so the gym there can be open for anyone who needs entertainment. This time of year, there isn't as much need for much beyond maybe a hot meal or a place to hang out on the weekends."

Natalie nodded, but before she could respond, the door opened and her focus was lost again. Mike stood in the doorway, greeting neighbors at the bar with a smile, and she couldn't take her eyes off him. How had so much changed in one day?

Chapter 4

Mike took his time walking through the crowded restaurant, greeting all the locals as if they were long-lost friends. Just seeing Natalie from across the room threw him off balance, and he needed the time to compose his thoughts. He had spent most of the night sleepless, replaying their kiss and what he could have done to make it last longer. Nothing had come to mind, and the thought of trying to recreate it was beyond anything he could comprehend. She could have anyone in the world, and he was just a regular guy.

"Hey," he said to his friends when he finally approached the table. He exchanged fist bumps and handshakes with his friends and nodded toward the women at the other end of the table quickly, avoiding Natalie's eyes.

"What took you so long? Not like you to be late," Patrick asked.

"Just lost track of time," he said.

"And then had to say hello to everyone and their brother," Liam quipped.

"Not my fault everyone we know is in one spot," Mike said with a grin. "Makes it easier. Now I don't have to send out hundreds of text messages wishing everyone a happy New Year."

"What's on the agenda for the day?" Dan leaned back in his seat as the server arrived to place platters of food on the table.

"I think we have enough food here for a week," Mike said as he was handed a plate to fill. "Might not be able to do anything after I eat all of this."

"Meals like this make me happy to not have a job that requires me to war tights," Jake said, poking his brother Patrick with his elbow.

"Spandex," Patrick said at the same time as Liam.

"And they look good in them," Emma said, leaning into Patrick.

"I'll work it off them," Mike promised. "Eat away."

"I say we eat all of this, and then spend the afternoon skiing," Liam proposed.

"I'm going to pass," Jake said. "Charlie has a hockey game, and I don't want to leave the baby with Stella for too long. As much as I appreciate the babysitting, I don't want to push it."

"I'll stay with you," Shea said.

Kendra pushed Dan to ski, suggesting he take their daughter Calle, who needed to burn off energy. Patrick and Emma also joined the ski party, but Mike was waiting for Natalie to reply before he committed either way.

"I'm not a good enough skier to stay with you guys," Natalie said finally. "And I'm not really sure I want to be around that many people."

"No one will know who you are, you'll be so bundled up. And it's outdoors, there's lots of space. Plus, Mike is a fantastic skier," Patrick said. "Maybe he can help you."

"That's okay," she blurted. "I don't want to put anyone out. And if I got hurt, it would set our filming schedule back quite a bit."

"A risk Patrick and Liam are clearly ignoring," Dan said with a laugh.

"You won't get hurt, and I'll keep you safe," Mike heard himself saying. "I promise."

Their eyes met for the first time since he sat down at the table, and he felt his heart skip a beat. She nodded slowly and smiled at him briefly. "Ok, I trust you."

***

Hours later, with his stomach so full he questioned his ability to make it down even the bunny slope, he was helping Natalie into her skis. She started to fall over as she moved to step into the second one, and he grabbed her waist to steady her.

"Thanks," she said. "Am I going to regret this?"

"No," he said, reluctantly letting go of her. "You'll be fine."

"Do you?"

"What?"

"Regret kissing me last night," she said, staring at the ground.

He tipped her head chin up with one finger, so she looked at him. "Not for one second. Do you?"

A lifetime seemed to pass before she answered, but then she shook her head slightly. "No."

His brain short-circuited for a moment, until a family surrounded them and forced them to move. "Let's start small," he suggested, pointing to the slope that was mainly filled with small children. "Have you ever skied before?"

"Yes," she said with a nod. "But it's been years, so a refresher before going too high up to turn around would be helpful."

They moved together to the conveyer belt that would take them to the top. She stepped on and then laughed as she nearly fell but smiled at him over her shoulder as she started moving away. He jumped on behind her, watching anxiously until she disembarked without incident. They crisscrossed down the small hill painfully slowly, but she stayed on her feet.

"This is fun," she said, once they were at the bottom. "Do you mind if we just practice a little more? I know this is small for you."

"I don't mind."

"Are you sure? I would guess you could be doing the black diamonds if I wasn't holding you back," she said.

"This is better for my knees," he said. Growing up in New Hampshire and then living in Vermont meant that skiing was as natural as walking for him, but there was no way he was losing this time alone with her.

After an hour of practice, they moved to the ski lift, where he got to spend an agonizing length of time pressed up against her on the tiny bench. He had never realized how much space he took up until he had her tight against him, his arm behind her back and her elbow resting lightly on his thigh. She disembarked with laughter and managed to stay on her feet, although he was ready to catch her if she fell. They skied down slowly, repeating the process until she was picking up speed and appeared more comfortable. When they got to the bottom again, her cheeks were pink, and she was smiling.

"This is fun," she said. "But utterly exhausting. I don't know if I can do it again."

"Want to get a hot cocoa and wait for everyone else?"

"That sounds perfect," she said.

They made their way over to the lodge, removing their skis and placing them on the rack outside the door. His watch said it was nearly four in the afternoon, and he realized how much time they had spent together. Somehow, when he was with her, time seemed to stand still, and when he was away from her, it was endless.

As she pulled off her helmet and ski coat, she smiled at him again. "I didn't realize how cold it was, but suddenly I can't feel my toes."

"Go sit by the fire and take your boots off," he suggested. "I'll go grab our drinks."

He ordered the two hot cocoas and a basket of popcorn, carrying them carefully to where she had captured two prize armchairs directly in front of the fire. From the way the crowd around them was behaving, it would appear everyone knew who she was, but no one wanted to be the one to approach.

"Thanks," she whispered. "I feel like everyone is staring at me."

"That's because they are," he told her. "Do you want to get out of here?"

"In a minute, when I defrost." She sat back and sipped her drink delicately, staring into the fire. "It's weird. I never thought much about it before. And then suddenly, I didn't want anyone to look at me. Now I don't know what to feel."

"You had a good reason to avoid people," he said.

"So did you," she pointed out. "And you didn't."

"I've lived here a long time, and I know everyone," he said. "It's different for you. I'm not a public figure, and I didn't blame myself for what happened."

She nodded but didn't respond, and he wondered how far he could push her.

"It's not your fault," he finally said. "I know I told you that before, and again last night, but I want you to believe it."

"I'm starting to," she said in a whisper. "Between you and my therapist, it's a pretty consistent message."

"I'm glad you're seeing someone."

"Jake helped with that. He goes to the VA, but his doctor was able to get me in to see someone quickly."

"Oh, I thought it would have been your management team."

"I'm sure they would have flown someone in," she said. "But this town is special. They seem to treat everyone as part of their family, and I guess I'm a part of that."

"What's the next step? You managed the party last night, and brunch today. Now skiing. What's next?"

"I don't know," she said. "I just know that I can't let myself shut down again. I need to push past this, somehow."

"I'll help you any way I can," he offered.

"Does that include yoga?" she said with a teasing smile.

He groaned and then smiled back at her. "If you insist."

***

The next few days passed in a blur, with nonstop appointments at the gym for private training. The first few weeks of the year were always slammed for him, as everyone had overeaten during the holidays and made a resolution to be healthier in the new year. He considered it his job to make the workouts fun and manageable, so they would remain clients past these weeks. In the last few years, he had managed to retain at least sixty percent of them, either as training clients or members at the gym.

Even with the demanding schedule and influx of new faces, there was one person he couldn't get off his mind. She took over his dreams, and he found himself looking for her everywhere he went. During a workout at Patrick's house that morning, he had learned that Natalie hadn't left her apartment since their ski trip. Now he was obsessed with thoughts of her and worry, and she was all he could think of as he drove home.

A sign distracted him, and he took a turn at the last possible second. He could be making a huge mistake, he thought as he unbuckled his seat belt, but it would be worth it if this worked.

***

He knocked on the door, second guessing himself with each moment that passed. When he didn't get an answer, he groaned, knowing it would mean he had to walk around and expose his foolishness to even more people. He rang the bell and knocked again, relieved to hear the click of the lock.

"Mike?" Natalie blinked at him, looking as though she had been woken up by his arrival.

"Hey," he said. The bundle in his arms began to stir, and he spoke quickly. "I'm sorry to barge in, but I have something for you."

"Come in," she said, stepping back and opening the door fully. "What do you have?"

"I was thinking about Rex, and how much he has helped Jake," he said. "And it seemed like when you are near the dog, it helps you relax. So I thought maybe you could use a friend yourself?"

He removed the jacket he had been using to cover the quivering puppy in his arms. The dog was still small enough to be carried but had the potential to be the size of Jake's Labrador retriever. She was black, with fur so soft it felt like holding a blanket. "The shelter doesn't know what breed she is," he explained. "They got some from down south a few weeks ago, just before Christmas. This little girl was slated to be put down, and the shelter here pulled her just in time. She's a little scared of everything and needs a friend to help her remember what it's like to be a dog. I thought you would be perfect for that."

"Me? I've never had a dog before," she whispered, reaching out to stroke the dog's head. "Does she have a name?"

"Not one she's attached to," he said. "She was part of a litter that never had a home, just bounced from shelter to shelter. I think her name probably changed every time, or she just had a number."

"How sad." Natalie reached for the dog, looking unsure of herself until the puppy licked her chin.

"If this was a bad idea, I can take her back," he offered.

"No," she said on a breath. "This is the nicest thing anyone has ever done for me."

He cleared his throat, suddenly feeling less sure of himself than when he was fifteen and had asked his crush to the school dance. "I, umm, also stopped at the pet store and got you some essentials.

Ralph suggested crate training, so I got one of those, and a bed to go inside because it looked uncomfortable. And I got the food that the shelter uses, plus some bowls. And a leash, of course."

"Should we take her for a walk now, do you think? Do you mind going with me? It's already so dark outside, and I—"

"Of course I don't mind," he said quickly. "I should have thought of that myself. I'll make sure to come by each night and walk her with you before bed, if that's alright with you?"

"I can always ask Liam," she suggested.

"No, it's fine," he said. He didn't want to lose the opportunity to see her every night. "I drive right by here anyway, and I created this problem, not Liam."

"She's not a problem," Nat said with a soft laugh. "I am."

"No, you're having a normal reaction to a trauma," he said firmly.

Natalie bent over and put the puppy on the floor before clipping the leash on and then stuck her feet into boots. He held the leash while she pulled on a warm jacket and hat, but she took it back before they stepped outside.

"I wonder if we should talk about it," she said.

"What?" His heart started racing, thinking she wanted to talk about their kiss on New Year's Eve. Although they had briefly discussed it while skiing, once they got distracted, it hadn't come up again. And it was all he could think about.

"The night when JJ was shot," she said. "My therapist thinks it's weird that I haven't talked to you, or JJ about it since it happened."

"Weird seems like a strong word for it," he said. "It's not like we talked all the time before it happened."

"No, you usually clammed up anytime I was around you," she said, a hint of a smile on her face.

"Can you blame me?"

"Why is that? How do you see me?"

"What do you mean?"

"I mean, why were you so scared to talk to me? Do I come across as rude or snobby?"

"Not at all. But you're a movie star," he said. "I didn't want to be one of the millions of people who fawns all over you. Patrick caught me off guard that one day when he had you on FaceTime in the gym, and I don't think I've ever recovered."

"But now that you know me, do you still think of me the same way?"

He considered her question as they walked in silence, the only noise the crunch of snow under their boots. The puppy sniffed along happily, stopping to mark her spot every few feet. "Here's the thing," he said finally. "You are hands down the most beautiful woman I've ever been in the presence of. And I know that would get me in trouble with all of Windsor Peak, so please keep that between us. And when we first met, that was all I could see. But that day, when we were hanging out and horseback riding, and actually talked, you became a real person to me. And I felt terrible that I had treated you like a pinup poster for a long time."

"I never felt like that from you," she said softly.

"Well, I think I owe you an apology for it anyway, so I'm sorry. Once we started talking, I could see why Patrick adores you, and why he wanted to protect you for so many years," he said. "You're smart, and funny, and a little bit shy, which was unexpected. It's almost like the character of Natalie Cloud and the person Natalie Cloud are two different people?"

"Well, they are," she said. "Natalie Cloud isn't a real person. My actual name is Natalie Jurgilewicz."

"Really?" He knew the shock he felt was on his face, because she laughed softly when she looked at him.

"Yes," she said with a nod. "It's not brought up much, maybe once a year someone will post an old picture and mention it, but it never gets a lot of traction. It helps that I grew up on military posts, and went to a lot of different schools. I went to one high school, but I was so shy and quiet, not many people paid attention to me. I had a few friends, but not a lot. One close girlfriend, but that fell apart before we graduated, and I haven't heard from her since. That means there aren't a lot of embarrassing pictures to haunt me, just a few yearbook photos floating around to haunt me."

"Are there actual bad pictures of you out there?"

"Oh, yes. I went through a very awkward phase," she said. "I burned most of the pictures, so don't get your hopes up."

"When did you change your name?"

"The first thing they told me when I was auditioning was that the name had to go," she said. "I did a few small commercials and bit parts under my real name, and then I got an agent. As soon as I walked into the office, he said it had to go. I tried to object, but he was adamant, and said that if people couldn't pronounce it, they would move on to the next. I needed a name that evoked sexy thoughts, not confusion."

They walked in silence for a few more minutes before he laughed, unable to help himself. "I have to say, your name could be Anchovy Sourmilk, and I would still have sexy thoughts about you."

Chapter 5

"I feel like I'm floundering," Natalie heard herself say, shocked at the honesty behind the words.

"You are." Dr. Jones adjusted her glasses while continuing her steady gaze on Natalie.

From the moment Nat had stepped into the room to start therapy, she had known there wouldn't be any coddling happening here. Her therapist in Los Angeles tended to let her get away with things that Dr. Jones had put an immediate stop to, and somehow it made Natalie feel safer. The doctor dressed in a gray suit each day, buttoned up tight to her neck. The flat shoes, lack of jewelry or makeup, and her hair in a tight bun all gave the impression that she meant business.

"What do I do about it?"

"Is that a question for me, or for you?"

Nat sighed, knowing that the doctor was right but hating it just the same. "Mike got me a dog."

"Did he now?" The therapist crossed her legs and leaned back in the chair. "Why did he do that?"

"He thought it might help," she said. "Jake has a service dog, Rex, that helps with his PTSD. Mike noticed that I tend to be calmer when Rex is around, and thought maybe having a dog of my own would be a good idea. She's just a tiny little puppy, not trained like Rex. But I did sleep better last night."

"No nightmares?"

"A few, but maybe not as bad? I woke up quickly. The puppy was crying, and it pulled me out of it."

"That's a good thing," Dr. Jones said. "Mike seems to be a supportive friend."

"He is," Nat said quietly. "I just can't figure out why I'm so traumatized by what happened and he's not."

"Do you know that he's not?"

"He seems fine."

"So do you, in a lot of ways. People show you what they want you to see."

"I told him about my real name," Nat said. "No one knows that."

"Which means you trust him."

"I do," Nat admitted. "With my life."

"You seem to be fixated on him today, rather than what we usually talk about." The doctor tapped a pencil on the top of the notepad she held.

Natalie nodded, realizing her thoughts had been more aimed at Mike, their kiss, and the kindness he showed when he brought her the dog. Consciously, at least, she wasn't thinking about the incident as much as she had been. "I know our time is almost up," she said to the doctor. "Do you have an assignment for me?"

"Yes," Dr. Jones said, snapping the notebook shut. "I want you to go out somewhere new. It doesn't have to be alone, but it needs to be somewhere other than your friends' houses or the Windsor Palace. You can go shopping, to a spa, or go out for a meal, as long as you go outside your comfort zone."

46

"Do I have to go alone?"

"No." Dr. Jones smiled at her. "Bring whoever will make you feel safe. I'll see you in two days."

***

Natalie was outside with the puppy when Holly pulled in the driveway. Holly was wearing scrubs and pulled on a down jacket as she walked toward Nat.

"Hey," she called to Nat. "Can you believe how cold it is? I thought Nevada was cold, but that was tropical compared to this weather."

"Patrick says it's because of how we're positioned between mountains," Natalie said with a laugh. "Makes no sense to me, and I'm frozen when it's sixty out."

"Want to come inside for a minute? I have some soup in the crockpot, if you want to join me for lunch." Holly waved to one of the workers from the youth center as they pulled out of the driveway, probably off in search of their own midday meal.

"Sure," Natalie said. She followed Holly into what was a mirror image of the apartment she lived in on the other side of the house. Liam would likely renovate the entire house when the youth center moved, but hadn't mentioned yet if he planned to keep the apartments as is. Natalie realized she should be prepared to move if that happened but stopped herself before she fully spiraled at the thought.

"You just drifted off somewhere," Holly commented as she pulled off her coat.

"I was just thinking that Liam would probably want to redo the house when the new youth center opens," Natalie admitted. "I wanted to panic over the thought of having to move, but I stopped myself."

"He hasn't mentioned anything about it," Holly assured her. "But I'm sure you'll eventually want a place of your own, or to return to your actual home in California."

"It seems further and further away," Natalie said. "I haven't thought of going back there in a while."

"Because of the guy who was stalking you?"

Natalie had originally come to Windsor Peak to escape the attention of a man who had been following her everywhere, and she realized she hadn't thought of him in months. What had seemed like a threat in California seemed less so after what she had been though once she got to Vermont. "No, I honestly doubt he would be a threat now, after everything," she said. "And he's probably moved on to someone else by now."

"How are you doing with all of that? It seems like you're making progress," Holly said with an encouraging smile.

"I need to. I'm tired of myself and being scared of everything. Something happened on New Years that made me realize how much I'm missing out on by hiding out alone," Nat said.

"What was that?" Holly looked intrigued as she handed Natalie a bowl of soup.

Natalie stirred the soup slowly, debating how much to share. It had been a long time since she had a true girlfriend, someone to confide in about her inner thoughts. Shea, Kendra, Emma and Zoe had been wonderful to her, but she had really gotten to know Holly over the last few weeks and felt closest to her. Deciding a second opinion would be helpful, she put her spoon down and met her friend's eyes.

"Mike and I kissed," she said quickly.

"Oh, this is interesting," Holly said, grinning at her. "Tell me more."

"It was at midnight, I don't even know which one of us kissed the other one. But…"

"You have to tell me," Holly prodded.

"It was the best kiss of my life," she admitted. "I always hear people talking about having their world flip upside down, but that was the first time it's ever happened to me. Did that happen with Liam?"

"Once I realized I didn't hate him? Yes. Definitely with our second kiss, because the first near kiss just left me wanting more," Holly said, her cheeks turning pink. "But we don't need to get into all that, or else I'll be calling him to run home."

"Where is he, anyway?"

"Working out," Holly said. "With Mike."

"Of course," she said. "They had to change the time because Patrick was doing a morning show in New York today. He must have just gotten back to town."

"That's so crazy to me, that you guys can just run off for a few hours and be on the Today show," Holly said. "Let's shelve that for later, because this is my lunch break and I'm on limited time. Tell me more about Mike."

"I don't know what to say. We had this amazing kiss, and it confused me. Old Nat would have been dragging him back here for the night, and the new me was afraid to have him come back because I would have been unable to send him home," she admitted. "We talked about it briefly, but he hasn't made a move since."

"He brought you a dog," Holly pointed out.

"Yes, he did that, and he has checked in with me every day. But maybe he doesn't want to get involved with someone like me?"

"A stunning, brilliant, successful woman?"

"You know what I mean," Nat said with a laugh. "I'm a mess."

"No, you aren't. You went through a traumatic event, and you're recovering. That's not your fault, and it's certainly not a reason that Mike would avoid you," Holly pointed out. "If anything, the experience seems to have made it possible for him to talk to you. Liam said that Mike used to fall apart when you came into the room, but that he seems calmer now."

"What do you think I should do?"

"Charter a plane and take him to Paris for a weekend?" Holly suggested, laughter in her voice.

"I'm being serious," Nat said. "He's going to come over tonight to walk the dog with me. I don't know what to do."

"You could make a move on him," Holly said. "Or ask him out on a date. That might be the only way to make progress, because he's never going to get the nerve up to ask you out."

***

Natalie spent several hours playing with the puppy and answering emails to her team. In Vermont, she just had Dan, who handled all her legal and contract issues. In California, however, she had an extensive list of people who demanded her time each day. Her manager wanted to book interviews, her agent was demanding that she decide on a few small projects she had been debating, and her assistant was overwhelmed with a list of tasks that kept growing the longer Nat stayed gone. Suddenly, Maggie was overseeing things that Natalie could normally check in on herself, and she knew a change had to be made. She couldn't keep asking Maggie to run her social media, respond to fans, deal with mail and paperwork, organize her calendar, and also run her house. It was simply too much for one person to handle, so she knew that she had to hire someone to just manage her three houses.

A soft knock on her door jolted her back into the present, and she realized it had grown dark outside. Winter in Vermont meant the sun was gone before the evening news started, so it could be anywhere from late afternoon to evening. She checked her watch as she walked to the door, shocked to see it was almost eight and the day had flown by.

Mike smiled at her as she opened the door and held up a takeout bag. "I was hoping you hadn't eaten dinner yet."

"No, I was on the phone and then got lost in my head for a while, she said. "But now that you mention it, I'm starving."

"I just grabbed some salads and grilled chicken from Palace Plates," he said, pulling containers out of the bag and placing them on the kitchen counter. "I needed the protein; it was a long day of workouts."

"It looks like you got enough for half the town." She laughed as he continued to pull things out of the bag.

"I don't know if you've noticed, but I'm a big dude," he said. "I need a lot of food, and I wanted to make sure there was enough for you too."

"I think we might have enough for a few days." She pulled plates out of her kitchen cabinet and gestured toward the small island that separated the kitchen from the living room. "Want to eat here or at the table?"

"There is fine," he answered. "I brought a bottle of wine too, if you're interested."

"That sounds nice. I can open it," she offered, holding out a hand for the bottle. "Do you want water as well?"

"Yes, please."

They worked in companionable silence for a few moments, and when she returned to the island with the drinks, he had everything open and ready to serve. They filled their plates, Natalie watching in amazement as he placed three chicken breasts on top of his salad before taking a piece for herself.

"How was your day?" She tried to ignore the butterflies that filled her stomach suddenly. Concerned that she was acting nervous around him, she went into overdrive trying to be normal. In reality, nothing about the evening was normal for her, but she made her living as an actor and had to rely on that skill now.

"Busy," he said. "This time of year always is. I have way more appointments than usual, but it will slow down in a few weeks. Some people will quit entirely, but I convince most to cut down on the number of sessions and just see me once or twice a month to check in. That keeps them active and accountable, without busting their bank or jamming my schedule."

"It's nice that you care more about the people than the income," she said. "That's not normal in my world."

"You don't feel like you matter as a person out there?"

"In Hollywood?" She stared at him in disbelief. "Not even a little bit. I'm interchangeable with the newer, younger, prettier version of me. The only thing that has staying power for me is my contract with the movie franchise, and even then, they could kill me off and replace me if they really wanted to."

"I think the fans would have an issue with that," he said. "And for the record, I don't think there's anyone who can replace you."

"You're biased because you're my friend," she said. "The reality is, we're all at risk of being tossed aside at any moment. No one looks at me like a person with feelings, I'm a body they are constantly evaluating. Imagine if you had to keep telling clients they needed to lose the two pounds they had gained, or that it was time for Botox because you could see a line on their face. Obviously, that's out of your scope, but you know what I mean. That's how they view me, not as an actual person. I'm someone to make them money."

"I try to look at the bigger picture and focus on their health," he said slowly. "I don't look at people as paychecks. I guess I also have way less riding on it."

"True, they do have huge budgets and producers who expect a profit," she said. "For the most part, it's normally fine. The people who care about me show it, and I know who the rest of them are. I learned early on to know the difference between someone I work for, or someone that works for me, and a true friend. It's easy to see through most people out there."

"Do you think you'll go back?"

"To California?" When he nodded, she sipped her wine and considered the question. "I do like it there, usually. But facing my mortality has made my priorities change. When I used to want to have access to great restaurants and shopping, parties that went on every night, now I care more about who I'm spending time with. Not the volume of people I can see in a day, if that makes sense."

"It does," he said. He pushed his plate back and looked down at the puppy, sitting hopefully between them on the floor. "I think this one might need a walk. Have you named her yet?"

"I was trying out the name Midnight."

"Why did you pick that? Because of her color?"

"That," she said slowly, unsure of how much to say. "Also, because of you."

"Me?" He looked surprised, and she would swear he was blushing. "Why?"

She ducked her head, feeling more nervous than she should. Taking a fortifying sip of her wine, she decided to barrel on. "Because that's when we kissed. And that, followed by you bringing her to me, are the two highlights of my life right now."

Chapter 6

Her words caught Mike off guard, and he swallowed the piece of chicken in his mouth the wrong way. Suddenly, he was coughing and making a huge scene, while wishing he had the capability to handle a situation with her smoothly even just once. His eyes watered, and she looked panicked as she pushed the glass of water towards him. After a minute that felt like an hour, he was able to breathe again.

"I'm sorry," he said. "That didn't go down right."

"I'm the one who's sorry," she said. "I shouldn't have said anything, just forget about it."

"No," he said forcefully, then quieted his voice when he saw her shock. "I mean, I don't want to forget about it. That's the best thing I've ever heard, honestly. I love the name, and the reason for it."

"Okay, Midnight it is," she said. She scooped the dog up and kissed her on the head before clipping the leash on. "We should probably walk her before you have to go."

He grabbed her jacket first and helped her into it, then pulled his own on. The entire time they walked the dog around the yard, he was kicking himself. She wouldn't have said anything if she didn't want to pursue something with him, right? Why did he have to blow any chance she gave him? Soon enough she would tire of his inability to talk to her without falling apart, and she would move on to someone smoother.

"I had an appointment with my therapist today," she said. "And at the risk of making you fall down the mountain, I wanted to tell you what she said."

"Are you making fun of me?" he asked in mock outrage. "I just almost died."

"Did you, though?" She arched an eyebrow, and he could see the smile she was hiding. "I promise, I'm not nearly as scary as you seem to think."

"I don't think you're scary," he said. "I just don't know how to talk to you about some things. I can be fine, but then you mention kissing, and I lose my mind."

"We don't have to talk about it," she said. "Consider it a closed subject. But what I did want to talk to you about was the challenge my therapist gave me."

He struggled again with a response. The last thing he wanted was for her to forget about kissing him, but how could he possibly bring it back up now? He forced himself to focus on what she was saying, pushing the issue to the back of his brain so he could stew on it all night. "What did she say?"

"She wants me to go out somewhere that I haven't been since the incident," she said. "Not a friends' house, or the Palace, or anywhere I have been able to go. I was doing some research this afternoon to decide what I wanted to do, and I kept thinking about what she suggested."

"Which was?"

"Once I decide where to go, she thinks I should bring someone that makes me feel safe. You were the first, and only, person that came to mind. I always feel okay when I'm with you."

"Is that true? I know Patrick and Liam would do anything for you," he said.

"They would," she agreed. "But they have done so much already. So have you, honestly, so it's fine if you want to say no."

"No," he said quickly. "I mean, no, I don't want to say no. I'd love to go with you."

"Even if I said I wanted to go to the hair salon?"

He rubbed a hand on his neck, where his close-cropped hair ended. He visited the barbershop regularly, and hadn't been in a hair salon probably ever, but he would go anywhere for her. "Sure."

"I'm only teasing you," she said with a soft laugh. "I was debating a spa for a massage, or a dinner out. Patrick and Liam have been raving about this restaurant near Stowe that I'd love to try. The massage would be easier, because it's more private, so I'm trying to decide how much I want to push myself."

"I'll do either. Or both," he said. "Whatever you want."

She smiled at him and then shivered. "It's cold out here. Do you want to come in and we can watch a movie?"

"I'd love to, but I have my first appointment at five," he said. "I should probably get home and get some sleep."

"Okay." He thought he heard disappointment in her voice but couldn't be sure.

"I'll check in with you tomorrow," he promised. "If you decide what you'd like to do, and when, just let me know so I can clear my schedule."

"I will," she said.

He walked her to the door and waited until she was safely inside, and he heard the lock click, before he walked to his car. The entire ride home he regretted leaving, and even more so, that he hadn't tried to kiss her goodnight.

***

By eleven, when he pulled into Patrick's driveway, he was exhausted. He had spent a nearly sleepless night considering all the ways he could have handled the situation with Natalie the night before, and in each one, it had gone better than reality. Even the one when he simply fell off his chair in shock that she apparently wanted to pursue something with him, an option that he just found hard to believe.

Emma opened the door as he walked up the front steps, waving for him to come in. "It's freezing out there," she said. "Patrick and Liam are already downstairs, I'm not sure if Dan and Jake are coming."

"Want to join us?" he asked as he pulled off his heavy coat. Emma rarely joined them for a workout, preferring quiet yoga to the raucous conversations that happened when they lifted.

"I'll pass," she said with a laugh. "Have fun."

He descended the stairs and found the two movie stars lounging in the theater room adjacent to the world class gym that Patrick had installed in his basement. "Let's get to work," he called to them. "No time to be lazy."

"Wow," Liam said as he stood and stretched. "New year, new you, huh? Taking on the drill sergeant persona this year?"

"I'm exhausted," he admitted. "And I'm short on time because I have another appointment at one."

"Didn't sleep well?" Patrick asked as he stretched on the floor.

"No."

"What's up? That's not like you," Patrick said.

Mike sighed, unsure of how much to say. He considered both men friends, but they were also Natalie's pseudo-brothers, and he needed to tread carefully. Not only did he not want them to be involved in what was happening between him and Nat, but he was also slightly worried about their response. Patrick and Natalie had a history, from what he understood, and he didn't want to step on his friend's toes.

"I'm not sure that I should talk to you guys about it," he said finally.

"It's about Nat, right?" Liam grinned at him from the bench he was sitting on. "And you're worried one of us will get all jealous and cause problems. Not going to happen, bud. If something finally happens between you two kids, I'll be happy for you."

"Same," Patrick said. "Don't stress over that at all. We both think of her like a sister and just want her to be happy."

"It's just crazy, though," Mike said. "The thought that she could even be interested in me."

"Not even a little," Patrick said with a laugh. "First of all, she's been going on about your looks since she first saw you on FaceTime. To the point that makes me uncomfortable, not to mention inferior because she's so impressed with your physique. But second, you're a good guy. And you went through a traumatic event together, so it makes sense you'd be drawn to each other."

"That's probably all it is," Mike said. "She feels bonded to me over that, once she recovers, she'll move on to someone more appropriate for her."

Liam stared at him and then laughed. "There is no one appropriate for Nat. She's a world class sex symbol, and she's a lot to handle."

"That's harsh," Patrick said. "I see her as fragile in a lot of ways. Be sure about this before you jump into anything. I don't want to see her hurt."

"I don't want to put you guys in the middle of anything," Patrick countered. "That's part of this, making sure it won't be awkward for us as friends if I do pursue her."

"We're all grownups," Liam said. "And we're both in happy, committed relationships."

"And we want that for you," Patrick added.

"You don't think it's a crazy idea for me to pursue her?"

"You've been doing it since you met, in your own super uncomfortable way," Patrick said. "It's made me cringe for months now, watching you be struck silent when she came into a room. If you're finally willing to start talking and make a move, do it."

"I did already," Mike admitted.

"You what?" Liam and Patrick spoke at the same time, then turned to point at each other before turning back to Mike.

"I kissed her on New Years Eve," he said. "Or she kissed me, I'm not sure. But she's kind of made it clear that she would like to repeat it. And I'd like even more, if I'm being honest. I don't just want a physical relationship with her, I want it all."

"You going to pull a JJ and propose out of the blue?" Patrick asked, causing Liam to laugh.

"No, that's not my speed. I was going to ask her to go to dinner, but she kind of beat me to the punch. She wants to challenge herself by going somewhere she hasn't been since the shooting," he said. "And she asked me to go with her. I'm not sure it's considered a date, but I'll treat it like one."

"Solid plan," Liam said. "Let her take the reins. That will be safer for everyone."

"You make her sound terrible," Patrick said with a shake of his head. "She's not like that."

"You would know," Liam said with a pointed look.

"Are you sure..." Mike's words trailed off as he looked at his friend, unsure of how to even voice the question.

"It was a long time ago and lasted for about ten seconds," Patrick said, answering the unasked question. "I am in love with Emma. There is no other woman in the world for me, and there won't ever be. You and Nat dating is not a problem for me. Unless you hurt her, which we'll have to deal with."

"I'm going to let you pretend you could actually hurt me and ignore that last part because we're on a time crunch here. Let's get started." Mike stood and clapped his hands. "I have two new clients right after you, who I'm guessing will be very demanding."

"Anyone we know?" Patrick asked, laying back on a weight bench.

"You know them well," Mike said. "It's your dad and Stella."

"Oh, good luck to you," Patrick said, laughing. "Can you do it here so I can watch?"

"I offered, thinking you wouldn't mind," Mike said. "But they wanted to meet me at the gym instead."

"Can you make a video?"

"No, I used up all of my storage recording you two so I can get more followers," Mike quipped.

They both stopped moving and looked at him, then at each other. "If we team up, we might be able to take him," Liam suggested. "I'll go low, you go high."

Mike arched an eyebrow and waited, laughing when they both sighed. "I don't really record you, and I don't care how many followers I have," he said.

"I take it all back," Liam said. "I don't want you to find any happiness."

Mike laughed and pulled out a barbell, placing it in the rack above Patrick before adding weight. Focusing on the task at hand, he tuned out their laughter, because the last thing he needed was to be distracted and have someone get hurt. He forced his brain to put Natalie on the back burner until he finished his workday, when he could see her again. He just had to get through the next seven hours, and then he could drive himself crazy some more.

***

The rest of the day was uneventful, with his favorite new clients being Ben and Stella Burrows. They had entered the gym in brand new workout gear and sneakers, evidenced by the tag still hanging off Ben's collar. When he sat with them for a quick consultation before their evaluation workout, he discovered they both thought they were there for the other person.

"Just between us," Stella had said in a pseudo-whisper, leaning across his desk. "Ben really needs to be more active. I'm worried about his long-term health if he continues to spend all his free time in that recliner."

"Me?" Ben had exclaimed, in mock outrage. "I'm here for you! You keep telling me that you want to lose ten pounds, even though I think you're perfect."

"Oh, you," Stella had said, swatting at his arm. "You just say that. I'm far from perfect."

"You're perfect for me," he had said. "I just wanted to keep you company. I didn't know you were worried about me."

"I want to make sure you stick around for a long time." Stella had pulled a tissue from the box on his desk and dabbed her eyes. "I feel like our lives together have really just begun. I can't imagine losing you."

"Oh, honey," Ben said, standing to pull her into his arms. "I'm not going anywhere."

Mike had cleared his throat to get their attention, reminding them both that they needed to schedule physicals before starting regular workouts. They agreed, and he walked them through a stretching routine and a light workout. They had kept him laughing along the way with their banter back and forth, pushing each other to work harder. When they finished, they had agreed to twice weekly sessions with him, rather than the five times they had originally signed up for. He knew they would tire out quickly if they tried to go that hard, and he wanted them to be comfortable. He stressed the importance of having a physical and a doctor sign off on the workouts before they started, and both promised to have it done within the week.

"How's your love life?" Stella asked as they were cleaning off their equipment.

"Mine? Non-existent," he replied.

"That's a shame. Such a handsome, nice guy being all alone," Stella had said. "I happen to know a movie star who is always looking at you when she thinks you won't notice. Not that I'm getting involved."

Ben had laughed, putting his arm around his wife. "All you do is get involved. I'm sure Mike will figure it out."

After they left, he had finished his workday with Stella's words rattling in his head. Maybe it was time to push past his own comfort zone, he decided as he drove toward Natalie's apartment. He spent his entire day telling people that they needed to do that to make progress toward their goals, and he was the ultimate hypocrite not practicing what he preached. It was time to make a move, once and for all.

Chapter 7

Natalie opened the door as soon as Mike's headlights turned off, smiling as she watched him walk in carrying a bag of food and a large bouquet of flowers. The delicate pink and purple blooms in his gigantic hand brought a smile to her face, because it was such an accurate representation of him as a person. Hard edges softened by kindness that she was lucky to be the recipient of.

He stomped up the steps, knocking the snow off his boots, which he then toed off as soon as he stepped into the apartment. He placed the bag of food carefully on the table next to the door where she left her keys and handed her the flowers before shocking her entirely by pulling her close.

"Is this okay?" His lips were so close to hers that his breath warmed her skin, and she nodded slightly before he closed the distance. The heat fused through her, making her feel dizzy. They stood in her doorway, making out like teenagers, until Midnight decided that she needed attention as well and jumped on Mike's legs.

He stepped back, looking as dazed as she felt, and then bent to pet the dog. Nat considered the flowers in her hand, which had been crushed between them, and laughed. "This was very sweet," she said. "I'm going to get a vase and see if I can rescue them."

"I didn't plan to do that," he called as she moved into the kitchen. "But I'm glad I did."

"Me too," she said, grinning to herself. She placed the flowers into water, trying to plump up the petals before deciding they looked perfect. Every time she looked at them, she would think of the passion behind the kiss. "I hope we'll do more of it."

He was on the floor with Midnight when she came back into the room, and her heart melted even more. When she moved to sit on the couch, he extricated himself from the puppy and joined her, gently taking her hand in his as he did. "I'm trying to forget that you're a movie star and just act like I would with any woman I was interested in." he said. "It's not easy."

"And I'm trying to pretend that you don't make me feel like a teenage girl again, afraid to talk to the quarterback of the football team," she said with a laugh.

"I was definitely not the quarterback. I was a lowly lineman who would have been more than happy to talk to you," he said. "I imagine you were a cheerleader?"

"No," she said, shaking her head. "Not at all. I played tennis and was in theater. I was not someone you would have paid much attention to, I promise."

"I find that very hard to believe."

She laughed, forced to be honest with herself and him. "Okay, maybe you would have noticed. I can't claim to have transformed overnight into what I am now, like Liam claiming to be an ugly duckling when he was in school. But I really didn't date much, that's the truth."

"Why not? I would think every guy there was trying."

"I moved a lot, don't forget, which made it hard for me to fit in. I was shy, still am in some ways," she admitted. "I know it doesn't appear that way, especially with what I've chosen as a career. But it's different when I'm on stage than in real life. When I'm acting,

I'm truly pretending to be someone else, and that person can be confident. If that fits the role, it's easy to put on. But in real life, I tend to wait until other people talk to me first, which probably made it harder on teenage boys."

"And full-grown men," he added.

"Tell me about your life growing up," she said.

"Want me to grab the food and I can talk while we eat?"

"Sure," she said. "What did you get tonight?"

"A chicken and veggie stir-fry," he said. "Zoe made noodles out of zucchini; it looks amazing. And it's still hot, so we don't have to reheat it."

She grabbed bottles of water out of the fridge and placed them at the kitchen island, where he had placed the containers of food. "Do you want a plate?"

"I can just eat out of here," he responded. "But if you'd rather, that's fine."

"I don't mind," she said, pulling out two forks and passing him one before taking the stool next to him. "Tell me about young Mike."

"I was a jock, as I'm sure you can imagine," he said. "I played anything I could, and my parents encouraged me because it kept me out of trouble. I was a hyperactive kid, and it gave me a chance to burn energy in a healthy way."

"What was your favorite?"

"No one has ever asked me that before," he said, smiling at her softly. "Everyone assumes football, which obviously I loved. But I also loved playing baseball as a kid. It was a simpler game, and we could all play, even the neighborhood kids who didn't play on a team. When it got more competitive later in life, I still just had fun and it was less pressure than anything else I did."

"What position did you play?"

"First base," he said. "I'm a lefty, and that's an advantage there. Plus, people run a little slower when they are heading in my direction."

"I can see that," she said, laughing.

"When I got serious about football, the coach wanted me to stop playing anything else. He was afraid I would get hurt and ruin my chances of playing in college, or beyond that. I didn't care, and fortunately my parents agreed," he said.

"And you ended up playing football in college?" She twirled some zucchini noodles around her fork as she asked, waiting for him to answer before popping it in her mouth.

"I did," he said. "I went to Alabama, got my degree in Kinesiology while I was playing. They wanted everyone to go into Communications, but I dared to be different."

"Good for you. It has obviously worked out well for you," she said.

"I knew I wasn't going to play football for long, and I wanted a backup plan. I have always been interested in exercise and how the body works, so it was a good fit for me."

"Clearly," she said, squeezing his bicep gently. "You know what you're talking about. Did you play football after school or move straight here?"

"Oh, it was a long path to Windsor Peak," he replied. "I bounced around the NFL for a few years, socked some money away. I grew up in New Hampshire, not far away. My family used to come skiing here when I was younger, and I always loved it," he said. "I came up to ski one year and got to talking to a guy on the ski lift. He was telling me he drove over a half hour to get to a decent gym, which is too far for most people. I finished my day skiing and then called my parents and told them I was staying."

"Wait," she said, wiping her mouth with a napkin. "Do you own the gym?"

He nodded, and she could see a faint blush appear on his cheeks. "I do. Not many people know that, though."

"Why not? That's amazing," she said. "Not only are you doing what you love, but you made it easier for people to be active."

"There's a lot to it," he said. He sat quietly for a moment, looking lost in thought, before he sipped his water and continued. "I'm not from here. I grew up in a different small town, and I saw how people were treated when they came in from nowhere and flashed money around. I didn't want to be like that. Most people here know that I played football, but they don't give a lot of thought to what I have or don't have. If they knew I owned the gym, it would make them feel weird to have me train them. And that's what I love, teaching people how to fall in love with fitness. Does that make sense?"

She nodded slowly, taking in his words. "It makes total sense. I can certainly relate to wanting to be judged on the criteria that matters. I feel like this town just accepts people for who they are as a person, not as a wallet. Have you ever felt unwelcome here?"

"No," he said. "Never. That's why I fell in love with it here. I don't know if I would have even built the gym if I hadn't fallen in love with the town first, but they just welcomed me. I never had a sense of not belonging or being pigeonholed into what people thought I should be. When I was a kid, I was both athletic and smart, and that meant I had friends in both groups. And I was the biggest guy in the school, which was intimidating to a lot of people. They either wanted to compete with me or were afraid of me. Plus, I was a little different from everyone else, because my mom was from Mexico and yelled at me in Spanish."

"That explains your gorgeous skin tone," she said. "You look tan all the time. Do you speak Spanish too?"

"Not as well as I should," he admitted. "I spent my childhood trying to avoid it, because it made me different. My mom had a thick accent and struggled with English and acted different than the other moms. I was too focused growing up on getting her to speak our language than to learn hers, I am embarrassed to say. Having a mom who wasn't the norm on the playground made me stand out too," he said. "I didn't want to be like that, I wanted to fit in with everyone. As an adult, I wished I had embraced it. Being bilingual would have been an asset."

"I am always so jealous of people who speak more than one language," she said. "Back to kid Mike. What else am I missing?"

"I was on the math team, and the captain of the football team, and no one really knew what to do with me. I was kind of the popular kid with no friends, if that makes sense. Being a little exotic in a rural town makes you stand out, and not everyone knows what to do with that. The other kids like me, with different ethnicities, thought I was a jock. The football team thought I was a nerd. The smart kids thought I was beneath them. But when I got the scholarship to Alabama, and then got drafted, people came out of the woodwork wanting to be my friend. But that didn't happen when I came to Windsor Peak. People just seem to like me for who I am."

"It's hard when you don't know who is around because they value you as a person, or because they want to use you for something," she said.

"Exactly."

"What are your parents like?"

"They're amazing," he said. "I'm one of four kids, the oldest and obviously the biggest. They joked all the time that if they knew how much I would eat, they would have had to stop after having me. My mom was a professional dancer who traveled to do shows, and my dad got dragged to one of them by a buddy who was dating someone in the company. He said they saw each other across the room and that was it for him. They got married two weeks later. They've been together for thirty years now and still dance in the kitchen."

She smiled at him, seeing the love on his face as he talked about his family. "That's amazing. That's what I want."

"Really?" He looked so surprised she had to laugh.

"Do I really give off the impression that I'm just looking for a good time?"

"It's not that," he said quickly. "But your life is so glamourous, I just didn't picture you thinking of simple things like that."

"That's all I think about now, if I'm being honest," she said. "The thought of going back to the spotlight alone is terrifying. Leaving this town, even this apartment, is scary most days."

"Speaking of," he said. "Did you decide what you wanted your challenge to be?"

"I'd like to have a massage, and my assistant said the spa isn't far from the restaurant that Liam and Patrick rave about," she said. "She offered to make a later afternoon appointment; we could have massages and then shower there and go to dinner?"

"I'm game," he said. "I can't tell you the last time I had a massage."

"I might have to ask for a male masseuse for you," she said teasingly. "I don't want to get jealous of some other woman just before our first real date."

"Trust me when I say this." He turned her chair so she was settled directly between his two massive thighs, and his arms rested on the back of her stool. "There is no other woman who could take my attention away from you. And I hope that doesn't come across as creepy."

"Can we make a deal?"

"Sure."

"I'll try to be braver, if you do too." She placed her hands on his neck, pulling him closer. "Stop assuming you're not enough for me."

She leaned in the rest of the way and kissed him, groaning when a sharp knock rapped on the door, causing Midnight to go crazy barking. The doorknob rattled as Liam called out to her from behind the door, followed by Holly hushing him.

Natalie crossed to the door, opening it to find the couple on the other side, standing in the common area between their two apartments. Liam grinned at her, the smile widening when he saw

Mike behind her. "Did you forget that everyone was coming over to talk about the fundraiser for the service dogs?"

"I did forget," she said, slapping her hand to her forehead. "Is everyone else here?"

"Not yet," Holly assured her. "But we thought you might want to come out and have a glass of wine with us first. We didn't mean to interrupt."

"No problem," Mike said from behind her. "We were just finishing up dinner. I'll take Midnight out quickly and meet you over there."

"I can do it," Nat offered. Holly and Liam headed toward the kitchen, heads together as they talked.

"I need a minute," Mike said. "In the cold. If you know what I mean."

She laughed and nodded, watching as he clipped the leash to the dog's collar and stepped outside. Heading into the main house, she left the door open so that Mike would know where to find her when he came back in.

"That's heating up, huh?" Liam asked her, his voice teasing.

"Stop it," Holly said, hitting him lightly in the stomach.

"I didn't do anything wrong," he argued. "Just asking Nat about her love life."

"That's intrusive," Holly said. "She'll tell us when she wants to."

"And what if she wants to right now?" Liam challenged his girlfriend.

"You two are too much," Natalie said with a laugh. "We are getting to know each other, and he's helping me to move past what happened. That's all it is for now."

"But we can hope for more, right?" Holly asked, causing Liam to laugh. She narrowed her eyes at him, causing him to take a step back. "Don't get on my bad side."

"You don't have a bad side, my love," Liam said, moving closer to kiss her.

"I'm going to open the door for whoever just pulled in," Nat said as the couple continued their embrace. She walked across the giant living room, pulling the door open to find multiple cars parking in the portico. Dan and Kendra emerged from one car, along with Ben and Stella. Jake and Shea were pulling a car seat out of the back of their SUV, while JJ and Zoe were walking hand in hand.

Calle, Dan and Kendra's daughter, rushed in first. "Hi," she said enthusiastically to Natalie. "I gots to come because everyone wanted to. It's even going to be past my bedtime. Charlie had hockey so he couldn't babysit, and Mom and Dad both thought they were the mostest important to be here."

"That's a lot of information to share," Dan said, guiding his adopted daughter into the house. "Maybe a little more than necessary."

"But it's all true, Daddy. And you said we could share anything as long as it's not lies."

"I did tell you that," he said. He leaned over and kissed Natalie on the cheek. "Did you say hi to Miss Natalie, or did you just start info-dumping?"

"I said hi," the little girl said, crossing her arms.

"Calle, I have popcorn," Liam called from the kitchen. "And I made sure the big TV has all your favorite movies ready to go. Come pick out what you want to watch."

"She's her mother's daughter," Dan said quietly to Natalie. "Don't tell anyone I said that."

"Said what?" Kendra asked, coming inside with a baby snug in a car seat carrier.

"How much I love you," Dan said smoothly, taking the heavy seat from his wife. "Take off your coat, I'll get this one settled and get you a drink."

Everyone else filed in after them, and the house was suddenly alive with voices and laughter. Natalie saw Mike join the crowd, carrying Midnight who he deposited with an overjoyed Calle on the couch. She was so lucky to have been brought into this amazing group of people, who had treated her with such kindness since she appeared in town. Liam and Patrick were like brothers to her, and the rest were quickly becoming family. As she met Mike's smile from across the room, she felt lighter and more hopeful than she had in a long time.

Chapter 8

"Can I steal you for a minute?" JJ's solemn voice pulled Mike out of the conversation he was in with the three Burrows brothers. They were arguing over who was the best golfer, and Mike had little to add to the case for any of them. They had finished their planning for the fundraiser, and everyone was enjoying a last drink together before heading in their different directions.

"Sure," he said, stepping back from the group. JJ nodded his head toward a nearby door, which led to a small library for the after-school program. The room had several bookshelves with books for all ages, and several small desks.

JJ closed the door halfway and leaned against a desk, making Mike feel nervous about what his friend wanted to discuss. There was no reason to feel that way, but JJ was clearly in official mode, and it made the air between them feel different. From the time he was a young boy, his mother had stressed the importance of him obeying what a law enforcement officer asked of him and remaining docile. As he grew in size, the lessons got firmer, with his mom fretting over a threat he didn't understand until he was a grown man.

"What's up, JJ? You're freaking me out a little."

"I'm sorry," JJ said quickly. "Nothing to do with you, or not about you. It's about Natalie."

"What about her?" Mike tensed even more, worried about her suddenly.

"Just before I headed over here, one of my officers, Jeff, called to let me know they had a strange call from the Inn," JJ shared. "A person checking in had a lot of questions, specifically about Nat and where she could be found. I sent Jeff over to ask some questions and see what it was about, but the person had already left their room. The front desk said they would call when he came back, but I felt like you needed to know. I don't want to say anything to Natalie if it's just a fan, because she finally seems like she's doing well. But I wanted someone to watch her back."

"Watch who's back?" Natalie's voice came from the doorway, and both men snapped their heads around. "What's going on?"

JJ met his eyes and gave a slight shrug of his shoulders, silently asking if Mike wanted to handle it or let him do so in his official capacity. Mike decided it would be better coming from him and stepped closer to her. "Someone checked into the Inn tonight and was asking questions about you," he said. "We don't know anything more, but JJ wanted me to know so I could keep an eye out. There's no indication that this is a threat to your safety at all."

Natalie paled and turned to JJ. "Do you know anything about them? Name, description?"

"Yes," he said, pulling out his phone. "Name is Dermott Locke. The clerk said he's mid-thirties, brown hair, average size."

"I know who it is," she said, sagging slightly. "He's a reporter. He's had a thing for me for a while now, tends to show up where he's not wanted. I'll call my publicist and see if she can deal with it. He's a complete nuisance, but I don't think he's a danger."

"Even if he's just a pest," JJ said, "I'd feel better if you stay aware. I know when you came out here originally, you were trying to put some distance between yourself and someone that was leaving threatening notes for you. For all we know, it could be Locke."

"He has no reason to," Nat said. "I mean, I don't care for him and the stories he puts out, but I can't imagine him trying to hurt me."

"I'll keep an eye out," Mike said. "Can you let us know as soon as you talk to him?"

"Absolutely." JJ stood and headed to the door, pausing before he crossed into the other room. "Call me if you need me, anytime. And Nat, if you would feel more comfortable staying with us, Zoe would love it. Just say the word."

"I'll stay here with her," Mike said quickly. "It's just for tonight. Hopefully you'll get some answers tomorrow. No need to pack up and move for nothing."

Natalie smiled slightly, waiting until JJ left the room before speaking. "So you're spending the night with me?"

"On your couch," he said.

"No chance you'll fit on my couch," she said, laughing.

Liam's voice called to them from the other room, telling them that the Burrows were packing up to leave. Mike followed Nat into the main room, where they spent the next fifteen minutes saying good night to everyone. They declined another drink with Liam and Holly, who quickly disappeared behind the door to their private apartment.

"I think Midnight needs to go out once more," Natalie said. "Then we can see about this couch situation."

Mike clipped the leash on the dog and frowned when Natalie pulled on her jacket. "Shouldn't you stay inside?"

"Isn't it better to stay with you?" she countered, and he couldn't argue with the logic. He nodded and opened the door for her, following closely behind.

"It's so quiet here," she said, glancing up at the sky. "I think I forgot what the stars looked like after living in cities for so many years."

"Where did you grow up? We talked about my childhood, but not yours," he said.

"Arizona," she said. "This cold weather is not at all what my body is used to."

"Makes us appreciate the warm days that much more," he said.

"So true." She tucked her hand in his arm while they waited for Midnight to finish sniffing around and then headed back into the house. "About this couch."

"I'll be fine," he said. "I promise. Worst case, I can move to the floor, but I've slept in worse places."

"You can share with me," she offered. "We can put pillows between us if that helps."

"No, I'd rather stay out here. Less temptation."

She frowned at him, and then the couch, then shrugged. "I'll get you some pillows and blankets."

She returned with an armful of linens and then stood watching as he put them on the couch. He glanced back at her, unsure of how to end their night. Her fidgeting suggested that she was feeling the same, so he smiled at her. "I'll be fine, I promise."

"I left an extra toothbrush on the sink," she said. "Do you need anything else?"

"I'm good." He stepped forward and hugged her before kissing her softly. "I know this is weird, but I'll feel better keeping an eye on things."

"I have a feeling that I'll sleep better tonight than I have in weeks," she whispered. She pulled back and disappeared down the short hall to her bedroom, leaving him alone.

He had just pulled off his shirt and folded it to place on the chair next to him when she returned, stopping short at the sight of him. "Oh, my."

"What's wrong?"

"I umm…"

"Yes?"

"Sorry, I seem to have lost my senses," she said. "You're a little distracting like that."

He glanced down at his torso and then smiled at her. "Now you know how I feel every time I'm around you."

"I just wanted to say that there is water in the fridge," she said. "And now I need to go back to my room, where some very sweet dreams are waiting for me. Otherwise, there is no chance I'll be sleeping alone tonight."

***

Mike woke up before the sun, as usual, and Midnight perked up immediately in her crate. After using the bathroom and brushing his teeth, he got the puppy out, who jumped joyously on his legs. He laughed as he pulled on his sweater and jacket before clipping the leash on Midnight. When he opened the door, a flash of light blinded immediately. He held up a hand to shield his eyes and once the stars cleared, spotted the culprit just beyond the porch. A man holding a camera was smirking at him as he leaned against a car.

"What are you doing?" Mike practically growled as he stomped toward the man, who had the good sense to back up and put the car between them.

"Just checking in on Natalie," he said. "Looks like she has a new man in her life. Want to answer a few questions for me?"

"I want you to get off the property immediately," Mike said. He pulled out his phone and started dialing, talking into it once it was answered. "Nick, it's Mike. I'm up at Liam's and there's a trespasser. Can you send someone up?" He hung up with the Sheriff's department and glared at the reporter.

"I'm not here to cause problems," the other man said. "My name is Dermott Locke, I'm just here to write about what our Natalie has been up to."

"She's not *our* Natalie," Mike said. "You need to leave. Or you'll be removed once an officer arrives."

"Explain to me the living situation here," the man persisted. "It's Liam Dorsey's house, and I heard in town that he lives with his new girlfriend and that Natalie also lives here. Do you live with her?"

"You need to leave."

"Just your name," Dermott said. "To go with the picture, of course."

A cruiser pulled into the driveway; the headlights left shining on the reporter as the officer stepped out of the car. Mike recognized Nick from the gym and knew that he and JJ were close and he would know what Natalie had been through. Nick stopped a few inches from the reporter, nodding to Mike before turning back to Dermott.

"Are you bothering these people?"

"No, sir," Dermott said. "I was just checking in on Natalie and Liam and met this nice gentleman. We were just getting to know each other."

"He asked you to leave," Nick said. "You obviously heard him call the police. Why are you still here?"

"He's not the property owner. For all I know, he's trespassing," Dermott tried. "He could be a danger to Natalie."

"If he was here to bother anyone, would he have called me?" Nick's voice got sterner, and he pointed to the car. "Get in your car and get out of here before I arrest you."

Dermott wasted no time climbing back into the sedan he had left running in the driveway and raced away. The two men stood silently in the driveway as his taillights disappeared before Nick turned to Mike. "Want me to run him out of town?"

"No," Mike said, sighing. "I feel like that might cause Nat more problems. I'll talk to her when she wakes up, see what she wants to do. I know Patrick has people who will deal with stuff like this. I'm sure she does as well."

"Okay, any more issues, give me a call. I'm on until seven, but JJ and Jeff will be in the office after that."

"Want a cup of coffee or anything before you go?" Mike offered, pointing to the house.

"No, thanks," Nick said. "I'll head to town and make sure our friend found his way back to the Inn."

Mike walked the puppy for a few more minutes before heading back inside, where he gave Midnight some water and wrote a note to Natalie. She knew he had to leave early for work and had said she would be fine once the sun came up. With the house being used for the youth center, it started filling with staff early in the morning, so he knew she would be safe. He sent a text to Liam, alerting him of the morning's events, and then headed to his first appointment. As much as he loved his job, he really wanted the day to be over so he could be back where he started.

***

His cellphone rang a few hours later as he drove from the gym to a private client's house. Seeing his mother's face on the screen caused him to smile as he hit the button on the steering wheel to answer. "Hey, mama. How are you?"

"How am I? My son has a movie star girlfriend and I'm the last to know. I'm the laughingstock of Lake Shore." His mom sniffed, which he knew was an attempt to make him think she was crying. It was a trick that had often had him racing home for a visit, only to find out that she needed help moving the couch.

"What are you talking about?"

"You and Natalie Cloud! I can't believe I'm the last to know," she said. "I have been answering the phone all morning. Your sister is beside herself. She called and woke me up. You'll need to call her and apologize when we hang up."

"Apologize for what? Mom, I have no idea what is going on here. Nat is a friend of mine, that's it. For now, at least." He slapped himself on the forehead the second the words came out of his mouth.

"Miguel. I taught you better than that," she said. The use of his birth name was rare and signified that she meant business. "You don't spend the night with women that you aren't in a relationship with. Of course, I would rather you be married first, but I'm told that I'm old-fashioned."

"Mother. Please focus. Where did this come from?"

"Your picture is all over the internet," she said. "There's an article on US Weekly's home page asking who you are. And let me tell you, you've been identified a few times over. I had to stop reading the comments. There were so many people claiming to have dated you. Not to mention doing *you know what*, which I can't even think about. High school, Miguel! Girls from high school are saying these things. Ay, Dios mío."

"I have to call you back," he said. He heard her sputter before he hit the red button and knew that he would pay for hanging up on her. But he needed to talk to Natalie first, and he was on borrowed time.

The phone rang four times and then went to voicemail, which was full and incapable of taking his message. He switched to text and dictated a message asking her to call him as soon as possible and sent it just as he walked into his client's house. The minimal amount of public relations training he had in college and his brief stint in the NFL had taught him it was best to say nothing. Let her professionals handle it and keep his head down. His phone chimed with incoming messages, none from Nat, and he groaned, knowing he was going to have a hard time staying quiet today. As much as he wanted to shout to the world that Natalie Cloud wanted to date him, respect for her mandated he stay quiet. At least for the next few hours.

Chapter 9

"Girl, what have you done?" Phyllis, her longtime publicist, moaned in her ear. Natalie had answered the phone finally after receiving three text messages and non-stop calls, which finally clued her in that something was wrong.

"What happened?"

"That paparazzi guy who has it out for you sold a picture this morning," Phyllis said. "He claims it's a man who was coming out of your place early this morning. The rumor mills are flying hard and fast. I expect this is a non-issue and we can get rid of it, but you need to be smarter."

"Smarter? I'm asleep in my bed and just got woken up to find out there are rumors about me online," Natalie said. "I really don't appreciate this."

"My job is to keep your public image what you and the studio want," Phyllis bit back. "You are a major sex symbol, and you stay coy enough that fans feast on any small amount of your personal life that gets out there. People are still reeling from your supposed breakup with Patrick and think you're deep in mourning over that relationship, and that's why you're hiding out. No one knows about what happened to you, which would explain the seclusion and distract from this hunk who came out of your bedroom early this morning. If you want to get in front of it, I'll book you on Jimmy for this week, and you can tell him about the shooting."

"I don't want to do that."

"Well, you can't keep hiding," Phyllis said. Her voice softened as she continued. "I know the last few months have been hard. And I also get that you're a healthy young woman and you can have as many lovers as you want. I just need to be aware so that I don't get blindsided at five in the morning with a crisis because you had sex."

"I didn't."

"That's between you and your sheets, honey," Phyllis said. "I need to know everything about him. Name?"

"Can I talk to him first?"

"Darling, that ship has sailed. I need to get in front of some people and explain that this is a friend who has been training you, and you had an early workout. To do that, I need his name, and I am praying that it really is the man who is a trainer," she said. "He sure looks it, but since he has a puppy on a leash, I'm not quite sure."

"That's my dog," Natalie said. "And yes, he is a trainer. But I don't want to lie."

"Our whole world is lies, we aren't getting a complex about honesty now," Phyllis said. "If you want to fall in love with him later and introduce him to the world, that's fine. It worked for Giselle; we can make it work. But for today, unless you want me to introduce him as your love interest, we are going with a workout."

"Fine," Natalie said, sighing. "I'll text you his information, okay?"

"Thank you," Phyllis said. "And answer your phone when I call."

Natalie shook her head as she hung up, and then quickly texted Mike's information to Phyllis. She opened a new text to send to

Mike and saw he had sent her one early this morning, asking her to call him. She hit the button before she could overthink it and was relieved when he answered.

"Hi," she said. "I'm so sorry."

"Don't be," he said. "This isn't your fault. And it's not like I haven't had a picture in the tabloids before. I just didn't know how you wanted to handle it."

"My publicist is going to tell people that we had an early morning workout," she said. "She offered to book me on a late-night show to talk about the shooting and explain why I've been hiding here, but I'm not ready for that yet."

"I get it," he said. "Workout is fine, I'll go with whatever you think is best. But I don't know that this guy is going to go away easily. He seemed pretty hung up on you. I called JJ and he sent someone over to chase him off the property, but I guess he was asking questions all over town yesterday. There's a good chance he'll find out about the shooting before you have a chance to say anything."

"I didn't think of that," she said. "Let me take a shower and get myself together, then see what my options are. Are you okay with me giving my publicist your name?"

"That's fine," he said. "Just so you have it, my first name is actually Miguel. People have just always called me Mike."

"Miguel," she repeated. "I like that. I assumed Mike was short for Michael."

"Most people do," he said. "But if they're going to link me to my past, it will come up anyway, so it's best if you knew."

"I'll talk to you later," she said.

"Okay, keep me posted if you hear anything else. Or if you have any run-ins with our friend."

She hung up and texted Phyllis with the corrected first name, then dropped her phone on the bed. After a quick shower and a cup of coffee, she felt more prepared to face the world, and knew the best place to start. Patrick had always been her sounding board, and she knew he would offer her advice that she might not want to hear but needed to. She bundled up and clipped a leash on Midnight before grabbing her car keys and heading out for the short drive to her friend's house.

Emma opened the door as Natalie climbed the stairs to the front porch, Midnight racing ahead of her. "Is it okay if she comes in with me? I should have asked before I just showed up with a dog," Natalie said.

"It's totally fine," Emma assured her. "We're a pet friendly house; we just haven't gotten around to getting a dog of our own. Horse rescue takes up a lot of time."

"Are you doing that full time now?" Natalie knew that Emma and Patrick had been helping a horse rescue raise funds, and that Emma had started doing more and more with the California-based rescue to help horses on the east coast.

"Yes," Emma said, nodding. "Patrick convinced me to give up the job at the bakery, and although Piper was sad, she knew it was coming. I've been so busy with our horses and helping other rescues find fosters or new homes, time was getting tight. It makes me nervous to not have my own income, but Patrick and I have had a lot of good conversations about that."

"I'm glad," Natalie said. "I know it's a touchy thing for you, but doing what you love without worrying about money is a blessing."

"It is." Emma beamed at her and pointed to the kitchen. "Want some coffee? Patrick will be down in a minute; he was just showering."

The two women had just settled at the kitchen island with their cups of coffee when Patrick jogged down the stairs. "Hey, Nat. Everything okay?"

"Yes," she said. "You didn't see the latest?"

"Latest what?" Emma asked.

"A photographer who follows me around in California appeared here yesterday," Natalie said. "Apparently, he was asking questions around town and then staked out my place early this morning. He got a picture of Mike coming out before dawn, and it's everywhere."

"Oh, this is interesting," Emma murmured. "But I have a feeling I'll need to wait for a girls' night to get the good details."

"He slept on my couch," Natalie said.

"Sure, he did," Patrick said with a wink. "What does your team say?"

"Phyllis thinks I should go onto a late-night show and talk about the shooting," she said. "Explain why I've been hiding out up here and change the storyline. For now, she's telling people that he's my trainer, but that won't stick for long. Especially because we just made plans for our first date, and you know how hard that will be to keep quiet."

"Lots to unpack here." Patrick poured himself a cup of coffee and leaned against the counter. "First of all, I think going on record about what happened is a good idea. Do you have any idea how many women out there have been through something similar who don't have the resources you do to get help? You did nothing wrong, and you have nothing to hide. Get out there and share what happened, it will be good for you in a lot of ways."

"You really think so?" Natalie had never opened up publicly, her entire image was aloof and mysterious. To go on a talk show and share a traumatic experience with the world was a lot to think about.

"Yes, I do. You've been pigeonholed your entire career because of the image people have of you. I know what roles you get offered, and every single one of them is wrong, because it's just about what you look like. You're a brilliant actor, and a good person, and you deserve to be seen as more than your body," Patrick pointed out. "Allowing the world to see you as a little softer is not going to be a bad thing. Maybe it will open some eyes about who you really are, make people realize you're more than what you look like."

"Okay, I'll think about it," she promised. "What else?"

"Mike is a good guy. I'd be happy for you both if you were able to make this work. Just be sure before you get too involved."

"What does that mean?" Natalie's voice was sharper than she intended, but her best friend's implied meaning was obvious.

"Nat, you know as well as I do that you don't keep guys around for long," Patrick said gently. "I'm not trying to be rude; it's just a fact."

"It's not a fact," she said, pushing her coffee mug away. "It's a show. I talk a good game, but I haven't been involved with anyone in a long time. Most of the pictures in the press are just me meeting someone for the first time, and the magazines assume I was dating them. You of all people should know that. I asked you to go along with the façade of dating me for so long, just so I could have a break from the constant speculation about who I was sleeping with. And while you were off still doing whatever you wanted, because you're America's golden boy, I was really alone. Did you ever consider that Mike could be the one to hurt me? That I could really fall for him, and he could decide I'm not worth it?"

"Nat, don't leave," Emma said, putting her hand on Natalie's arm as she stood up.

"I need to, I'm sorry," she said. "I didn't come here to be insulted."

"I wasn't trying to insult you," Patrick said. "I'm just telling you what the world sees. The Natalie who was draped all over me a few months ago and flirting her way across the globe to recover from our so-called breakup, that woman would hurt Mike. I'm hoping the Nat that I know and love won't."

"Of all people, you know why I have to act that way," she said. Tears threatened, so she busied herself with picking up Midnight and grabbing her bag. She rushed out of the house before she could start crying in front of them, although she wasn't sure why his words had hurt her so much.

"Nat." Emma's soft voice broke through her thoughts as she unlocked the car and pulled the door open. "Please, wait."

Natalie turned around to see that only Emma had followed her from the house and was rushing toward her over the icy walkway. Getting in the car and driving away was too rude to consider, so she placed the dog in the car and waited.

"Thanks," Emma said. "I thought for sure you would drive off. He didn't mean to hurt you, but I can see why it would have."

Natalie sniffed and wiped away a tear, unsure of herself suddenly. Female friendships were new to her, and she felt the need to tread carefully. "It's okay."

"No, it's not. But he's a dude, and they don't think," Emma said, smiling at her. "Let's do a girls night tonight, okay? We can do it early, I'll pick you up at five. That way you can be home before it's too late."

"If we go out in public, there are going to be pictures taken of all of you," Natalie warned.

"So what? They already post pictures of me all the time, I've gotten pretty used to it. And no one else will mind," Emma said. "Be ready at five."

***

"I agree with Patrick," Shea said. "Not about the public image of you, or that you would hurt Mike. That's all ridiculous, we know you better than that. But that you should get out and talk about what happened."

Natalie had just finished recounting the day's activities to the circle of women and was surprised by Shea's response. Jake's wife was usually one of the quietest in the group, and the last Nat would have expected to encourage her to go public with her struggles.

Kendra frowned, then nodded slowly. "My first instinct is to disagree," she said. "But as someone who felt the need to hide my domestic violence situation, I think I would have been comforted by someone like you speaking about what you went through. It normalizes it a little, makes it okay for women to speak up when they are victims of violence."

The women were all sitting around a high-top table in Kendra and Zoe's business, Palace Plates. During the day, they sold pre-made meals and meal kits to busy families, as well as ready-to-eat lunches. In the evenings, they offered cooking classes, nights for meal prep, and events. The space was not being used this evening, so Kendra had texted them all to meet there. Natalie knew it was an effort to shield her from both the public eye and the nosy reporter that everyone had seen around town. The kindness and friendship these women had shown her over the last few months was unlike anything Nat had ever experienced in her life.

"What are you nervous about? Just sharing the story, or being back in the spotlight?" Zoe asked Natalie, pouring more wine for everyone as she did.

"That's a good question," Natalie said. "I've gotten so comfortable here, away from everything. It's been like staying in a little bubble, and I know that if I go public, it will pop."

"It won't," Emma said. "We'll all still be here, and Windsor Peak won't change. You know Liam and Patrick will have your back no matter what. Not to mention Mike."

"Speaking of," Kendra said. "Am I the only one wondering what's happening there?"

The rest of the group laughed and shook their heads, making statements that they were also in the dark. "Spill," Zoe ordered. "We're a safe space, you can tell us."

"I know," Natalie said. "And for the record, I've never had friends like you all. I'm so grateful to have you in my life."

"That's very sweet," Holly said. "Now spill."

"I like him. I know that sounds juvenile, but it's true," Natalie shared.

"He spent the night last night?" Zoe asked.

"He did," Nat said with a nod. "But not in a romantic way. We knew that someone was in town asking questions about me, and he didn't want to leave me alone. He slept on the couch, believe it or not. It was the first good night sleep that I've had in months, just knowing he was out there."

"And nothing happened between you two? The sparks that fly when you're near each other are obvious to everyone," Zoe said. "I feel like you resisting him is the same as when I tried to avoid my feelings for JJ."

"No one fought against love like you," Emma teased her sister. "That was painful for all of us."

"Oh, stop. It wasn't that bad," Zoe said.

"It was," Kendra said with a nod. "But back to Nat."

"I don't know that I'm the one resisting it," she said slowly. "He was afraid to talk to me until New Years Eve. We had a good conversation, and then kissed at midnight, and that changed everything."

"Did we all miss it?" Zoe glanced around at the other women. "I can't believe this kiss hasn't come up before."

"Well, to be fair, you were all busy kissing your significant others," Natalie said. "But it finally broke the ice between us. I think I came on a little too strong when I first met him and scared him. Then he couldn't talk to me for months, except to ask me if I was okay and to work out after the shooting. But that night, he said something that caused a shift in my perspective, and then the kiss really changed things."

"You've been through a lot," Kendra said kindly. "It's nice that you have each other to relate to. Just be careful that it's not trauma bonding, because I don't want either of you to get hurt."

"When we kissed the first time, it was like nothing I've ever experienced before," Natalie said, smiling slightly as she remembered the moment. "It sounds so silly, but it's true. I have kissed a lot of men on and off set, and none were like this."

"The first time?" Shea perked up. "Has more happened?"

Natalie laughed and ducked her head before nodding. "Yes, but it's like we're in middle school. Nothing more than kissing."

"It sounds like a trip to New York might help speed things along," Kendra said. "A few days away did wonders for Dan and I."

"Us as well," Zoe said. "We came back married."

"That might be a jump," Natalie said with a laugh. "I think I still scare him too much for that. But it's definitely worth considering."

Chapter 10

"The women get to go out and have a fun night, and we have to work out?" Dan griped as he put the weights back on the rack.

"It was the only free time I had," Patrick said. "I was busy all day."

"Busy counting money?" Jake asked from across the room.

"Don't be ridiculous," JJ said. "He has people that do that for him."

"You guys are really struggling, being away from your better halves like this," Patrick said. "This is why we should always do things as couples. They keep you in line."

"Now that Mike has a woman in his life, we can," Liam said. "We didn't want to leave him out before."

"I don't know about that," Mike said. "Jumping the gun a little."

"I don't know," Dan said. "My early morning texts from half of Natalie's team says otherwise."

"Why are they texting you?" Mike stopped and stared at Dan, his attention pulled back to Patrick on the weight bench when he loudly cleared his throat. He grabbed the weight and put it back on the rack before looking to Dan again.

"I'm her lawyer," Dan explained. "And I'm here. They all thought I would have some insight into what was happening. She's vanished off the face of the earth for months, avoiding all contact with Hollywood, and then suddenly she's thrust back in the spotlight with a picture of a strange guy coming out of her house at dawn."

"And he is strange," Liam said. He ducked behind Patrick when Mike took a step toward him. "In the best way possible. Or not strange at all, I take it back. Don't hurt me."

"Oh, you'll pay for it when it's your turn on the bench," Mike said. "In the meantime, you are overdue for some time on the treadmill. The happiness diet is making it a little hard to see those abs."

Liam immediately lifted his shirt to look in the mirror, then frowned when Patrick nodded. "I have a photoshoot in two weeks," Liam said with a moan. "And of course it's shirtless. Why didn't anyone tell me?"

"I'm pretty sure I tried to tell you that sitting in the corner texting your girlfriend wasn't a good workout," Mike said.

"I don't do that," Liam objected. They all turned to stare at him, and he shook his head, walking to the treadmill. "I'll be over here for the next three days if anyone needs me. And I left my phone over there on the table."

"Where's the shoot?" Patrick asked.

"Italy," Liam answered. "I'm trying to talk Holly into coming with me. It's only two days of posing, then we could explore a little."

"She doesn't want to go? I'll take her place," Dan offered.

"She took a new job at the hospital," Liam said. "She feels bad taking time off so quickly."

A baby fussed in the pack-and-play set up in the corner, and Jake went over to pick his daughter up. He held her to his chest, and Mike was caught off guard for a moment. Jake was the toughest guy he knew, and seeing him hold the small baby and kiss her on the head was a show of tenderness unlike his persona. An image of Natalie holding his baby flashed into his head, and he quickly pushed the it away. Fantasizing about a future with her, settled down and happy with a family in a small town in Vermont, wouldn't end well for him. She lived the same life as Patrick and Liam, constantly off to film something or do a commercial, and he had a life here. He couldn't imagine leaving this town or his business behind to follow her around the world, but he also couldn't ask her to stay for him. He was so far ahead of himself, he realized, trying to push the thoughts away. He needed to have a first date with her, then figure out how to remain in her life forever. One step at a time.

***

After they finished their workouts, Dan and Jake disappeared with their infants while Patrick, Liam and Mike showered. They had decided to go to the Windsor Peak Palace for a quick dinner, and then hopefully be in the right place to offer rides home to the women. Mike knew that they had all ridden together in Kendra's large SUV, so he had already texted Nat to let her know he could drive her home.

As they walked into the Palace, JJ's brother Desmond waved them to the bar. He was bartending several nights a week to help Kendra out, although they all knew that the ability to flirt with the available female tourists who came to ski was the real reason for his second job.

"Hey, guys," Des said, leaning across the bar to speak quietly. "Heads up, that reporter is here. I called JJ to let him know, but he said he can't stop him from visiting local establishments unless he's causing a ruckus. If he bothers you, I'll call over and get them to come remove him."

"Thanks for the heads up," Patrick said. "Maybe we should go next door?"

"No," Mike said. "He can't dictate how we live our lives. What's the worst thing he could do?"

His two movie star friends laughed and shook their heads. "You have no idea," Liam said. "But I'm game. Want to sit at the bar?"

They settled into three barstools at the end of the bar, where they could still see anyone approaching and the wall behind them offered some protection from a crowd forming. The restaurant was half full, primarily with local residents but a handful of ski groups that would likely go crazy when they spotted Liam and Patrick together. Both men kept their heads down and studied the menu as if they hadn't read it a thousand times, the baseball hats they wore covering most of their faces. Mike sat on the stool closest to the other people, blocking them further with his size.

Des slid three bottles of beer in front of them, then nodded at the menu. "Know what you want?"

"He wants a salad, dressing on the side," Mike said, before Liam could speak. "And grilled chicken."

"No, I want a big, fat burger. And fries. But I'll have what he said," Liam said glumly.

"There's a story here, but I'm on alone and don't have time to hear it," Des quipped.

They finished placing their food orders and got halfway through their beers before JJ came in to join them. He greeted everyone and took the stool next to Mike, shaking his head when his brother held up a beer. "I just wanted to stop in and make sure this guy isn't giving you guys a hard time," he said.

"If you mean Mike, yes, he is," Liam said. "He made me order bland food instead of the amazing things your wife makes. You should arrest him."

"I would, but I don't think my handcuffs would fit his wrists," JJ said. "Any trouble other than that?"

"No," Mike answered. "Nothing."

"You'll be driving Natalie home, I assume?" JJ asked, taking the soda his brother handed to him.

"Yes, she's going to text me when they're done next door," he said.

"I walked by on my way in, and they sound like they're having a great time," JJ said. "Nice to see Nat out and having fun."

Mike nodded his agreement as their food was delivered, and JJ excused himself to get back to work. The three of them ate in silence, watching a hockey game on the big screen TV. Liam stabbed at his salad as if it was trying to attack him, making Patrick and Mike laugh. As they finished and pushed their plates back, a small group of fans approached to get pictures with the two celebrities, during which Mike got a text from Natalie that the women were wrapping up. He made a signal to the other two to get moving and paid the bill while they took their last few selfies. The best part of his day was starting, and he wanted to get to it.

They cut through the kitchen to avoid getting swarmed by a bigger crowd on the way out, cutting down an alley and knocking on the back door to be let into Palace Plates. Emma answered the door and was immediately in Patrick's arms, making Mike and Liam wait until they were done before they could all move inside. Natalie was sipping on a glass of wine once he got inside, and when she put her glass down and smiled at him, he felt a shock run through him.

She stood as he walked closer, tucking her arm into his and leaning against him slightly. "I'm a little tipsy," she stage-whispered. "But I had so much fun."

"I'll get you home safe," he promised. "Do you want to finish your wine?"

"No, that's okay," she said. "I'll see you all later, my ride is here."

They waved goodbye to everyone else and quickly ducked out the front door, and he couldn't help but hope she wanted to be alone with him as much as he did her. Normally leaving the group would take at least a half hour, and here they were on the sidewalk not even three minutes after he had gone in to get her.

"I parked right over here," he said, pointing to his truck. "Watch out for ice, it's a little slippery."

"That's why I'm hanging on to you," she said, smiling up at him. "I know you won't let me fall."

The picture of them beaming into each other's faces was online before they even pulled into her driveway, along with a shot of him at the bar next to Liam and Patrick. As she unlocked her door, both of their cell phones started ringing, and she looked at him with a question mark on her face.

"We can answer them, or hide them in the oven," she said. "Your choice."

"Why the oven?"

"Because there is no chance that I would ever turn it on and ruin the phone," she said. "And it's the last place anyone would ever look."

"You don't think we should answer?"

"What I think," she said slowly, trailing her fingers down his chest. "Is that I missed you today. And I want to curl up on the couch and hear about what you did and tell you what I've been thinking about."

He smiled down at her then handed over his cell phone. She quickly silenced it and then put it alongside hers in the oven, closing it with a slam. When she took his hand and led him to the sofa, he forgot all about the phones, his family, her team, and any creepy photographers hanging around in his little town.

***

He was awake early, the pains of two nights on the couch forcing him to get up and stretch before taking Midnight outside. Although there were no photographers outside, he frowned when he spotted an envelope tucked under the doormat. They had been up late talking, seeing her more relaxed and happy had made his day even better. He debated tucking the envelope into his pocket to prevent anything from bursting her bubble, but refrained. It wasn't his place to be making those decisions for her.

After retrieving his phone from the oven, he sent a quick text to Natalie's explaining that he had walked the dog and left for work. Just before bed she had asked if he would want to have their date tonight, so he let her know he would pick her up mid-afternoon to head to the spa. It meant juggling things around on his calendar, but it was worth it to spend more time with Nat.

His morning flew by, and his last appointment before going to shower and head out was scheduled with Ben and Stella. He claimed two treadmills on the floor for them, checking his emails while he waited for them to arrive. When Ben came in alone, Mike frowned, looking behind him for his wife.

"Where's Stella?"

"She couldn't make it," Ben said. "Needed to go back to the doctor for some reason. I swear, they just want to get another co-pay out of you. You'll be happy to know that I had my physical and my doctor thinks it's a great idea for me to work out a few times a week."

"Hop on here and we can get started," Mike said, pointing to the treadmill. "You sure everything is okay with Stella?"

"I'm sure," Ben said. "She'd tell me right away if not. They forgot to run some labs or something, but she said it was no big deal."

"Alright, if you say so," Mike said with a grin. "I'm not messing with Stella."

"Nobody in their right mind would," Ben said. "She's a tough cookie, putting up with me all these years."

Bens was the last workout of his day, and the first one who hadn't spent the hour trying to get information out of him about what was happening between himself and Nat. The town gossip was on fire with this development, and everyone wanted to be the first to know. Of course, they all promised not to post it on social media, but he knew better than to open his mouth. Within a day or two, something else would happen that would take the attention off him, he just needed to wait it out.

Chapter 11

"They want me to go to New York and do a few shows," Natalie told her therapist.

"Who does?"

"My agent and publicist," she said.

"What do you want to do?"

"I don't know," she said, shrugging. "The old me would have gone without thinking about it. Now I'm nervous, and worried I'll break down on TV."

"Would that be a bad thing?"

"Yes," she said quickly.

"Why?"

"What do you mean, why? Because millions of people would see me being a blubbering idiot," she said.

"Millions of people would see you being open about a tragic event that you were an unwitting part of," Dr. Jones said. "Any reasons other than that not to go?"

"I'm scared."

"But you've been going out more, correct?"

"A little," Nat said. "Mike and I are going out tonight to a place I've never been."

"What is motivating you to consider going to New York?"

"My team is relying on me to go. It's not just affecting me, it impacts all of them as well."

"In what way?"

"Well, they have to deal with a lot of questions," Natalie said. "It causes them stress. And if I were to just go away, Hollywood will forget about me eventually. That impacts their jobs."

"You're just one person," Dr. Jones pointed out. "Do you think the owner of a giant company considers all his employees when he makes a decision?"

"That's different."

"Why? Because you know them all? Do you really think they wouldn't move on to the next big thing if you decided not to act anymore?"

Natalie considered the question. Most of the people who worked for her had only taken an interest in her when she got her big break with the movie franchise. Only her agent, who had gotten her the audition and had believed in her, was with her from the start. "I'm sure they would," she said.

"If you were to get sick tomorrow, who do you see at your bedside?" Dr. Jones changed tactics suddenly, throwing Nat off.

"Mike," she responded without thinking. "My parents. My friends here. And maybe…"

"What?"

"I got this letter this morning," she said, pulling an envelope out of her pocket. "It took me two hours to decide if I wanted to read it or just pretend I didn't get it."

"Tell me more," Dr. Jones prodded.

"I had a best friend in high school who I thought I would be friends with forever," Nat shared. "We did everything together. She was the popular, attention-seeking one, and I had fun tagging along. When we were seniors, I had a boyfriend, my first ever. I had been so shy, I had barely talked to boys before I met her, but she encouraged me. Then right before prom, she told me she had made a mistake and slept with him. I was horrified, because I trusted her. Looking back now, I see she was always trying to keep me in check, doing things like that to make sure I didn't outshine her, but I didn't see it then. I begged my parents to let me leave for California immediately, and I told her not to come crawling back to me if I made it."

"Is that how you see the note? As her contacting you just because you're famous?"

"No, I don't think so." Natalie toyed with the corner of the envelope, which was already worn down. "I've been famous for a few years now, so this was unexpected."

"What does the note say? Do you mind sharing?"

"Just that she misses me. And that she heard from my mom about what happened, and wanted to check in," she said. "She's here, though. In Windsor Peak."

"How does that make you feel?"

"That's such a generic question, I'm disappointed," Nat said jokingly, but Dr. Jones just frowned and waited for an answer. "I don't know for sure. I feel like that version of Natalie is gone, the one she knew. And now even the Nat who lived in a bubble in Hollywood is gone. I don't know who I am right now."

"We've been talking about that for weeks now," Dr. Jones said. "You do know. You just need to be confident in enough yourself to embrace it. You're strong. You're a good friend to those you care about. You are famous. You are good at what you do. All of those things can be true at the same time."

"You think I should talk to her?"

"I can't answer that any more than I can tell you if you should go to New York. But I think you already know the answer to both of those questions."

***

When Mike knocked on her door shortly before three, she had changed outfits and her mind at least five times each. She had packed a small bag so that she could shower and change at the spa after their massages, rather than having to make the trip back to the house to get ready for the evening, and she had swapped out what she had packed several times. She felt and probably looked frazzled, but he smiled at her as he walked in, and she immediately felt better.

"Are you all ready to go?" he asked, smiling down at her.

"I think so," she said. "I brought Midnight over to Liam. He said he and Holly would watch her for the night. I think I have everything I need."

"You okay with this? We don't have to go if you're not up for it," he said gently.

"No, it's not that at all. I'm really excited about the massage, and I've heard Liam and Patrick rave about the food at this restaurant, so I'm excited," she said. "My assistant called and worked out all the details for us, so we should be all set."

He opened the door again and picked up her small bag, letting her lead the way to his truck. She climbed in after he opened the

112

door for her, smiling when she saw how clean it was. He'd obviously put as much thought into this first date as she had, and it helped her relax. He tucked her bag into the back seat before getting in and starting the drive, reaching over to take her hand in his as he drove slowly through Main Street.

"I'm excited about our first date," he said, sounding shy. "I feel a little ridiculous, like I've never been on a date before, so if I act weird, that's why."

"It's funny, isn't it?" She turned slightly to face him as she spoke. "I feel like we have known each other forever, and I'm more comfortable with you than almost anyone else, but I'm nervous too."

"At least we have that in common," he said, smiling at her. "I debated all day if I should tell you how nervous I was."

"I changed five times and switched the outfit I packed at least that many times," she said with a smile. "And I'm wearing leggings, so it really didn't require much thought for this outfit."

"You look amazing," he said. "But you always do."

He parked in a spot near the spa entrance, grabbing both of their bags before coming around to open the door for her. She had no idea why she had stalled getting out, but something about him opening the door and holding out a hand to help her with the big step touched her. It was old fashioned and romantic in all the right ways, and she couldn't help but be charmed.

The receptionist at the front desk almost fell over when Natalie walked in the door, staring at them open mouthed as they approached the desk. Natalie smiled at her, hoping to complete the check-in process with as little attention as possible. The lobby was empty, but it was only a matter of time before other clients would come in and spot her. "Hi there," she said. "We have appointments for massages."

"I'm sorry," the young woman said. "Let me find them."

Before she could start typing, another door opened and a well-dressed woman entered the lobby. "I've got this, Alex," she said to the receptionist. "Hello, I'm the manager, Allison. We are so glad to have you here. If you'll just follow me, I'll bring you back where it will be more private."

They followed the manager into a hallway that led to private treatment rooms. Elegant signs on the wall directed guests to locker rooms, the sauna, and other areas for services offered. They saw no one as they followed the manager to a large suite at the end of the hall, which offered sunlight from windows set high enough to maintain privacy. The room they entered was a sitting room, with a couch in the corner, with a bookcase next to it full of books and magazines. A credenza held several bottles of water, two bottles of wine, a fruit basket and a selection of snacks. Double doors were open, revealing the two massage tables set less than a foot apart, covered by sheets. There were several plants lining the walls, and soft classical music played from unseen speakers. Another door was open to reveal a changing area and makeup table, behind which was a private full bathroom.

"I thought you would be more comfortable in here than using the locker rooms," Allison said. "You can have this space for as long as you'd like, no rush to leave after your massages. The bathroom has everything you could need to prepare for your night out after. I'll step out and let you both disrobe as much as you're comfortable, and just press this button here by the door when you're ready for the massage therapists to come in."

Allison left, closing the door quietly behind her, and Natalie burst into laughter at the look on Mike's face. "I'm so sorry," she said. "I had no idea they booked us for a couples massage. I can ask them to do a second room if you'd rather."

"No, I don't mind," Mike said. "Do you?"

"Not at all, but you looked shocked when you came in here," she said.

"I'm fine with this," he said. He pulled off his shirt in one move, then took a step closer to her. "Are you?"

She took in the chiseled physique in front of her, taking the time to run her hands up his torso before standing on tiptop to rest them on his shoulders and pull him closer. "This feels like a dare," she whispered. "And I've never turned away from a dare." She kissed him lightly before stepping back, pulling off her own shirt as she did. He hissed a breath in and then closed his eyes.

"I give up," he said. "You win."

She laughed, disappearing into the bathroom to finish removing her clothes and wrapping herself in a towel. When she emerged, he had done the same, and he took her breath away again. The towel was slung low on his hips and looked dangerously close to falling off. She took a step closer to him then changed her mind, hurrying to the button on the wall and pressing it. "If I don't do that right now, we're not having massages."

He laughed, a husky sound in the quiet room, and she shivered. Mike wasn't playing hard to get, she believed that he was truly shy and a little intimidated by her. But it had been a long time since anyone had valued her company without also expecting things to get physical quickly, and it was refreshing.

***

Two hours later, Natalie felt as though she was sinking into the table, a languid, relaxed mass of former muscle. The massage therapists had thanked them quietly and left the room, leaving her and Mike face down on the table, fully covered by sheets. She glanced over at him at the same time he turned his head, looking as relaxed as she felt.

"That was amazing," he said. "I don't know if I can move though."

"Same," she said. "Do you think they would mind if we lived here now?"

His stomach rumbled, making both of them laugh. "I don't think they have enough snacks out there to tide me over that long," he said. "Want me to shower quickly while you keep relaxing, and then I'll be out of your way in the bathroom?"

"That's perfect," she said. She turned her face back to the soft pillow cutout, closing her eyes and savoring the relaxation she felt. She must have fallen asleep, because the next thing she knew he was back, softly touching her shoulder.

"I'm all done in there, whenever you're ready," he said. He kissed her on the nape of her neck, making her very aware of the lack of clothing she wore as heat surged through her.

"Thanks." She sat up, pulling the sheet with her. He was dressed in black dress pants and a button-up shirt that had to be custom-made to fit his chest and shoulders. A tie was hanging loosely around his neck, and he only wore socks on his feet. "I'll be quick, I promise."

"No rush, honestly. I'll make good use out of the snacks they have here. Do you want me to open a bottle of wine?"

"Not unless you want some," she said. "I'm going to have some water, and I'll hold off on anything more until dinner."

"Sounds good to me." He walked over and grabbed two bottles, handing her one. "I'll relax here, take your time."

Her bag was on the small dressing table when she entered, and she pulled out the dress that thankfully hadn't been wrinkled. The bathroom looked fully stacked with luxury bath products, so she left hers in the bag and stepped into the shower. As much as she wanted to enjoy the hot water, the man outside the door was far more interesting, and she was anxious to start her night with him.

Chapter 12

"Would you consider going to New York with me tomorrow?"

The question caught Mike off guard, and he paused with his bite of an appetizer inches from his mouth before putting the fork back on his plate. An hour before, he had been knocked senseless by her emerging from the bathroom in a royal blue dress that clung to her in all the right places. She had held her heels in one hand, her bag in the other, and had smiled at him, making him feel like the luckiest man alive. He had spent the drive to the small, intimate restaurant trying to compose himself and adapt to the idea that he was on a date with Natalie Cloud, and he needed to not act like an idiot. They had been led to a private table near a roaring fireplace, where he had managed to pull out the chair for her without embarrassing himself. The owner, Wyatt, had introduced himself and offered to send menus to the table or send them his choices, which they had accepted. After a glass of wine and a bacon wrapped fig, he had started to feel more like himself, but now he was caught off foot again.

"Do what?"

"Go to New York. I have been back and forth on whether I should take the advice my team keeps giving me and going on a few shows to talk about what happened. I decided midway through the massage that I needed to do it. I've let that guy steal months from me and take away my confidence. I need to do something to get it back," Nat said.

"You are the last person who should be lacking confidence," he said with a soft laugh. "You're the most beautiful woman I've ever seen, and so accomplished."

"It's more than that, though," she said. "I lost sight of who I am, I think. I'm scared of everything and nothing, and I hate that."

"You feel ready to be back out in the public?"

"Dermott kind of determined that for me," she said, referring to the paparazzi pictures that had been posted of them over the last few days. "People are going crazy asking why I'm here, making up rumors about me and Patrick. I even saw one that said I was in a thruple with Liam and Holly. I need to set the record straight."

"Yeah, the last picture of us coming out of Palace Plates had my phone blowing up," he said. "People I haven't heard from in twenty years somehow got my number and were texting asking what I was doing with you. But that doesn't mean you have to go public with anything you aren't comfortable with."

"I think what's motivating me is more the thought that I could help other victims of crime and violence, not the personal stuff," she said. "Not that I'm going to pretend you don't exist, but if I tell my story and one person is able to feel better because it happened to me? That's pretty powerful."

"I think more than one person will relate," he said. "You're brave to do this."

"My manager wanted to hire a bodyguard," she said. "I told her I would be more comfortable with you than a stranger. She agreed because she saw the picture and said if she hadn't talked to me, she would have thought that I had hired someone already."

"Maybe I should expand my business," he said. "Although right now, yours is the only body that I'm interested in guarding."

"Are you okay with being thrust into the spotlight? There's a lot of pressure that comes with dating me, and we've only just begun. I can go alone, or ask Liam or Patrick go to with me."

"No, I'm fine. I dealt with pressure when I played football, so this is not a big deal," he said. She raised an eyebrow and looked as though she would object, so he continued quickly. "I know it's not the same, but I'm a big boy. And I have a deep-seated interest in making sure that I'm fine with whatever happens, because at the end of the day, it means I get to be with you. And I happen to be crazy about you, in case you hadn't noticed."

"Oh, really?" Her cheeks flushed slightly, and she reached for her wine, looking at him from under her lashes.

"Yes, and I admit that when it started, it was primarily about how you looked," he said. "But over the last few months, it has become much deeper than that. You make me laugh, and I find that I want to talk to you about what's going on in my life. You care about your friends and your employees, even if it means putting your feelings on the back burner. And you're an incredible puppy mom."

"Thank you for that," she said softly. "I feel the same way about you, for the record. You make me feel safe, and like I matter."

"You do," he said. "You're more than a movie billboard, don't ever forget that."

"So, New York," she said. "Are you game?"

"I'd follow you anywhere," he said. "Just tell me when."

"I was thinking of flying out tomorrow afternoon, so I won't disrupt your schedule too much," she said. "Then do the circuit the next day, and we could fly back that night?"

"I can have people cover my clients," he said. "Don't rush it on my account."

"Maybe an extra night would be nice," she said. "Let me think about it."

Wyatt approached the table with two plates as another woman came and swept away the dirty ones. "How was that?"

"Delicious," Natalie said, beaming at him. "Patrick and Liam were right; this is the best meal I've had in a long time. And we're only one course in."

"I have even more for you," he promised. "Next up is a lobster bisque. I'll leave you to it."

"Tell me about your family," Mike said. "I don't know much."

"My dad was career Army, and my mom was a teacher," she said. "They encouraged me to follow my heart, but I think they both would have been thrilled to see me follow their path."

"What did your mom teach?"

"Kindergarten," she said. "She has the patience of a saint, and the kids love her."

"I hope I meet them one day," he said.

"Me too." She smiled at him as she pushed her soup bowl back. "Do you think that's where we're headed? Meeting the families?"

"I'd like it to be," he said honestly. "I would take a page from JJ's playbook and propose right now, but I feel like that happens to you all the time. I'm trying to be different than anyone else you've dated."

"You already are."

"Because I'm not an actor?"

"No," she said, shaking her head. "Because you're kind. And you make me feel like more than just a movie star. You seem to like who I am, and you respect what I say. And when you appreciate how I look, that gives mem confidence and doesn't make me feel like that's all that matters to you. That's not common in my world."

Wyatt interrupted them again, delivering a main course of filet mignon with truffle butter and risotto that looked almost too beautiful to eat. They both dug in, savoring the meal and talking about their families. When he was done, he had to resist the urge to lick the plate and was happy to see that she had eaten just as much as he did. When Wyatt returned to offer dessert, Natalie glanced at Mike before turning to the chef.

"If it won't be ruined, I'd love to take it home with us," she said. "I'm so stuffed right now, but I just know that I'll want a sweet treat in an hour or so."

"Not a problem at all," Wyatt said, beaming at her. "I'll box it up for you."

Mike slid him a credit card discreetly before he left the table. Wyatt nodded his thanks and disappeared, taking their empty plates with him. "Does this mean our night isn't over?"

"I hope not," Natalie said. "I had a nice little nap at the spa, so I'm not tired yet. You?"

He shook his head slowly, smiling at her. "Not at all."

Wyatt returned with a bag containing their dessert, and a bouquet of flowers that Mike had arranged to be delivered to the restaurant. He handed both to Mike along with the credit card slip and then wished them both a good night before vanishing again. Mike handed the flowers to Natalie, who looked stunned.

"I want you to know that this has been the best date of my life," he said.

"When did you order these?" she asked, sniffing them.

"When we made the date," he said. "I asked Wyatt to recommend a florist and made sure it was alright to have them delivered here."

"Why not give them to me when you picked me up?"

"I don't want to be forgettable," he said. "And I already knew that this would be the best night of my life."

"Don't you have a Super Bowl ring?"

"I do," he said, grinning at her. "Still second to this."

"Well, that makes the rest of the night interesting," she said coyly as he helped her into her jacket. She turned suddenly, placing her hands on his chest as she looked into his eyes. "This was also my best night. I would have remembered it forever even without the flowers."

They drove home in silence, anticipation seeming to thrum through them. Unless it was just him, which was entirely possible. She was humming along with the country songs on the radio, holding his hand on the center console. When they pulled into her driveway, he rushed around to help her out, remembering to grab her bag from the backseat as she took the bagged dessert.

"I'm going to change out of this dress," she said as she slipped off the heels inside the door. "Want to help?"

***

Awakening the next morning with Natalie curled up next to him put the day in second place as the best day ever, even before his eyes fully opened. Midnight had spent the night next door with Liam and Holly, so he didn't need to jump up for any reason. He had texted the gym manager late the night before asking her to find coverage for his appointments all day, and texted Patrick to cancel their usual session. It was the first day off he had taken, other than holidays, and it felt strange to have nothing on the agenda. And as much as he wanted to be able to go back to sleep, Nat's warm skin against his made that impossible.

"Why are you awake so early?" Her eyes never opened, but he heard the words loud and clear.

"Sorry, I'm a morning person," he whispered. "Ignore me."

"Kind of hard to do," she said, snuggling closer. "But I'll try."

An hour later, he had convinced her that sleep was overrated, and the rumble in his stomach had her laughing again. "I can't help it," he said. "I need a lot of calories at this size."

"There's no food here," she said. "Want me to order something?"

"That's ridiculous," he said. "I'll run down to the bakery and grab us food and coffee."

"If I have to be awake this early, that sounds delightful. When you get back, we can talk about what time we want to leave for New York," she said.

125

He slipped back into the clothes he had worn to the spa the day before and stuffed his feet into sneakers before grabbing his truck keys and calling out to her that he would be right back. He watched his speed as he headed downtown, aware of the kids waiting at school bus stops even as he wanted to race there and back as fast as possible.

"Hey, Mike," Piper called out as he walked in.

JJ, standing at the counter, turned around and started laughing. "Oh, man. I can't wait to tell the guys about this."

"What?" Mike and Piper spoke at the same time.

"You don't see it?" JJ asked Piper, pointing at Mike.

"No," she said.

"You're losing it," Mike said, hoping to put his friend off.

"Nope," JJ said. He leaned back against the bakery case and crossed his arms. "I guess the first date went well? I know you cancelled workouts for today and tomorrow, what's that about?"

"You really never take a break from interrogations, do you?"

"What is happening?" Piper's eyes darted back and forth between them. "Is this about Natalie? Are you really dating her?"

"No comment," Mike said as JJ burst out laughing.

"You can order first," JJ said, gesturing for Mike to go ahead of him. "I want to hear this."

Mike sighed and stepped up to the counter, avoiding Piper's gaze by studying the menu. To throw JJ off, he ordered enough food and coffee for ten people, and struggled enough that his friend had to give in and help carry it to the truck. "You're killing me, man," he said under his breath as they walked down the sidewalk. "I'm trying to be discreet."

"I'm just happy for you," JJ said. "I didn't mean to blow your cover. Piper won't say anything. I guess things are going well between you two?"

"Yes," he said. "That's all I'll say."

"What's with canceling the appointments? That's not like you."

"We're going to New York," he said. "Nat is going to do some press, try to end the rumors flying around and just get her face back out there."

"Good for her," JJ said, closing the passenger door after placing the box of donuts on the seat. "Have fun. I'm happy for you, honestly."

"Thanks," he said. "It's all a little hard to wrap my head around."

"Tell me about it," JJ said. "The girl of my dreams is my wife, and I still have to pinch myself every day to check if it's real."

Chapter 13

A sharp knock on the door startled Natalie as she was swiping on mascara. It was one thing for him to see her without makeup when they woke up and another for them to have breakfast with her skin still bare. She had assumed he would let himself back in, but perhaps he felt like it would be presumptuous to walk in without announcing himself. She hurried to the door and pulled it open, shocked to find her former best friend on the porch.

Brie Williams had been the blonde, beautiful cheerleader who dated the quarterback in high school. She was still beautiful, but in a softer way now. Her hair was pulled into a ponytail, and her skin was paler than back in their tanning days. Her soft blue eyes filled with tears when she saw Natalie, and she held up two hands.

"Please don't slam the door in my face," she said. "I know you should, but please don't."

"I shouldn't, and I won't. I'm a little shocked," Natalie admitted. "Please, come in."

"I thought I would be waking you up," Brie said. "When you didn't respond to my note, I decided to play bad cop and drag you out of bed. I planned to refuse to leave until you would talk to me."

"Well, this simplifies things. I had to think about it, and actually would have called you today," Nat said. "You saved me the trouble."

"I'm sorry," Brie said. "What I did was unforgivable. I can only hope that the old saying about age bringing wisdom is true, and you can find a way to forgive stupid, teenage me. But even that sounds terrible. You should tell me to leave."

"I'm not going to tell you to leave," Nat said. "Come and sit down. I know we have a lot to talk about, and I can't promise it will all happen today. I'm leaving for New York in a few hours."

"I can come back," Brie said, starting to stand up.

"No." Natalie put a hand up to stop her. "Let's talk. You came all this way."

"When that picture went online and said where you had been hiding out, I thought it was a good opportunity to try and catch you," Brie said. "You aren't usually within driving distance of me."

"Where are you living?"

"Connecticut," Brie said. "My husband works in New York, ironically enough."

"Oh, you probably could have taken the shorter drive to see me there," Nat said.

"I've tried before, but by the time I found out you were there, it was too late. Once I got as close as the hotel you were staying at, but they wouldn't give me any information or even take a note from me for you."

"I'm sorry," Nat said. "I probably wasn't there, though. I have an apartment, but the studio always makes it seem like we're all at the hotel to save us some trouble. That way a crowd forms at the hotel, not where I actually am."

The door opened suddenly, causing Brie to jump when Mike walked in. He was carrying a tray of coffee cups and a big bag of food, way more than the two of them could have eaten. "Did you buy everything Piper had?" Nat asked, jumping up to help him.

"Just about," he said. "I have more in the car."

"Mike, this is Brie Williams. We were friends growing up," Nat said.

"Nice to meet you." He stepped forward and shook her hand, then pointed at the door. "I'm just going to get the rest."

"Is that Mike Collins?" Brie asked as soon as the door closed.

"Yes," Nat responded. "Do you know him?"

"My husband is a huge Alabama football fan, not to mention the Patriots. Mike played for both."

"Yes, he did. I'm just learning about that time in his life," Nat said. "I didn't know him then."

"Austin is going to freak out when he finds this out," Brie said, reaching for her phone. "Would it be totally creepy to ask him for a selfie?"

"A little bit," Natalie said with a laugh. "Maybe give it some time."

"Oh, Austin is going to be so mad he didn't come with me," Brie said, tucking her phone away. "Are you two together?"

Before Nat could answer, Mike came back in, this time carrying a box with a dozen donuts and another bag of food. He deposited both on the small kitchen counter before selecting one of the cups of coffee and handing it to Natalie. "Would you like one?" he asked Brie, pointing to the cup. "The rest are all black, but I have cream and sugar. I got you a skinny latte, Nat."

She beamed at him and took a sip, noting that he got it exactly right. "What else did you get?"

"Just about every pastry option, and some bagels and cream cheese," he said. "Plus a few breakfast sandwiches and some of those omelet bites that Piper does. What would you like?"

"I'll come look," she said. "Brie, do you want anything?"

"No, I'm fine with coffee."

Nat stood and walked to where Mike was standing, peeking into the bags. "Oh, you got some of the frittata, I'll have that."

"We might have too many baked goods," Mike said, looking around at all the bags. "I panicked when JJ started asking me questions."

"That's okay, I can bring them out to the youth center employees," she said. "And if anything is left over, the kids will finish it off in minutes when they arrive."

Mike took out a smaller bag and repacked it with most of the hot food before picking a donut out of the box. "I'm going to take this to go, so you can talk to your friend. I wanted to run home anyway to pack a bag and make sure my clients are all set. Are you okay for a while?"

"I'll be fine," she said. "Want to plan to leave at two?"

"That works for me. I'll be back then," he said. He leaned down as if he were going to kiss her, then quickly stood up again, glancing over at Brie. He cleared his throat and spoke to the other woman as he approached the door. "Nice to meet you."

"Same," Brie said. "I hope to see you again."

Natalie sat back on the couch after placing a plate of pastries on the coffee table. "I'm famished," she said. "Please, dig in. And tell me about your life now."

"I feel like we should talk about what happened?"

"Why? What good will it do to go back and revisit history? Can we just get to know each other again as adults and start fresh?" Nat bit into the frittata, savoring the flavors as she did. Brie reached over and picked out an almond croissant, placing it on a napkin and then on her lap.

"You really feel like we can just forget our past?" Brie looked at her hesitantly as she sipped her coffee.

"I do. And that's what I'd prefer," Nat said confidently. "Tell me about your life."

"Well, I married Austin two years ago. No kids yet, but we're going to start trying soon. He's an investment banker, he works long hours in the city. I try to go in one night a week to meet him for dinner, but it's hard," she said. "I'm working part time, just to give myself something to do other than clean the house and go to lunches at the country club."

"Are you happy?" Natalie couldn't tell and had to ask. Brie's recitation of her life sounded almost scripted, and her friend had remained emotionless throughout. When they were younger, Brie was a bundle of energy and high emotion, and this was a major shift. Although Nat knew that everyone probably changed as they got older.

"I am," Brie said. "A little bored, if I'm honest. I envy your life, or at least what I see of it."

"The things you see are not reality," Nat said. "You see me at movie premieres or glamourous events. That's not every day. This is more my speed now, being here in Windsor Peak and taking it slow."

"You won't go back to acting?" Brie looked horrified at the thought.

"I will, I have a contract," she said. "We have years left of filming the series, and there are some other things in the pipeline that are intriguing. But I had thought about leaving it all behind, finding a way out of the contracts and just living a quiet life. The thought has never been far from my head."

"I'm shocked. This is all you talked about when we were younger, I never thought you would want to stop," Brie said. "Is it because of him? Mike?"

"Maybe a little, but we just started dating," Natalie said. "I went through a traumatic event a few months ago, and it's had me reset my priorities quite a bit. You realize what matters to you when your life flashes before your eyes."

"What happened?" Brie stared at her, slightly bug-eyed, and Nat thought about the interviews the next day. This was what she was going to face on camera, in front of the world. She briefly debated going into it before deciding against the idea.

"You'll hear all about it on TV tomorrow. That's why I'm going to New York, for the talk show circuit," she said instead. "I don't feel like going down a dark path right now, if that's okay."

"Of course it is. Want to tell me the details on you and Mike instead?"

Brie's enthusiasm as she asked set Natalie on edge a bit. This had been her closest friend, but they hadn't talked in years. She hadn't even discussed the night before with Holly or Emma, who she was very close to, and it felt weird to share with Brie first. Natalie felt herself start to close off from her, without fully being able to put her finger on what was making her feel that way.

"I really should pack," she said. It wasn't true, but it was a believable and harmless lie, she decided. "Can I call you when I get back from New York? We can make plans to get together."

"Maybe we could meet you guys in New York for dinner?" Brie suggested. "I know Austin would love it."

"That might work," Natalie said. "Give me your number and I'll text you once I have my schedule. They were still working out the details when I talked to them last."

Brie typed her number into Nat's phone, sending herself a text before handing it back. "That way I'll have your number too," she said. "I'll head out and let you get to it. Unless you need help?"

"No, thanks," she said. "It was good to see you."

"I'm so happy that we reconnected," Brie said. She hugged Natalie, and when she pulled back, there were tears in her eyes. "I've missed you."

"Me too," Nat said. She opened the door and watched as Brie walked to her car, then closed and locked it before settling back on the couch. Something about the entire experience was off, and she couldn't put her finger on it. She sent a text to Holly, and minutes later there was a knock on the door that connected her apartment to the main house. Holly was on the other side, hair in a messy bun and wearing what looked like one of Liam's hoodies. Midnight was at her feet and she started happily scratching at Natalie's legs to be picked up.

"You can't text me that you have a load of goodies from Piper and then keep the door locked," Holly said with a laugh. "I even smell coffee, and we just ran out, so this is really a miracle."

"Help yourself," Nat said. "Mike brought all this over and then ran back to his house. I'll have to bring it all out to the main kitchen soon."

"Mike did, huh?" Holly looked at her with a smirk. "He just popped by before nine in the morning, did he?"

"We had a date last night," Natalie said. "Our first official one."

"Oh, tell me more." Holly settled in, coffee and a muffin in hand, and Nat felt herself relax in her friend's presence way more than she had when Brie was in the same room.

"It was amazing. The best first date ever, really," Nat said. She stroked the dog's soft fur as she spoke, smiling as the puppy licked her hand. "Although we've spent so much time together, it's hard to even think of it as a first date."

"You went to Fireside? That place is amazing."

"First, we went to the spa in Stowe," she said. "We had a massage, and I honestly thought it would be in two different rooms. But my assistant booked us for a couple's massage, which could have been really awkward. But it was amazing, and I realized how comfortable with each other we already are. Then we both showered and got ready for dinner."

"Together?" Holly asked, muffin halfway to her mouth.

"Not showered together," Nat said, laughing. "Just that individually we showered and got ready for dinner."

"I already know the food was amazing, so you can skip that part," Holly said. "What happened next?"

"We came back here and—"

Natalie was interrupted by the door opening and Liam sticking his head in. "Do I smell coffee?"

"They must have some brewed in the kitchen out there," Nat pointed out. "Maybe that's what you smell."

"No, it's a distinct smell of Piper's coffee."

"You texted him, didn't you?" Natalie asked Holly.

"I did," she said, laughing. "Just come in and get some goodies. Mike bought out half the bakery this morning for reasons unknown."

"Oh, are we gossiping? I want in," Liam said. He grabbed a cup of coffee and a donut and settled in next to his girlfriend.

"I'm not talking about this with you," Natalie said. "And I have to get ready. We're going to New York this afternoon."

"We are? That's fun," Liam said. "How much should we pack?"

"Not we as in us," Nat said, pointing between the three of them. "We as in me and Mike. I was hoping you guys could take care of Midnight again."

"Of course, we can puppy sit," Holly said. "A romantic getaway sounds fun.

"No, it's a work trip for me," she said. "And I asked him to come along."

"Work in what way?" Liam asked, standing to get another donut. He selected one, then picked up the whole box and carried them back to the couch.

"I'm doing the talk shows tomorrow," Nat said. "It's time to share what happened and why I've been hiding out."

"Good for you," Holly said. "Reclaim yourself."

"What does that mean?" Liam asked.

"Something happened to her," Holly explained. "It doesn't define her. When she puts it out into the world, she makes it a shared experience, so it won't feel like it makes up such a big part of who she is."

"You're so smart," he said, leaning over to kiss her. "I love when you do that."

"I hadn't thought of it like that," Natalie admitted. "I was just thinking that it would help other people and maybe help with the constant fear that I have. It's like when we had to fly home after that plane crashed in Austria, remember?"

Liam nodded. "We were all terrified."

"But we all said if we didn't fly then, we never would again. That's how I feel now, if I don't get back in front of the public, I might never be able to. And that the fear that's keeping me locked up in this apartment might keep growing, and keeping me here longer," she said. "I don't want to be afraid of the world anymore."

"You're doing a brave thing," Holly said encouragingly. "I'm proud of you."

"We're proud of you," Liam said. "We're a *we* now, my darling."

"Yes, I forgot that I always speak for both of us," Holly said with an eye roll. "Now *we* must go to the grocery store, since we are out of coffee and most everything else."

"Oh, that could probably be a you—" Holly cut him off with one look, and he was on his feet instantly. "I'll just shower first, and then we can go. Want me to bring some of this out to the main kitchen? No way are you going to eat all of this."

"Yes, please," Natalie said. The three of them loaded up the boxes and bags of baked goods and brought them out to the kitchen, where the staff enthusiastically dug in and offered their thanks. Holly and Liam disappeared behind their door, leaving Natalie to go back to her apartment and prepare for the trip to New York. As soon as the door closed behind her, she glanced at the empty room and then her watch, trying to decide what to do with herself for the next several hours alone. Deciding there was no time like the present, she texted Mike and asked how soon he could be ready to leave. His reply was instant, telling her he would be by to pick her up in fifteen minutes. Her trip back to her real life was about to start.

Chapter 14

Mike had what he considered to be an abnormally high balance in his portfolio from his years of playing in the NFL. He had gotten fairly used to Patrick's wealth, at least what he saw of it at his mansion in Vermont. But flying on a private jet from Vermont to a small airport near New York City, only to then be whisked via helicopter to a high rise downtown, was a new world. Natalie had explained that the studio had planned their travel, but when she opened the door to her apartment, he was stunned again.

It took up an entire floor of the high-rise. Natalie had scanned a keycard to have the elevator stop at the floor as they descended from the helicopter landing pad on the roof. The elevator doors opened to a small foyer, where she unlocked another door to enter the apartment. Floor to ceiling windows overlooked Central Park, and he could see a large balcony visible outside. The massive living room featured hardwood floors, a baby grand piano, plush looking white couches and chairs in two separate cozy seating areas, and a massive crystal chandelier hanging from the ceiling. A kitchen was to his right, where he could see gleaming stainless appliances and marble countertops. Stepping inside, he noted a large dining room off the kitchen, with seating for at least a dozen people. From the living room, hallways were visible in either direction, which he assumed led to bedrooms.

"This is amazing," he said. "I don't even have words. Why are you living in a tiny apartment in Vermont when you have this?"

She shot him a look. "You know why. Come this way."

He followed her down the hallway on the right, where open doors revealed a study and at least two bathrooms before double doors revealed what had to be the primary suite. A king size bed looked small in the room, which also included a lounge chair, a desk, an armoire and doors leading to a bathroom and closet. The bed itself was artwork, the headboard carved to resemble a tree growing out of the wall with the base a tree limb. The linens and many pillows were a mossy green color, giving the impression of a nest.

"Wow," he said. "It's like you brought some of Central Park right in here."

"I grew up with lots of trees around me and always wanted a treehouse," she said. "When this design was shown to me, I fell in love with it."

"It's beautiful," he said. "It suits you."

"Thanks," she said. She crossed to one of the doors and opened it, revealing a massive walk-in closet filled with clothes and shoes. An island in the center held a safe in the center, which he assumed was filled with jewelry. Apparently satisfied with what she saw, she closed the doors and turned back to him.

"I don't want to make presumptions," he said. "Do you want to show me the other bedrooms?"

"No," she said with a soft laugh. "I mean, I will. But you don't need to see them unless you'd prefer to sleep alone."

"Not even a little," he said. He stepped closer to her and pulled her in, feeling calmer once he had his arms around her. "We have an early wake up tomorrow morning. I need to make sure you don't oversleep."

"You mean you need to make sure I get some sleep, right?"

"Hey, we all have our priorities," he said, making her laugh. "You have anywhere you need to be right now?"

"I'm exactly where I need to be," she said, meeting his eyes.

***

The sun was getting dimmer when her phone rang for the fifth time in ten minutes. "I need to get that," she said. "I know it's my publicist freaking out because I haven't checked in about tomorrow."

"I'll go take a shower and unpack a little," he said. "Give you some privacy."

She answered the phone as he closed the bathroom door, and he could hear several other voices as she talked on speaker phone. He flipped on the shower, placed a towel on the heated rack, and stepped in. By the time he was done, she was up and pacing the room in a bathroom, looking at him wild-eyed.

"Why did I agree with this?"

"Because you're brave and it's a good idea," he said gently. "But if you change your mind, we can be back in Vermont in a few hours. Less if you do the whole helicopter and private plane thing."

"They have me booked on two morning shows and a late night," she said. "That's a lot of talking."

"How many do you usually do in a day?"

"A lot more," she said. "That's what Phyllis said, too. I should think of this as an easy day, not too much to handle. Are you sure you're not a plant from the publicity team?"

143

"I don't think I'd be able to pull that off," he said. "I just know that I hated when I had to go to a press room after a big loss, but I knew I had to do it. I heard once that if you do the thing you fear the most first, it makes everything else easier. What's scarier, going out in public or being on the talk shows?"

"Public, for sure," she said.

"Alright, then, where are we going? Just for a walk? Dinner? I think you should go somewhere that you'll be seen," he said. "Go big or go home, right?"

"I have a stomachache," she said with a groan. "But I know you're right. "Let me text Phyllis, she flew in to be with me tomorrow. She would have already made reservations at the best possible place hoping I would agree to go out. She can also let the right people in the press know where we'll be so they can get pictures."

"And here I thought it all happened naturally," he joked.

"Nothing about Hollywood is natural," she said. "Let me shower and by the time I'm done, we should have a plan."

"Do you have a TV here? I can catch up on some Sportscenter while I wait," he said.

"Follow me." She walked back down the long hall to the set of couches that were facing a fireplace. When she pushed a button on a remote control, an enormous TV rose from the credenza against the wall.

"I need one of those."

She laughed and handed him a different remote before heading back down the hall. He sank onto the couch and flipped to the sports station, content to wait as long as he needed to. An hour of

NFL highlights and multiple personalities talking about who would win the Super Bowl later, and Nat was back. Her hair and makeup looked done, but she was in leggings and a tank top rather than a fancy outfit he had been expecting.

"We have a little time to kill," she said at his expression. "Phyllis has a car picking us up at eight."

"PM?"

She laughed. "I know that's late for you, I'm sorry. But New Yorkers don't eat dinner early."

"I might pass out before then," he said. "Maybe I should run out and get us some snacks?"

"No need, I'll be right back." She disappeared into the kitchen and came back with a large charcuterie board. "I had some food delivered earlier when the housekeeper was here. I knew you couldn't go more than two hours without eating. All your favorites are in the fridge. Do you want water, wine or beer? Or I have whiskey."

"I need to be awake for eight, so I'll stick with water," he said. He leaned forward and stacked a piece of pepperoni and a slice of cheese on top of a cracker. "This is great, thank you."

"Can I talk to you about something that's bothering me?" she was perched on the edge of a chair next to him, and looked so unsure of herself it had him instantly worried.

"You can talk to me about anything."

"Yesterday, there was a letter outside my door." When he nodded, she paused. "You saw it?"

"I did. I wasn't sure what to do, but I didn't want to overstep or be too protective."

"I appreciate that," she said with a slow nod. "That was exactly the right thing to do. It was from Brie. We were very close throughout high school but had a major falling out just before I moved to California, and we haven't talked since."

"The fight was that bad, or just lives took different directions?"

"It was that bad. I was hurt and angry, and I told her never to contact me again. When I got the letter, I realized that the anger had faded, and I thought it would be nice to see her and reconnect with an old friend," she said. She picked a cashew off the tray and popped it into her mouth, looking lost in thought as she chewed.

"Did you call her and ask her to come over today?"

"I didn't have to," she said. "She just showed up."

He paused, a handful of mixed nuts frozen halfway between the tray and his mouth. "That early?"

"I know," she said. "That threw me off too. It felt weird."

"I'd say. I'm a morning person, and I would never show up at someone's house before eight. Unless they invited me."

"I thought it was you coming back from Pipers," she said. "It really caught me off guard, but then I decided to embrace it. I figured the opportunity was there. I had planned on talking to her anyway, so go with it."

"It didn't go well, I take it." He took a long swig from his water bottle and watched her as she considered her response.

"I don't know. In some ways, it was fine. We talked about her life in Connecticut, and her husband. He's a big fan of yours, by the way," she said.

"I'd guess he's a bigger fan of yours, but thanks."

"She was kind of nervous, and also a little intrusive. I think that's how I would describe it. She started asking me about you, and I hadn't even talked about that with Holly and Emma yet, who I feel closer to," she said.

"Have you since? I'm happy that I'm worthy of some girl talk," he said with a grin.

"Maybe a little," she said in a teasing voice. "But Brie and I haven't been in contact in over ten years. It was weird for her to be asking me questions about my love life, don't you think?"

"Maybe," he said. "Or she just thought it was something that would break the ice more. Who knows? You're going to have your guard up around anyone who isn't in your inner circle right now, and that's reasonable. Let her earn her way back in if you decide to give her a chance."

"You're right," she said. "I don't want to blow her off entirely, but I also can't instantly be her best friend again. I don't even know her anymore, and she certainly has no idea what my life is like."

"I get this from old high school teammates all the time," he said. "People who think they were better than me like to try to put me down somehow. The ones who never liked me try to be buddies now, thinking I'll get them good tickets. The only ones who are sincere are the ones who were always there for me. And a few who I never noticed but are just genuinely nice people. Moral is, most people reveal their true colors pretty quickly. Just sit back and see what she does next."

"You aren't supposed to be so wise," she said.

"Why not?"

"I don't know. It's not what people would expect out of a football player."

"And you caring about people's feelings isn't something people would expect out of a bombshell, but here we are," he said. He tugged on her wrist to pull her onto his lap. "I'm going to pretend to be really upset that you just called me dumb so that you can make it up to me."

"I think I said you were the opposite of dumb," she said, giggling as he tickled her and kissed her neck.

"Hmmm, that's not what I heard. You might need to convince me a little more."

"I already did my hair and makeup," she said. "I think maybe you need to convince me that it's worth it to mess them up."

"Challenge accepted," he said. He glanced around the room and then back at her. "We are alone here, right?"

She laughed and nodded. "We are all alone."

***

They were fifteen minutes late to the car waiting downstairs, but Natalie was fully relaxed and glowing as they stepped outside. She held his hand and didn't look the least bit worried as they slid into the car. The drive was short, and he was helping her out when the first lightbulb flashed. Soon there was a small crowd of photographers and fans surrounding them, and he tucked Natalie tightly against him and pushed his way through the crowd to the door. The manager of the restaurant was holding it open and gestured for them to go first before pulling it shut behind him.

"I apologize, Ms. Cloud. Are you alright? I don't know how they knew you would be here. I assure you our staff did not say a word," he said.

Mike studied her face, relieved to see that she hadn't checked out mentally. She looked a little rattled, but when she met his eyes, she smiled. "I did it."

"You did," he said. He kissed her, refraining from picking her up and spinning her around. "I'm so proud of you."

"Excellent," the manager said, looking confused. "If you'll follow me, your guests are already seated."

"Our guests?" Mike and Natalie looked at each other in confusion, both shaking their heads to indicate they had no idea what was happening.

"Oh, dear. I didn't foresee this at all. Austin is a frequent customer, and when he said they were meeting you, I assumed it was arranged," the manager fretted. "I can move them or send them away."

"No need," Natalie said, shooting a look to Mike. "I do know them. It's fine."

Chapter 15

Mike followed Natalie to the table, which was set up a few steps and overlooked the restaurant. They would be very visible to everyone else dining there, as well as the numerous paparazzi on the sidewalk. He wasn't sure who Austin was, or why he had surprised Nat on her first night out, but he would follow her lead. When they approached the table, he recognized Brie from that morning, and realized the man must be her husband.

"This is a surprise," Natalie said, briefly embracing Brie and offering her hand to Austin. "It's nice to meet you. This is Mike Collins, I believe you know of him."

"I'm a huge fan," Austin said, pumping his hand enthusiastically. He was in a suit and tie, dark hair slicked back, and fairly generic looking overall, Mike decided. He could be any of the many corporate men that they had regularly been paraded in front of at NFL events, especially Super Bowl week.

"Nice to meet you," Mike said, extracting his hand so he could pull out a chair for Natalie. The round table was small, almost as if it had been set for two people and then hastily had two more chairs and settings when the other couple arrived. Brie and Austin had taken the seats overlooking the restaurant, forcing Mike and Natalie to have their backs to everything. He knew it was causing him to feel itchy, not knowing who was looking at them or approaching, but he was trying to stay calm for Nat's sake.

"How did you find us here? My assistant just made the reservation a few hours ago," Natalie asked.

"Pure luck," Austin said, his voice just a little too loud. "I happened to be here for lunch with some clients and overheard the receptionist talking about the phone call. She was asking to stay late so she could see you."

"How fortunate," Natalie murmured. She smiled at the waitress as she approached the table, offering a wine list.

"We ordered some champagne," Austin interrupted. "I thought it would be nice to celebrate you and Brie reconnecting."

"I'll take a whiskey on the rocks," Mike said to the waitress. "Not much of a champagne guy."

"Of course, of course," Austin said loudly. "I should have done the same. I'll take that too. The girls can have the bubbles."

"Do you want to look at the wine list?" Mike asked Natalie, ignoring the other man. It wasn't Austin's decision what Nat would drink, and Mike wasn't going to let her get railroaded by a loudmouth.

"I'll have a glass of the champagne first," Natalie said. She squeezed his hand under the table, which he took to mean she appreciated his support.

Austin started bombarding Mike with facts about his years of playing football, including things he hadn't thought about in a long time. "Do you have any of your rings with you?"

"No, I keep them in a safe," Mike answered.

"Do you keep in touch with Brady? Or any of those guys?"

"A little," Mike admitted. "I'm happy to have a quieter life now. I don't want to be in the spotlight and have no interest in broadcasting."

"That's so cool. You have his number though, right? Maybe we could call him."

"It's a little late," Mike said. "Maybe another time."

"Sure, sure. Maybe we can catch a game together one day. Take the girls to the Super Bowl even," Austin suggested.

"Maybe." Mike glanced over at Natalie and saw that she was struggling not to laugh. At least this was all causing a nice distraction for her on this first night out in the city.

"What shows are you doing tomorrow?" Brie asked.

"The Today Show, so we'll have to eat and run," Natalie said. "I need to be up early for hair and makeup. Then I'll be on Kelly Clarkson's show, and Jimmy Fallon."

"All in the same day?" Brie looked shocked.

"Yes," Natalie said, nodding. "It's easier that way. Kelly and Jimmy film in the same location, so that makes it simple."

"What are you promoting?" Austin asked.

"Nothing right now," she said.

"Then why go on?" he pressed.

The waitress returned with the champagne and whiskey and took their orders. Mike was relieved that when Natalie went first, she ordered her starter and entrée at the same time. That meant a few less minutes sitting at this table, which made him happy. He felt his phone buzz and glanced down to see a text from Patrick, showing a picture of Mike and Natalie entering the restaurant. "Nice work" the text read. When his phone buzzed again with a text from his mother asking why he was in New York, he switched on do not disturb and returned it to his pocket.

"What game was it when you picked up the guy and carried him back about five feet?" Austin's voice brought Mike back to the table.

"Which one?" he asked in an easy voice, making the rest of them laugh. "It was a long time ago. I don't remember."

"Oh, man. Do you have that CTI thing people talk about?" Austin referred to the brain injury that occurred to many long-term football players, some of whom Mike knew well.

"It's CTE. And no." His voice sounded sharp, even to his own ears, but he couldn't stand it when people brought it up around him. He glanced over at Nat again, willing her to change the subject, and she jumped into action.

"Tell us about your work, Austin."

"I'm an investment banker," he said, puffing out his chest as he spoke. "For Morgan Stanley. I'd be happy to talk to either of you about your portfolios. I think I could be a major asset to your bottom line. What do you think?"

"I have a business manager who handles all of this," Natalie responded. "I'm afraid it's out of my hands."

"It's your money," Austin insisted. "Wouldn't you feel better having a close friend manage it for you?"

"My business manager is a close friend who has been with me for the last ten years," Nat responded.

"Mike, your money must be sitting in the bank. I can make it worth a whole lot more."

Mike had been raised to never bring up politics, religion or money at a social event. This was someone he had known for less than a half hour, trying to get into his wallet. He finished his glass of whiskey and turned to Natalie. "I'll be right back. I need to use the restroom."

Brie got up from the table and followed him, forcing him to slow his pace to allow her to keep up. The manners hammered into him at a young age allowed nothing less, and he listened to her chatter as they walked down the stairs. "Austin is so good with money," she said. "You should talk to him. I bet he could make your net worth get closer to what Natalie must have."

"Thanks for the idea," he forced himself to say before disappearing into the men's room. Once inside, he took his time using the facilities and using a hand towel to put some cool water on his face, waiting until his pulse had slowed down before making his way back to the table.

When he returned, Natalie was sitting stiffly, her chair noticeably closer to his and further from Austin's. He searched her face and saw something he didn't like, and when Brie returned, he reached for Nat's hand. "I'm not feeling well," he said. "Would you mind terribly if we had to cut this night short?"

"Not at all," she said quickly. "Let's get you home. I'm so sorry, Brie. We'll have to do this again another time. I'll be in touch."

They rushed down the stairs, stopping to talk to the horrified manager at the bottom of the stairs. Mike passed him a credit card and asked him to settle the bill for the table, and to pack up their food and deliver it to the car.

"It's not your fault at all," Natalie said soothingly. "We just decided we would prefer a quiet night in. We will come back soon, I promise."

Mike texted the driver that they were ready to be picked up and was relieved to see the town car pull up to the curb minutes later. He and Natalie repeated the process of getting through the crowd with her secure next to him, and he opened the door for her before battling his way around to the other side. A waiter appeared outside a moment later, carrying a bag that he passed through the passenger window to the driver, and then they were peeling off into the busy traffic.

"I'm so sorry," Natalie started to say. He cut her off by picking up her hand and kissing the back of it.

"You have nothing to be sorry about. I'm sorry that I can't stand your friend's husband," he said. "And I feel like something happened when I went to the bathroom. Why were you acting weird when I came back?"

"Oh, it's nothing," she said, but he could tell she wasn't telling the truth.

"Please, tell me."

"He hit on me." Her words were quiet, and she stared out the window as she spoke them.

"He what?"

"Put his hand on my thigh and tried to kiss me," she said.

"Why didn't you tell me that there? I would have handled him. What makes a guy think he can do that?" Mike was seeing red, and leaned forward to tell the driver to turn around.

"Don't," she said, tugging on his arm. "It happens all the time. I don't know why, but some guys just think it's okay to paw at me. It's my public image, I guess, or that's what my manager says. I know how to shut it down, and now we know that we're not going anywhere near them again. If Brie wants to be my friend, I'll figure out how to do that without her creep husband around."

"I still think I should deal with it," he grumbled. "For the record, it's never okay for a man to put his hands on a woman like that."

"Thanks," she said, kissing him softly. "I do know that, but it's hard in my work, you know?"

"No. Do people do this to Liam and Patrick?"

"Kind of," she said. "Liam got swarmed at the store over Christmas and came home with scratches on him and said women were all over him. We don't seem like real people to fans, I guess."

"That's absurd," he fumed.

"You mean to tell me that in your football career, no one tried anything like that?"

"It's different," he said. Women had flirted with him, sure. But no one tried to force themselves on him.

"Well, you're a giant," Natalie said with a smile. "That probably helps. And I'm thinking you're hungry, and that's making this all feel worse."

"Starving," he admitted.

"There's a small diner on the same block as my apartment," Natalie told him. "They make the best milkshakes and burgers in the world. Want to continue our night out in a more low-key spot?"

"Absolutely, I do," he said, forcing himself to relax and match her mood. He would not ruin her first night out in the city with his dark mood.

The driver gratefully accepted a large tip from Mike, as well as the gourmet food that had been bagged up at the restaurant. "My wife didn't expect me home for hours," he said. "This is a double treat. I get an early night, and I can bring her home dinner."

They waved goodbye to him before walking the short distance to the diner. It was half full, but no one looked in their direction as they entered. The waitress behind the counter grinned at Natalie when she walked in and came around to hug her.

"My girl," she said. "It's been too long. And you brought me some fresh beef. I love it."

"Gina, this is Mike," Nat said. "Mike, Gina owns this place and makes it so I need to keep up with my workouts."

"Go grab your booth," Gina said to her. "It's empty and waiting for you. I'll be over in a minute."

They slid into the booth at the far end, where Natalie could be obscured by the high back. It was the only one that didn't have windows facing the street, instead a small TV was on the wall playing reruns of I Love Lucy. Natalie smiled when she saw it.

"This is my favorite show ever," she told him. "Gina keeps it on all day and night, just in case I come in. I've spent many lonely hours sitting here, passing the time with Lucy and Ethel."

"I'm glad I'm here with you," he said.

"Me too," she said. "I'm not so lonely anymore."

***

Mike was disoriented when he woke up in an unfamiliar bed, the sky still dark outside, before he realized where he was. The sliver of light under the bathroom door suggested Natalie was in there prepping for the busy day, so he flipped on the lamp on the bedside table and sat up to check his phone. The text messages were full of people who had seen pictures of the two of them out the night before, with more than one person asking what was happening between them. Pictures of him helping her to the car were all across social media, her tiny frame tucked against his, so close they looked attached. But the prime spot was reserved for a shot taken through the restaurant's glass door, where they were embracing and kissing. It was going to be hard to deny a romance with that floating around, and he kicked himself mentally for giving in to the moment. Natalie was likely going to answer for it all day, and he hated putting her in that position.

The bathroom door opened, and Nat looked surprised to see him propped up in the bed. She was in the familiar leggings and tank top he was growing used to seeing her in. Her hair was wrapped in a towel, and her skin was scrubbed and bare of makeup. She looked amazing.

"I'm sorry if I woke you up," she said. "I had planned on letting you sleep, since we were out late last night."

"That's why they make coffee, right? I don't mind being up early."

She moved to climb back onto the bed but was stopped by the cell phone in her hand chiming. "That's the team," she said. "I'll go let them in. We'll stay out in the living room, so take your time getting ready." She started to leave the room then looked back at him. "You're coming with me, right?"

"Couldn't keep me away," he promised. When the door closed behind her, he climbed out of bed and headed for the shower.

Fifteen minutes later, he was showered and headed to the coffee stand downstairs with a list of orders from everyone in the room. He emerged from the elevator to find the doorman arguing with no other than Dermott, the annoying reporter.

"He knows me," Dermott insisted, pointing at Mike.

"I do," Mike said. "And I know you don't belong here. Please leave and stop giving this gentleman a hard time."

"Did you spend the night here? That's four nights in a row, if I'm counting right. What's the story behind this getaway? Who did you have dinner with last night?" Dermott fired questions at him as he tried to walk by, the smaller man getting in his way.

"Why are you following her?" Mike demanded, stopping to stare at the reporter. "Don't you have other stories you could be doing?"

"I've been covering her for years," Dermott replied. "Normally, she will give me a picture and a quote, which will pay my rent for a month. This time is different, and I have a feeling something is going on that would be my big break. You need to understand what it's like for me. I have to be one step ahead, and if I sense there's a story brewing, I need to follow it."

"And if we tell you there's nothing happening? Or that she doesn't want to talk to you?"

"It's my job, man. I don't know what to tell you," Dermott replied. He stepped between Mike and the door to the street, pulling his phone out at the same time. "If you want to answer some questions, I could leave her alone."

"I'm not going to do that, and I need you to leave. I'll tell you this one time, and one time only," Mike said, deliberately keeping his voice low. "I'm here to protect her. You do not want to get in my way."

The reporter scurried out of his path and moved back toward the door to Natalie's building. Mike turned around and pointed at him. "And stay away from her. I don't want to see you here when I get back."

He stormed off to the coffee shop, relieved to find it open and not busy. Pacing back and forth as the orders were made seemed to make people nervous, so he forced himself to calm down. Why would Dermott show up here? And why was he trying to get into her building before dawn?

He pushed the thoughts out of his mind as he walked back to the building. Today was about celebrating Nat's reemergence into the spotlight, and her bravery in telling her story. Any other distractions were going to be kept at bay, no matter what he had to do.

Chapter 16

The lights blinded Natalie for a moment as she sat on the couch waiting for the hosts to join her. They were setting the stage during a commercial break, and a stylist was fussing with her hair while someone else fiddled with her microphone. She forced herself to take a deep breath as she searched the shadows for Mike. When she caught sight of a shadow that was broader than everyone else, she knew it had to be him. He was just behind the camera, likely ready to run to her side if she needed him.

Savannah walked across the stage, notecards in her hand, smiling at Nat. They hugged briefly before both sitting back down as the countdown began.

"You ready for this?" Savannah asked.

"I think so," Natalie said, forcing a smile.

Savannah welcomed the viewers back, introducing Natalie while pictures flashed across the screen of her various movie roles. "We know her as a fierce superhero, but the real-life woman has undergone quite the scare and is here to talk about it with us. Natalie, welcome."

"Thank you, Savannah. I'm happy to be here."

"Pictures recently surfaced of you in a small town in Vermont," Savannah said. "Fans had been asking questions on your social media for several weeks, wondering where you had gone. You're well known for your attendance at charity events and parties, so what brought on these weeks of seclusion?"

"As you may know, my close friend Patrick Burrows grew up in Vermont," Natalie said.

"Oh, yes, we all know and love Patrick," Savannah said with a laugh.

"I went to visit him a few months ago, wanting a change of scenery. Just before I got to town, there were a series of armed robberies that were concerning for the local police," Natalie said. "When I arrived, Patrick asked me to keep a low profile, afraid that I could be in danger if I was too visible."

"If I could ask," Savannah interrupted. "What made you need a change of scenery?"

Natalie paused, then took a sip of the water that was on the table in front of her. "I was receiving some unusual messages, and gifts were arriving at my home. I didn't feel safe in California, and thought being out of sight would help whoever was behind it all move on."

"How frightening," Savannah murmured.

"It was," Natalie said. "I thought it was the scariest thing that could happen to me, but I was wrong. Two days after I arrived in Windsor Peak, I was held at gunpoint. The man decided that he was going to take me with him and get his lottery payout, and there was nothing I could do to stop him."

"That's terrifying," Savannah said. "Were you alone?"

"No," Natalie said, shaking her head. She debated whether to include Mike in the story, and then decided he deserved the recognition. "Patrick's good friend, Mike Collins, had spent the morning with me. We had gone for a horseback ride and were just going back into Patrick's house for lunch. When we opened the door, the man was standing there, pointing a gun at us. He said he had been hoping to find something valuable at the house of a movie star, but what was more valuable than a movie star herself? Mike kept me behind him the entire time and wouldn't let the guy near me. He stood between me and a gun, and I know I'm here today because of that. He was my hero."

"That's amazing," Savannah said. "How did it end?"

"I was able to press the distress button on Patrick's alarm panel," she shared. "The local sheriff got the signal and came in ready for battle. The two of them shot at each other, and thankfully JJ had better aim than the other man. Although he went through a few scary days, he is now recovered and doing well. The other man was not so lucky."

"You must be traumatized from witnessing all of that," Savannah said.

"I have been," she admitted. "I've been seeing a therapist several times a week, and my friends have been amazing. They have shown me what true friendship looks like and rallied around me in so many ways. And Mike has been there for me every step of the way."

"Do I sense a romance blooming?" Savannah's voice was teasing, and it was all Nat could do not to let a goofy smile spread across her face.

"Mike is my friend. He makes me feel brave, and safe, and I needed that on this trip," Natalie said. After a long discussion with her publicist and Mike, they had all decided not to address a romance immediately, but to say he was with her as a friend. It was farfetched, especially after the kiss was caught on camera the night before, but his size and former profession led credence to the idea.

"You won't be the first person to fall for their best friend," Savannah said with a laugh. "And I doubt you'll be the last."

"I'll just say that Mike is one of the most remarkable people I've ever met, and leave it at that," she responded. "He makes me feel safe even when I'm terrified. He's a hero who literally put his life on the line for me once, and I have no doubts that he would do it again and again. And he also encouraged me to share my story so that other victims of violence won't feel alone. There is no shame in what happened to me, to us, and I needed to embrace that. If you're out there watching this, and scared or ashamed because of something that happened to you, you need to hear this. Whatever it was, it happened to you, not because of you. It doesn't define you. You can turn it around and use it to be stronger. Embrace what you've already overcome and how strong you are. We are not our trauma; it's just a blip in our story."

"What a great message for our viewers," Savannah said. She thanked the audience for watching and letting them know where they could find Natalie online. When they went to commercial Savannah stood and embraced Nat. "That was wonderful. You did amazing."

"Thank you," Natalie said. She suddenly found herself overcome and fighting back tears. "I am so relieved. I feel like I just got a piece of myself back."

Savannah waved at someone behind Nat. "You did, and you are a pillar of hope for women around the world," she said. She looked up at something behind Natalie before she spoke again. "Good luck to you both."

Natalie turned and found herself in Mike's arms, so she let the tears fall. It wasn't grief she was feeling, but something different that she couldn't explain. She wasn't feeling fully like herself again. The fear was still pushing at her to get back to her safe place, but she managed to take a deep breath and push it down. It helped to have Mike holding her, and she let him lead her off the stage and back to the green room where they had sat pre-show. She heard compliments from people as she walked by but wasn't able to focus enough to do more than nod and try to smile.

Once the door closed, Mike tilted her chin up to meet his eyes. "Are you okay?"

"I am," she said, nodding. "That was hard, and it didn't cure me. But it's a step in the right direction."

"You're my hero," he said, kissing her on the top of her head. "I'm so proud of you."

"You're going to get even more press now," she said. "I didn't mean to bring you into the conversation. I'm sorry. We thought I could brush past it, but I went on and on. I think I gave my feelings away there."

"Sorry that the world knows that I'm the luckiest man alive? Don't be ridiculous," he said. "I can handle anything you throw at me."

"Oh, yeah?" She laughed, looking up at him. "I'll have to think of something that will throw you."

"You do that," he said. "Want to get out of here? We have a couple of hours before the next one. I want to get some food into you."

"You mean you're hungry."

"Well, that's a given. But I also noticed that you just drank your coffee and didn't even take a bite of the muffin I got you," he said.

"And you barely ate last night. I figured the nerves were getting the best of you, but now you know you'll be okay."

"Let me just check my messages quickly, then we can get out of here," she said. Her phone was on a small table next to the couch, where she had left it when she went onto the set. She scrolled quickly through messages from her team, pausing when a new one came on her screen that made her roll her eyes. "Brie just texted me."

"I'm not surprised," Mike said. "What did she say?"

"She just watched the segment, and that I did good."

"That's nice," he said.

He was right, but something was still putting her on edge regarding Brie. It could be that her husband had been trying to solicit both her and Mike as customers ten minutes after meeting them, and just the whole blindside that happened with them crashing the dinner. She wanted to give her friend the benefit of doubt, but fame had taught her to be careful of anyone new around her. She had been burned many times by new friends who were suddenly asking for favors, proving that was their interest in her. They wanted to be introduced to an agent, or a casting director, or could she please ask if there was some small part in a film they could have. And that wasn't even the worst. The worst was when people asked her for money, either through a money-making scheme or a sad story. It was why she had a business manager, because she would fall for every sob story and hand over all her money if it was up to her.

"Anything exciting on your end?" She pushed the thought of Brie aside and turned to Mike, who was scrolling on his phone.

"Lots of messages," he said. "Some clips of me missing a tackle, so my quarterback got sacked, suggesting that you could find a better protector for your amazing body. A few of my old teammates are suggesting they would be better suited for you than I am, and want me to give you their number."

"I'll pass, but thanks," she said with a laugh.

"Alright, food. Let's get moving." He pulled her to her feet and helped her into her jacket.

"Let me just tell Phyllis that we're leaving," she said. "She can meet us at the next one."

***

Five hours later, she was done with her talk show circuit. All had gone well, with hosts that she had known for years and was comfortable talking with. Phyllis reported that there was a lot of positive press about her, and that most were focusing on the reason for her appearing on the shows rather than speculating on her romantic life. Overall, it was seen as a huge success by her team.

"What's up next?" Mike asked as he climbed into the back seat next to her.

"I need to change," she said. "And maybe a nap. Unless you want to get back to Vermont, in which case I can just change and we can go."

"I'm in no rush," he said. "Want to stay here for an extra night?"

"Really? I thought you'd want to get back."

"I'm enjoying the alone time with you," he said. "And it's good to see you back out in your element."

"It's strange," she said. "I haven't felt as nervous as I thought I would be being here. I had a few moments when I was about to panic, and then I looked over and saw you, and knew that I was okay. It was harder than I thought to be around so many strangers, but I guess that's going to take time. Or maybe being in a different place made it easier to avoid panic?"

"Maybe it's like your therapist thought. When you faced it head on, it became less scary," he suggested.

"True." She glanced out the window at the city streets, filled with people from all walks of life. Parents with strollers, white-collar workers dressed to the nines, health care workers in scrubs, homeless people on the sidewalk, police officers and teenagers. All independent and yet a part of the heartbeat that New York seemed to have. "I do love being here, where it's so alive. But I have really grown to love the slower feel of a small town. Of knowing everyone and just having a quieter life."

"What made you think of that?"

"I don't know," she said. "I guess today has me thinking about what comes next. Do I go back to Los Angeles?"

"Do you need to?" he asked lightly, but she knew there was more behind it that they needed to talk about. Her life wasn't in Vermont, and it was going to be a problem at some point.

"I will," she said. "We film again in a few months. And we have a premiere soon, which I'm expected to be at. Life goes on, doesn't it? Whether or not we're ready, it's going to keep moving."

The driver pulled up outside her building, and she waited for Mike to open the door for her. At each stop, he had told the driver he had it and rushed to help her out himself. He didn't even wait for his door to be opened; he was so unused to having things handled for him; she wasn't even sure he knew the driver was expected to do it. As she took his hand to climb out, she felt him tense up, and looked up to see Dermott outside the door.

"I told you to leave her alone," Mike said. "Why are you here?"

"It's my job," Dermott said. "How are you feeling, Natalie? You've been doing press all day. Want to answer a few questions for me?"

"I'm exhausted," she said. "And ready to change. You can talk to my public relations team."

"I'm just trying to make a living," Dermott persisted. "You had dinner last night with Austin Williams. I've been doing some research on him and there are a lot of rumors on Wall Street. Someone suggested that he's mismanaged some accounts to favor a female client that he's involved with romantically. Any comment on that?"

"I don't even know the man," she said. "I grew up with his wife. We were with them briefly last night."

"Does he handle your money? Or yours, Mike?"

"No," Nat answered for both of them. "He does not."

"Any romantic history between you and Austin?"

"Absolutely not," she said, stepping through the door that Mike held open. "That's ridiculous."

"Where are you guys going tonight?" Dermott called out as the door started to close.

"Staying in," she called out. "I'm exhausted."

They got into the elevator, ignoring Dermott as he took pictures of them through the glass doors, waiting to speak until the doors closed. "I hate that guy," Mike said.

"I know," she said with a sigh. "But it is his job. I can't fault them for wanting to get a paycheck. It would be nice if I wasn't such a frequent target of his. I hope telling him we were staying in will make him go away."

"Does that mean you want to try going out tonight?"

"I need some time to decompress. That was a lot of people to be around after being so isolated for months. She opened her door and stepped out of her heels, letting her jacket drop off her shoulders at the same time. Before Mike could lean over to pick it up, she grabbed his hand. "Let's see where the day leads, shall we?"

Chapter 17

"We set the date for the service dog fundraiser," Patrick said. He was on a Peloton next to Liam, who had on headphones and was paying more attention to the instructor. Mike had arrived early for their workout and was waiting for them to finish their ride, killing the time by checking his email on his phone.

"Oh, yeah? When is it?"

"The last weekend in March," Patrick shared. "It's usually a slow time up here, so we can fill the Inn with some heavy hitters without disrupting the ski tourists."

"But they'll still be able to get some skiing in," Mike said. "Good plan. I wasn't sure if you would want to wait until spring to make things easier for travel."

"We debated that," Patrick said. "But according to Jake, there is a long waiting list of veterans in need of service dogs. That means the charity has some urgent needs for funding, and we can alleviate that. Liam and I could just make donations of our own, but it would make more sense for us to say we'll match what is raised."

"That's very generous of you," Mike said.

"It's the least we can do. You've seen the difference with Jake, it's remarkable."

"It is," Mike agreed. "When I got Midnight for Natalie, I didn't know what to expect. But it's definitely helped her, and I've seen the benefits with Jake. I can see how a properly trained service animal can improve lives."

Patrick stopped pedaling as Liam pulled off his headphones and reached for a towel. They both climbed off the bikes and moved towards the weights, so Mike tucked his phone away. "Speaking of Nat," Liam said. "How did it go in New York?"

"Did you watch the interviews? She killed it," Mike said.

"Not what he means," Patrick said. "How did it go between you two?"

"Things are good," he said. "We had a lot of fun. The first night her old high school friend showed up at our dinner with her husband, and it was really weird."

"No one cares about that," Liam said, laughing.

"I'm not going into details with you guys," Mike said. "It's like talking to her brothers. But things are good. That reporter guy is annoying."

"You keep changing the subject," Patrick said. "But you mean Dermott? He can be a lot."

"I'd say," Liam said. "He follows her around to the point that it's creepy. It's been going on for years now, and no one can get rid of him."

"What are the odds that he was the one who freaked her out before she came out here? Leaving the flowers and notes?" Mike asked the question that had been on his mind since seeing the reporter in New York. His interest in Natalie seemed to go beyond professional, and Mike wasn't sure what to do about it.

"Maybe run it by JJ," Patrick suggested. "I honestly can't see him doing that. He definitely has a thing for her, but he seems to want the story more than her, if that makes sense. She's pretty private and avoids the press most of the time, but she's always been kind to him. I think him latching on to her has more to do with his paycheck than malice, but I could be wrong."

Liam agreed, but Mike still sent a text to JJ to share the thought. It was worth having a professional look into it, especially since the guy didn't seem willing to leave town on his own.

***

He arrived at the gym a few minutes before his appointment with Ben and Stella, allowing him time to pop in on his gym manager to check in. Ashley was behind her desk in her small office, dressed for a workout.

"Hey," he said, leaning a shoulder against the door frame. "How's it going?"

"Good," she said. "Welcome back. Did you have a nice trip?"

"We did," he said. "It was quick, but good to see Nat back in her element."

"I watched the interviews," she said. "You're going to get a little attention now because of it."

"I know. We talked to her press team last night for a long time. For now, it seems better to just ignore it."

"What do you want to do about the reporters calling here for you?"

"Is that happening a lot?" He was shocked, no one had said anything to him.

"Yes," she said, nodding. "I didn't want to bother you with it, but we were getting five to ten calls a day before the interviews. Yesterday was even worse."

"I'm sorry," he said. "I can have the calls directed to a call center and filtered if that would help?"

"Let's give it a few days and see if it dies down," she suggested. "I have the calls coming in here, so the front desk doesn't get overwhelmed. I'm making quick work of figuring out if they are an actual client or a reporter."

"Just say the word if you want it to change," he said. "And thank you for covering my clients yesterday."

"That's never a problem," she said. "Nice to see you take a couple days off for once."

He laughed and looked over to see Ben coming in the front door. "My next client is here. I'll talk to you later." She waved and went back to her computer as he walked toward Ben.

"Hey," he said. "No Stella again?"

"She went to Boston with her sister," he said, sounding annoyed. "No notice or anything, just told me two days ago she needed some girl time. I've barely heard from her since she went."

"That's not like her," Mike said.

"Not at all. Don't get me started," Ben grumbled.

"You miss her," Mike said, smiling at him.

"Of course I do," Ben said. "Come on, make me so tired I'll be able to sleep tonight without her next to me."

Mike got him set up on a treadmill for a quick warmup before moving over to the weights. Ben worked in a stony silence for the first half of the session before sighing loudly.

"I'm used to her being around," Ben said. "She makes my life easier. I think I take her for granted, and that's why she went away."

"I see Stella as someone who shows her love by taking care of those around her," Mike said. "You know how they talk about love languages? I think that would be hers."

"That doesn't mean she wouldn't get sick of taking care of an old grump like me."

"You're hardly old," Mike said with a laugh. "And I never see you as grumpy, at least until today."

"You in love with that nice Natalie?"

The sudden shift of conversation caught Mike off guard, and it took him a second to respond. "I don't know," he finally said. "Maybe."

"There's no maybe about love, Mike. It's either all in or not," Ben said. "It seems like she has a lot going on in her life. As you know, we never know what curves are ahead for ourselves or anyone else. You might not want to be caught up thinking for too long and miss your chance."

"I'm not sure if I've ever been in love," he admitted. "I've said it to women before, but now that I'm with Nat, it changes things. Gives me a different perspective."

"That doesn't mean what you felt for the ones before wasn't important," Ben said. "Don't diminish other relationships for this one. It's okay to have loved more than one person in your lifetime, and it's okay for it to feel different every time."

Mike knew Ben spoke from experience, having been widowed when his three boys were very young. "You're right," he said. "I feel bad that I even said that. It's just that everything with Nat is so all-encompassing, if that makes sense. I want to be with her all the time, and I think about her constantly. I see something that would make her laugh, so I want to tell her right away. Or I worry about her and want to check in or have something on my mind that I want to talk to her about. I'm going on too much, but you know what I mean."

"I sure do," Ben agreed. "She seems like a nice person, and she's had a hard time. I'm glad you can be there for her. It sounds like you have the right reasons to be around her, so enjoy it. See where it takes you. I've made a lot of good and a lot more stupid decisions by following my heart, but I don't regret a one of them."

"Good advice," Mike said. "Now, should I help you figure out how to win Stella back?"

"Oh, she never stays mad for long, if that's what's happening here," Ben said. "One thing I've never had to doubt is that woman's love for me. I just need to figure out the best way to get her to come home."

"We can talk it over while you do some curls," Mike said. He selected the weights off the rack and handed them to Ben, catching a glimpse of Dermott walking in the door as he did. Mike was about to excuse himself to go deal with it when Ashley marched out of the office and turned the man around, escorting him back outside in record time. He needed to give her a bonus, Mike decided, grinning as he watched.

***

"Miguel." His mom's voice came through the speaker of his truck, her tone and the use of his formal name making him wince.

Rosalita Collins was upset with him for something, and he would never not be afraid of his mom.

"Hi, mom," he said. "How are you?"

"None of that nonsense," she said. "Why am I finding out more about your love life from the magazines than from your own mouth?"

"Mama—"

"Don't you mama me," she warned him. "I'm not going to be sweet-talked."

"I was just going to say that half of what you're seeing probably isn't even true," he tried. "You know magazines will say anything to sell a copy."

"I have people calling me too," she said. "Reporters asking me for pictures of you as a young boy or wanting to know more about you. One of them invited me to dinner at a fancy restaurant, but your father said no to that."

"If you want to go to a fancy restaurant, I'll send you to one," he said. "I'd appreciate if you didn't talk to reporters. They'll move on soon enough."

"Miguel," she said, her voice softer now. "Is she worth it? All this attention and them digging into your life? I know how you hated the attention when you were in the NFL."

"That was nothing compared to this," he said with a sigh. "They barely paid any attention to me. I was lucky to have some high-profile guys on the team who took the heat off me. No one cared about the big guy on the offensive line."

"I did," she said.

"Other than you," he said, making sure the eye roll didn't make its way to his voice. "You know what I mean."

"I do, which is why I'm asking again if she's worth it?"

He paused, wanting to convey his thoughts so that his mom would understand. His parents had been married a long time, and he admired the love they showed each other every day. He had grown up feeling secure in knowing his parents were in a strong relationship, and it had made him want the same for himself. "I think she is, mom. She really is a remarkable person. You'll see."

"Will I? Is that an invitation for your dad and I to come meet her?" she asked. "We could make it there this weekend."

"No," he said quickly. "Let's give it a little more time, okay? Patrick is planning a big fundraiser in March, why don't you come over for that instead? You'll be able to meet Nat and see some of your favorite celebrities."

"That's a long way off," she said. "Are you sure we can't come sooner? I miss my baby."

"I miss you too, mom. Even though we FaceTime and talk all the time, so you make it hard to miss you."

"You'll miss me when I'm gone," she said. "You never know when our last conversation will be."

"That's a horrible thing to say."

"I speak the truth," she said. "You know my friend Meryl? Her husband just keeled over the other day. Gone in a second. You just never know what life will bring. I have a physical coming up next week. Who knows what they could find."

"You're perfectly healthy and you know it," he said. "Are you doing the exercise routine I sent you? Both you and dad?"

"We do. I'm more flexible than he is, if you want to know the truth. And I think I could lift much heavier weights, but you insist I stay with those little ones," she said with a sniff.

"You aren't trying to bulk up, you're just trying to keep everything working," he said. "You're one broken hip away from the nursing home."

She gasped loudly. "I can't believe you just said that," she said, then laughed. "I guess it's what I deserve, after all I just said to you."

"I've got to run, mama. I'll call you later," he promised. "Love you."

"I love you too. Please be careful," she said.

She clicked off, and he was left in silence to consider her words. He knew she was overly protective of him and his siblings and would have been happy to have them all still under her roof. Each week when he played football, she had worried about him, and he knew from his siblings that she watched games through her fingers. When he was injured the last time and was being carted off the field on the back of a golf cart, he could feel her eyes on him the whole way. She was a big reason he had chosen retirement over trying to get back out there, because he knew she would never ask him to stop playing but would continue to worry.

Now her worries were focused on his relationship with Natalie, and he knew she would stew over that until they met. If he knew her at all, he would guess she was watching Nat's movies and reading every bit of press about her, and he mentally kicked himself for not discouraging that. The press had not been as favorable towards Natalie as her male costars, and he knew it was all lies. She was nothing like what they painted her, and he needed his family to know that. But calling his mother right back would show his cards too soon. He needed to wait and figure out how best to approach it. Without his mother sensing that he was already in love with a woman she hadn't met yet.

Chapter 18

Natalie had enjoyed a quiet day back in Vermont, nestled on her couch with Midnight for most of the day. It amazed her how much she had missed the puppy while she was in New York, and the feeling seemed reciprocal. They were content watching Bravo when Holly knocked on the door midafternoon before letting herself in.

"I can't believe this is unlocked," Holly said as she walked in. "You never leave it open."

"I went out a few hours ago to get a cup of coffee from the main kitchen," Nat explained. "I ran out and didn't feel like going into town. When I came back in, I decided to test myself and leave it unlocked."

"No one out there would hurt you, and they wouldn't let a stranger in," Holly said. "How did you feel?"

"Nervous for the first hour," she admitted. "But then we settled in for a Below Deck marathon and I forgot about it until you just came in. That's progress."

"It sure is," Holly exclaimed. "I'm proud of you."

"If all I need to do to get praise is leave a door unlocked, I should have started a long time ago," she said with a laugh.

"You know this is a big deal," Holly chided her. "Don't put yourself down. Every little step is one closer to being back to yourself. Speaking of, I need the full update of New York, but I'm not alone. All the girls want to hear about your trip. I told them we would meet them at the Palace."

"I'm not even dressed," Nat said, looking down at her leggings and baggy sweater.

"Not right this instant," Holly said. "I know you better than that. We'll go down to meet them at five."

"Which gives me about an hour?" Nat glanced at her watch and noted the time.

"Yes, but for the record, you look amazing just as you are. You don't need to dress up for us or even put makeup on."

"What are you wearing?"

"I'm changing out of scrubs, that's for sure," Holly said, gesturing to the work clothes she was wearing. "But I don't want to get dressed up. I'll either be wearing jeans or leggings and a sweater. You can stay casual, I promise."

"I'll see," she promised. "I'll be ready in an hour. Do you want me to drive?"

"No," Holly said quickly. "Not to be rude, but your driving leaves something to be desired. I'll drive us all down, and if we need to leave a car there, Liam can take me in the morning to pick it up."

"Sounds good," Nat said. "And I'm not insulted. I don't drive much anymore, so I know I can be frazzled behind the wheel."

"Trust me, if I could have a driver everywhere, I would be too," Holly said. "I'll see you in an hour."

Natalie went to her closet and examined the options. During her time in Windsor Peak, she had moved from risqué outfits to tame clothes that fit in with the town but still made her feel good. What Holly didn't realize was that she didn't dress for the other women, or for the crowd. She dressed to make herself feel confident. For her, clothes were a way to put on the persona that she needed to be out in the public eye. Bold clothes made her feel brave, skimpier or tight outfits made her feel sexy, and high-end fabrics made her feel worthy. It was something she should probably examine with Dr. Jones, because she should be able to throw on jeans and a sweater and feel good about herself, but it was more of a struggle. All the years of standing in a costumer's office, having every little thing she wore critiqued, had made her more sensitive than she would like to be. Finally, choosing a pair of butter soft, suede leggings and a warm cashmere sweater, she felt the perfect combination of confidence and sexiness while still looking tame enough for Vermont.

She applied just enough makeup with expert strokes, having learned from the best. Debating over her hair, she finally opted for a high ponytail, which saved her from having to get the curling iron out. Once equipped with her armor, she felt ready to face the public again. Just as she slid on knee-high boots and grabbed her jacket, she heard a knock on the door and Liam popped his head in.

"Hey," he said. "I wasn't invited to the festivities. Want me to take Midnight while you're gone?"

"That would be great," she said. "And if I'm out late, maybe you can keep her for the night?"

"Sure," he said. "We love having her. Holly wants to go down to the rescue soon to find a dog for us, but we just haven't had the time. Tomorrow, hopefully."

"Oh, that would be great. Then Midnight will have a playmate," she said. "You have a key to this door in case you need to get her food and crate?"

"I do," he said. "Have fun tonight."

"Thanks." She stretched up and gave him a kiss on the cheek. "For everything, really. You've been such a good friend to me over the last few months."

"Not before that?" he asked in a teasing tone.

"Well, back then you were either trying to sleep with me or running off to some party with Zane," she reminded him. "Being with Holly has really helped settle you down."

"When you find the right fit, it just works," he said. "I'm the luckiest man in the world that she took the time to see who I am on the inside. I made such a bad impression on her to start, and she was still able to fall in love with me. She made me want to be a better person, as cheesy as that sounds."

"You're a good guy. You just needed to find the right person to grow up for," she said.

"True," he said with a nod. "And I'm hoping that you found your person. I like him a lot. He's a solid dude."

"Thanks," she said. "We'll see what happens. I'm a lot, as you know."

"Nat." He waited until she met his eyes before he spoke again. "You are not too much. I've heard you say that for years, and I want you to know it's not true. You're loving and kind and fun and smart, all the good things. Just because the press has painted you as this seductress who is difficult doesn't mean it's true."

"Are you sure?" Her voice was barely a whisper, but he had just said her deepest fears out loud, and she was shocked at his insightfulness.

"More than sure. I'm positive. You're one of the best people I know, and if the world doesn't see that, it's their loss." He hugged her tightly. "And I think Mike sees it, maybe even more than anyone else."

"Thanks, Liam. I love you," she said, wiping away a tear.

"Hey, I'm taken," he said. He backed up with his hands up, making her laugh.

"You're still a goof, but I do love you. Like a brother," she said.

"Love you too. You're the little sister I never thought I wanted," he said. "Get out of here, go have fun."

She walked through the busy center of the house, where she was stopped three times by young students racing through the house. One wanted a book suggestion, another asked her if she would help them with the play they were putting on, and a third complimented her boots. By the time she got to Holly's car, she was laughing and had almost forgotten the nerves about the night out.

"What's so funny?" Holly asked, clipping on her seat belt.

"I just made the mistake of walking through the house to get to your car," she said. "It's busier than Grand Central Station in there."

"I know, but it's so fun," Holly said. "Except when kids get sent in for quiet time because they were in trouble or if they get hurt. I can't handle hearing them cry."

"Luckily, that didn't happen today," she said. "I got roped into helping with the play they are putting together."

"Oh, so did Liam," Holly said, laughing. "He's horrified they don't want him to star in it, or even direct. They want his help to build the sets."

"I think I'm going to be in charge of costumes," Nat shared. "Which is fine. I love being around the clothes."

Holly drove through the streets to the small downtown area, pulling into a parking spot right in front of the restaurant. "This was lucky," she said. "I think it's going to be a good night."

They walked in to find the rest of their friends already seated in a small area tucked in the corner, designed by Kendra for groups to sit and chat. Comfortable furniture, a low coffee table, and a half wall gave it privacy. During the day, moms could sit and relax with lunch while their young children played with the small selection of toys Kendra kept tucked into a toy chest in the corner. At night, book clubs frequently took over the area, or groups of friends wanting to relax. The other women had saved a seat in the corner for Natalie, so she would be hidden from view but also able to see anyone who approached, and she appreciated their thoughtfulness.

Kendra, Shea, and Emma were already sipping cocktails as Holly and Nat pulled off their jackets. Holly gave her sister Shea a hug and took the seat next to her before looking around. "Where's Zoe?" Holly asked Emma.

"She's making us food," Emma shared. "She doesn't trust anyone else to get it just right. Once she brings it out, she'll sit and relax."

"Good," Kendra said. "She works way too much."

"Pot, meet kettle," Shea said, smiling kindly at her sister-in-law. "Maybe you two could learn to relax together."

"Hey, I just took maternity leave," Kendra said. "And I've cut back on hours. Having Des work at the bar has freed up most of my nights. I thought he would only want to do one or two, but apparently, he's having so much fun that he works most nights."

"It helps that he's right upstairs," Emma said. "If he wasn't working, he'd probably be sitting at the bar."

"True, that was my problem when Calle and I lived in the apartment upstairs." Natalie knew that Kendra and her daughter Calle had moved into the Burrows family home after she and Dad had been married, leaving the apartment upstairs empty. JJ's twin siblings, Desmond and Finley, had moved in, allowing Des to help Kendra out. "It's hard to be up there, hearing all the laughter, and not want to be part of the fun."

"And for a single guy, it would be twice as hard," Shea said with a laugh. "Des seems to have a regular following of single women who probably double your bar profits now."

"That's a good point," Kendra said. "I wasn't back there flirting the way he is. He is certainly good for business."

"At least you weren't until Dan came back," Shea corrected her.

"Would you call that flirting?" Kendra countered. "I thought of it more as avoiding."

"Whatever you say," Shea said with a laugh. "It all ended up good in the end."

"That it did," Kendra agreed.

They all looked up as Zoe approached, carrying a tray of food. "I made a bunch of appetizers, thinking you all didn't want full meals," she said. "Dig in."

"This is enough food for a football team," Holly said.

"I had some new ideas I wanted to try out, and who better to taste test them than my friends?" Zoe sat next to her sister and started handing out plates and napkins. "I'll know if you're lying to me about liking something."

"We would never dare," Emma said. "I love everything you make."

"You have to say that, we're related," Zoe said. "It's the same with JJ. He has to love it because we're married. But everyone else here will be more honest."

"Speaking of," Holly said. "We need to get the scoop on Nat and Mike, and the trip to New York. How are things going between you two?"

"That was not a smooth transition," Natalie said with a laugh. "But I know you've been patient way too long. New York was good. I was nervous, and it was a lot to overcome, but being on familiar sets and around hosts I've met before made it easier. The night after the interviews I needed a long time to decompress, so we spent the night there just relaxing in my apartment rather than flying back."

"Relaxing is good," Shea said encouragingly. "And you faced your fears, so you deserve that time. I'm so happy for you."

"I'm definitely not back to myself yet, but it's good to feel like I'm making progress," Nat said. "I have a therapist appointment tomorrow, so I'll see what she thinks. I took her challenge and went a step further."

"That's right. Your first date with Mike was the challenge, right?" Holly asked.

"Yes," Nat said with a nod. "We went for massages and then dinner."

"How was that?" Zoe asked, pausing in her quest to fill her plate.

"It was amazing," she admitted. "Ever since New Year's Eve, he's been less shy with me. For months, he would clam up as soon as I came into the room. Even after the incident, he would ask me if I was okay, but I could tell I made him nervous. Whatever clicked for him that night, it really changed things."

"It must have been the kiss," Holly said.

"You kissed that night? I didn't know that," Zoe said. "I must have missed it that night."

"You were all busy at midnight," Nat said. "But yes, he kissed me, or I kissed him, and things changed. I know it sounds cheesy, but the kiss rocked me in ways I have never experienced before. And it's only gotten better since."

"That's amazing," Shea said. "I'm so happy for you both."

"Me too," Emma said. "Mike is a stand-up guy, and obviously I think the world of you, so I couldn't be happier. And it seems like he makes you feel safe, which is even better."

"He does," she said. "He literally put himself between me and a gun. Who does that? Especially because I was almost a stranger to him. And now he's the perfect blend of protective without being overbearing. It's like he just knows what I need."

"He's been paying attention," Emma said. "Do you see this working out long term? Please say yes."

Natalie laughed. "I don't know. My life isn't here, and his is. That's a lot to overcome."

"You're talking to two people who already do that," Emma said, pointing to herself and Holly. "Patrick's life was in California, and so was Liam's. We've been able to adjust, and they seem happier having this be their home base."

"Could you do the same?" Holly asked. "Live here when you're not shooting? Or would you get bored?"

Natalie glanced around at the circle of women who had become her closest friends, far more than anyone in Hollywood. Or anyone since she was a young girl, really. Then she thought of Mike, and his willingness to work through her troubles with her, and the other men who had surrounded her with support and friendship. "I can't imagine leaving any of you," she admitted. "I feel like this is home now. I just can't screw things up with Mike, because then I'd have to leave."

"Don't say that," Holly said. "First of all, you won't. That man is crazy about you. Secondly, this is your home, as long as you want it to be. And we will all be there for you, no matter where you live."

Natalie nodded, unable to speak. The kindness she had been shown since she arrived in Vermont, and especially since she had been held at gunpoint, was unlike anything she had ever experienced before. She was so grateful to Patrick for sharing his inner circle with her, and no matter what they all said now, she wouldn't do anything that would risk them being torn apart. Protecting her friends was even more important to her than protecting her own heart.

Chapter 19

The phone he had just pulled out of his pocket chimed with an incoming text, and Mike grinned when he saw it was from Natalie. He had been just about to reach out to her himself, so she saved him from debating what to say. It didn't matter how much time they spent together, or how well he felt like he knew her, he would probably always be a little tongue tied around her. And that was okay with him, because she was worth fighting through the discomfort he felt as long as she wanted to spend time with him.

He read her text quickly and laughed. She had asked why she hadn't seen his house yet, and he responded asking her if now was a good time. He kept his house tidy, and the housekeeper who came once a week to do the bathrooms and floors had been by the day before, so he knew things would look good. He hadn't really thought about inviting her over, just because she seemed so content in her own space. But if she wanted to see his house, he was game. Her response came in immediately asking him to pick her up at the Palace when he was done for the night, and he told her he was on his way.

Lights flashed behind him as he drove too fast towards town, and he cursed himself under his breath. His rush to get to her had made him get pulled over, which meant it was going to take twice as long. He needed to remember to be patient, he thought as he rolled the window down. He recognized the officer as Jeff, a good friend of JJ's, and sighed with relief.

"Hey, Mike," Jeff said easily. "You're going a little fast, and you rolled through that stop sign back there. Everything okay?"

"Sorry, Jeff," he said. "I'm on my way to pick up Nat, and I just lost myself. I should have been paying better attention. I have no excuse."

"Nice of you to own it. We don't get that much," Jeff said with a smile. "Danielle would kill me if I got between you two lovebirds. Just drive a little slower, okay?"

"Will do, tell your wife I said thanks," he said with a laugh.

"JJ told me about your concerns regarding that reporter," Jeff shared. "We're all keeping an eye on him, and so far, all he's done is ask a lot of questions."

Mike thanked him for the update before driving at a much slower pace towards town. He parked and ran across the street, grateful that none of JJ's officers were nearby to see him jaywalking. Inside, the restaurant was packed, but he could see the women in the corner. He waved to Desmond and some familiar faces at the bar before heading to where he knew Nat was.

"Fancy meeting you here," Emma said in a teasing voice. "Your Natalie radar is strong."

"I texted him," Natalie said. "Sorry, I didn't mean to disrupt girls' night."

"No worries," Shea said, reaching over to pat Natalie's hand. "Mike, grab a drink and sit with us. We have to polish off all this food, so you're just in time."

He went back to the bar and returned with a beer, glancing around at the full chairs. Deciding to be bold, he went to where Natalie sat and gestured for her to stand up. Once she was, he took her spot in the chair and pulled her down on his lap. The women around them all sighed.

"That's romantic," Zoe said. "I need to see where JJ is."

"Don't all go running off when I just got here," he said. "I wanted to get the gossip."

"It's all about you two," Emma said with a laugh. "You're taking the pressure off the rest of us."

Zoe passed Mike a heaping plate full of appetizers and then sat back in her chair. "I'll have the kitchen make you a full meal to bring home if you want," she offered.

"This is fine, thanks," he said. "I'm glad I caught you all together. I was talking to Ashely earlier, and she mentioned wanting to run a self-defense class. I said I thought I could convince all of you to attend."

"Absolutely," Kendra said quickly. "After getting knocked around by my ex-husband, I want make sure I can protect myself and my kids. I took a class a few years ago, but I'd love to do another one."

"I'm in," Zoe said. "Maybe then JJ will relax about me walking to the car or the house alone at night."

The women all agreed and started talking about how they could utilize their skills in the drop-off line at school, but he felt the tension easing out of Natalie's body. She hadn't responded about the class, and he had felt her tense up, so he didn't want to push her. As her friends agreed, he knew she was coming around to the idea.

He finished the plate of food and his beer quickly, placing the empties on the table next to him. "Want to get out of here?" he said quietly into Nat's ear, earning him a nod.

They both stood and said their goodbye's quickly, and he helped her into her coat. "Anyone else need a ride home?"

They all shook their heads and went back to their conversation, so he took Natalie's hand and led her out of the restaurant to his truck. Although heads had turned when they made their way out, no one stopped them and he hadn't seen any pictures snapped, so he hoped this would stay out of the press.

"Do we need to run to your place and get Midnight?" he asked as he put the truck into drive.

"No, she's with Liam now, and he said he could keep her overnight if needed," she said.

"He was trying to plant the seed early for me? I have to go easy on him tomorrow."

"No, I asked him," she said. "Feel free to work him hard."

"You did?" he tried to hide the surprise he felt, but it was a nice shock to know that she had planned to end her night with him.

"Yes," she said with a nod. "I hope that's okay."

"Of course it is," he said quickly. "I was just about to text you and see if I could come over when I got your message. It's always okay."

"Same." The one word from her lips brought him such joy. He had to look out his window to hide the big grin that was on his face. Getting excited over her signs that she had feelings for him would never get old, he decided.

He pulled into his driveway nervous and excited for her to see where he lived. His house was nestled in a quiet neighborhood a few blocks from the main street area. His street contained six houses, all set on an acre or more and set back from the road. His house was on the end, surrounded by three acres of open land. He had a pool for the few months of a year that it was warm enough to swim, a putting green, and a pickleball court, still leaving plenty of empty space around him. He enjoyed the seclusion, but also liked knowing there were neighbors close enough if he ever had an issue.

A two-level craftsman style house, the exterior was done in deep blue siding with stone on the base. Three garage bays were at the end of the driveway, but he parked outside so that Natalie could enter the house from the front door for the first time. Double doors opened to the foyer, with his office behind a sliding barn door on the left, followed by a staircase. On the right, a formal dining room mainly collected dust, but looked nice thanks to the recent visit from the housekeeper. They took a few steps in, and the house opened up in front of them. He watched as she took in the granite countertops and shining appliances in the kitchen before turning to the great room, where plush couches faced a fireplace and TV.

"Come on, I'll show you the rest," he said. He pointed out a butler's pantry that led to a mudroom, where a door opened to the garage. He opened another double French door off the great room, which led to an outdoor area complete with two sofas, a fireplace, an outdoor TV, and a full outdoor kitchen. When she shivered in the cold, he brought her back inside and showed her a large bedroom on the first floor. "I keep this one for my parents. As they get older, the stairs will get harder, so I wanted to have a nice bedroom down here for them."

"This is beautiful," she said, peeking into the attached bathroom. "They must come a lot to take advantage."

"They sure do," he said with a laugh. "I had to fight to keep them from coming this weekend. "Let's go upstairs first, and then I'll show you my favorite place."

He followed her up the stairs, where he showed her two more guest bedrooms, and then his master. He flipped a switch as they walked in to light the fireplace, and she smiled at him. She took in the king-size bed and then looked into the bathroom and sighed.

"This is my dream bathroom," she said. "I never want to leave here."

The room was as long as the bedroom, with two large windows facing the mountains. A large jacuzzi tub was under a window, between two sets of sinks. On the opposite wall, a sauna and shower were behind a glass door, the toilet hidden behind another door. A vanity and bench were against the third wall, where Natalie sat down.

"That's never been used," he said. "I tried to put my deodorant over there and it just felt wrong."

"It's perfect," she said, flipping the lights on. "Oh, this is heaven. And I miss having a bathtub."

"Do you want to take a bath?" he offered, gesturing toward it. "I can run it for you, if you want."

She looked to be considering the offer and then shook her head. "As much as I would love to have you draw me a bath, because that is the most romantic thing anyone has ever offered, I'd rather see what you consider the best part of the house."

"Oh, right," he said. "Follow me."

He jogged down the stairs and then opened the door to the basement, gesturing for her to go first. At the bottom of the stairs, a large room held a full bar, a fireplace, an enormous TV and a sectional sofa. Another room held exercise equipment, a water cooler, and a small shelf that held towels.

"Of course, this is your favorite," she said with a smile. "A true man cave."

"It really is," he said. "I have the guys come over and watch football, and this is where I spend most Sundays just lazing around."

"I can see why," she said. She sank into the sectional, pushing the button to lift the recliner portion. "This is comfortable, I like this room. I also love the outdoor space and can't wait to be able to use that in the spring. But the bathroom wins the prize for me. I could happily live in there."

He had to stop himself from asking her to do just that, move in with him immediately. It was way too soon to think that way, and he had to get it together. Just because he couldn't imagine his life without her in it didn't mean she was on the same page, and he didn't want to scare her off. It was enough that she was talking about still being around in a few months, when they could sit outside. Focusing on the moment at hand, he cleared his throat and gestured toward the door. "Want to go back up to the kitchen and open a bottle of wine?"

"If you insist," she said, smiling at him. "I love your house." She kissed him and then ran off down the stairs, leaving him to chase her like the lovesick puppy that he was.

***

Their phones both started beeping an hour later, almost at the same time. Natalie frowned as she looked at him, then back to where their phones were nestled in his oven. "It's weird, right? We don't get this many text messages after eight."

"No, we're officially in the 'don't bother me after Jeopardy phase of life," he said. "Should I get them?"

"I guess so," she said. "Something big must be happening."

He retrieved their phones but didn't open his until he had handed hers off, and heard her gasp. "You have got to be kidding me."

He swiped the phone open and saw multiple texts from friends with a link to the same article, which accused Natalie of having an affair with Brie's husband. Pictures of the four of them at dinner in New York were posted, including a closeup that made it look as though Natalie and Austin were kissing at the table when they were left alone. They had placed a glamourous picture of Natalie next to a picture of a tear-stained Brie, the other woman appearing soft and vulnerable. The headline claimed Natalie had swept into town and ruined her friend's life, announcing she was having an affair with Austin. Mike scrolled through the article quickly, finding that he was described as her bodyguard and not her boyfriend. The reporters suggested that Natalie had been using her hired help to make Austin jealous.

"Did she agree to this?" he asked, holding his phone up.

Natalie looked at him with a stunned expression on her face, then held up her finger as her phone rang. He listened to her half of the conversation as she paced in front of him. "Hi. I know. None of it's true, you know that. No. No. No, I don't want to do that. It's not fair to him. Please, just make this go away."

"Your publicist?"

"Yes," she said, nodding. She sank back down on the couch next to him before getting up and pacing again. "Why would she do this?"

"You think she was a part of it?"

"Of course she was," she said. "Look at the picture. She was right in front of him. And she left the table when you did. I have to wonder if that was intentional to let him try to make a move."

"That's disgusting," he said. "But we know it's not true. You pushed him away. Even the photographer must have seen that."

"It doesn't go as well with the story to say some random sleazeball got shot down by me," she said. "It sells magazine to portray me as a vixen, destroying relationships."

"But that's not true. Just put out a statement."

"I don't even want to acknowledge it. It just adds fuel to the fire, you know? And besides, no one would believe me."

"What does your team want to do?" he asked gently, knowing whatever he hadn't heard was upsetting to her.

"They want us to go public," she said. "Make a big fuss, shove you in their faces. But I won't do that."

"Why not?"

"Because it's not fair to you," she said. "We've barely just begun dating, and now I'm going to have you face the media like that? You've seen how they'll dig into your life at just the suggestion that we're involved. Imagine what it will be like if it's confirmed?"

"Well," he said, pulling her closer to him. "We haven't just started dating. This has been going on since November. I'm just not good at it and it's going painfully slow."

"You aren't good at what?" She looked confused, making him laugh.

"I wasn't, but I'm getting better. At talking to you, making it clear that I want to be with you," he explained. "I don't think you've missed it, but I've been crazy about you since before you even came to town. When you used to FaceTime with Patrick during workouts, it made me crazy. I can't tell you how many hours I spent in cold plunge tubs, or running on a treadmill at a ridiculous rate, just to get you off my mind."

"That's so sweet," she said softly. "I didn't know you took me seriously."

"I was terrified of you," he admitted. "It didn't get better until New Year's Eve, when I saw the real you. Although that day, when we went riding, before the gun? I was going to ask you out that night. But then everything happened, and I felt like I lost you. I'm not making any sense."

"You are," she said, encouraging him to continue.

"Anyway, I'm crazy about you," he blurted out. "Completely, madly, all-consuming, crazy. I can't stop thinking about you. I just had to stop myself from asking you to move into my bathroom. That's how crazy."

She laughed and then leaned over and kissed him. "I might have taken you up on that."

"It's been four months, according to my math," he went on. "I know we've only been on a few official dates, but we've been together just about every day for four months, in some way. And the last few weeks have been the best of my life, being with you every day and waking up with you in the morning. Which all goes to say, I have no problem being dragged in the press, as long as it means I'm with you."

"I have been enjoying just keeping this between us," she said. "And the rest of the town, of course. But once it's out in the world, everything we do will be commented on and criticized."

"Who cares?" he challenged her. "We don't have to listen to them. I don't ever look at comments on social media, or read tabloids. I don't think you should look at it as allowing the world into our relationship. It's just us, living our lives and not hiding. We can do that and ignore any noise that's created, can't we?"

"Let me think on it, okay?" She kissed him again. "Maybe you can take my mind off it for now. Tomorrow, I'll deal with this."

Chapter 20

Natalie woke up as the sun was rising, unable to sleep any longer. It had been a long time since she had felt a betrayal as deep as what she was experiencing at Brie's hands, and she needed to get to the bottom of it. She dressed quickly and then headed down the stairs, only to realize that she didn't have a car. A note on the counter from Mike brought a smile to her face, as if he had predicted this moment. *I loaded the coffee maker for you, so it's ready to go. These keys are for the Jeep in the garage. Just hit the button on the visor to close the door once you pull out. I'll call you later.*

She made the coffee and sipped it for a moment, studying the family pictures he had on shelves around his great room. Early shots of him and his siblings, pictures of him in a cap and gown with his parents on two different graduation days, and then of him on a football field with his entire family. It looked as though it was just after a Super Bowl win, and she made a mental note to ask him. They all looked loving and happy to be together, all wearing his jersey showing their support, and she realized she was excited to meet them.

Once she had finished her coffee, she rinsed out the cup and grabbed the keys, ready to figure out what was happening. Backing the Jeep out of the garage was scary, but once she was on the road, she enjoyed driving it through town. Most of the businesses were still dark, just the coffee shop and bakery had lights on this early. She eased down the street carefully and made her way up to Liam's house, where she let herself in. Only once she was in her own space did she pull out her phone and start scrolling through messages again.

On Instagram, she was being portrayed as a home wrecker, a sex fiend diva willing to stop at nothing to get what she wanted. Comment after comment slamming her for an act that she hadn't even committed and was completely out of character for her. She had never once felt even remotely tempted to engage with a man who was in a relationship already, never mind married. And she certainly had her share of them who had hit on her over the years, so she had plenty of experience turning them down. The sight of a wedding ring on a man's finger as he tried to proposition her was enough to turn her stomach, and being accused of it was just as bad.

It was five a.m. in California when her phone rang, and her publicist's name appeared. Phyllis had been with her long enough to know that she would be freaking out about this, and Nat was grateful that she had called so early.

"Morning," she said. "I'm sorry. I know you probably don't want to be up this early."

"Up? I haven't slept yet," Phyllis said. "And I'm in New York still, so it's not as bad as you think."

"What's the latest?" Natalie braced herself for the information, knowing it was going to be difficult to hear.

"The husband is doubling down on this," Phyllis said. "Nothing more from the wife. I have no idea where this story came from, but I'm putting pressure on the head of that newspaper to tell me. From what I can gather, it was Austin or Brie. My money is on Austin."

"Why? Why would he do this to me? And to his wife?"

"He's drowning in debt," Phyllis said. "He made several bad decisions that cost investors millions, and himself almost everything. He was about to be fired from his job, and this may save him, because it's bringing publicity to the agency. Did he solicit you for money?"

"Both Mike and I," Natalie said. "He wanted to handle our investments."

"And you said no?"

"Of course, I did. So did Mike. There was no way we would have trusted that guy with a hundred dollars, never mind more," Nat said. "You think this is retribution for saying no?"

"I'm not sure if it's that, if he sold the story, or if he hopes to make money off of it," Phyllis shared. "But I'll keep working on it. In the meantime, I need to know what you're willing to do. Obviously, a well-placed picture of you and Mike would go a long way. We don't have to say much, just make it clear that you are involved with someone, and you would never do this."

"People won't believe that," she said quietly. "I've been portrayed as this for so long, it's what they expect. Making it look like I was with Patrick for years helped my image, and kept men away, but I was still the trampy girl that he slummed with. I don't know why my male counterparts can do whatever they please and still be considered good guys, but I can't even have a fake relationship on screen without being a slut. It's infuriating."

"I get that," Phyllis said, her tone soothing. "But we aren't reinventing the wheel here. The only way to fully soften your image is to get married and have a baby, but you'll still have people who assume the worst of you. It's jealousy, and a whole lot of other things inside of people that they don't want to identify, so instead they look at you like that. I hate to say it, but society would rather believe someone as beautiful as you is evil than believe you have a good heart."

"Why can't that be true of Patrick, then?"

"I never said it was fair," Phyllis said. "I don't know why men get a pass when women don't, and I'll never understand it. All I can do is mitigate the situations as they arise to the best of my ability. I don't think you can ignore this. This man is doing everything he can to ruin your image, and I don't want it to cause problems in the first happy relationship I've ever seen you in. Let the world see you with Mike. Be proud of your love for him."

"We aren't quite there yet," Natalie admitted. "The love thing, I mean."

"I'm not going to bother asking you about your feelings, because you clearly aren't ready for them. But that man loves you with every fiber of his being," Phyllis said with a laugh. "He wears it all over his face. I was with you for a few hours in New York, and I saw that. You aren't a big enough fool to miss it."

"Phyllis, you know what I mean," she said. "Putting this out there on blast, it steals it from me. What if I am falling in love with him? And the internet makes it ugly?"

"You ignore the internet. People go there to be cruel, to say things they would never say to your face. It's fueled by unhappiness with their own lives, and jealousy. It's the worst of people," she said. "That's not a true mirror of who you are. Look around you, at the people who know you and care about you. Those are the only opinions that matter."

"Can I call you back in an hour?"

"Please," Phyllis said. "Not much longer. I need to know what our response is."

Natalie hung up and then hit the one number that was listed on her favorites page. When her mother's sleepy voice came on the phone, she started crying. "Mom, I'm sorry I woke you up."

"Honey, what's wrong?" The sound of sheets rustling and Marilyn whispering to Natalie's dad, Bruce, came through the phone.

"I don't know what to do."

"Are you in danger?"

"No, it's not like that," she said quickly. "Do you remember Brie, from high school?"

"Yes," her mom said. "She was just up to see you not long ago. You told me all about it."

Natalie quickly filled her mother in on the dinner in New York, and the accusations being thrown at her now. Her mom listened in patient silence, and Natalie heard the beep of the coffee maker starting as she finished her story.

"That is horrible," her mom said. "But as I've said to you for as many years as I can remember, you can't control what people think of you. You can only control what you think of yourself and how you conduct yourself. Did you do anything untoward with her husband?"

"Mom! No," Natalie nearly screeched. "You know me better than that."

"I do, yes. But it's nice to have you get mad," her mom said. "Stop looking at this as a perception of you. It's not. Only the narrow-minded people in the world will read one article and determine that you are guilty of this, especially when it's one person's claims and no evidence. I'm assuming your press team wants to attack this with guns blazing."

"Yes," she said. "They've calmed down enough to settle on just having a picture of Mike and I together circulate, without commenting on the story."

"What do you think of that?"

"I feel like I'm using him," she admitted.

"Do you care about him?"

"Very much," she said softly.

"He seems to be very protective of you, and willing to do whatever you want," her mom said. "I'm eager to meet him, but from what you've told me, he seems like the kind of person who would be unphased by any of this. Including having his picture come out with you. Especially considering there have been pictures of you two already, and lots of speculation about your relationship."

"They said he was my bodyguard in the article," Natalie said. "That was almost worse than saying I would have anything to do with Brie's husband. Insinuating that Mike is a paid employee, that feels wrong."

"Then you need to make a decision," her mom said gently. "What feels more wrong? Letting this story go unchallenged, and having Mike portrayed as an employee? Or conveniently sharing a big kiss in public that can circulate everywhere?"

"I feel like it cheapens what we're forming," she said. "I'm proud to be with him, and I love the way he looks at me. I don't want that to change."

"Will you be less proud of him if you're seen publicly with him?"

"Not at all," she said. "But I might be less proud of myself. You know they'll come after him. Every girl he's ever kissed will want to speak to the press or make a TikTok about him."

"That doesn't mean that it's true," her mom said. "Or change how you feel about each other. That's outside noise. You need to focus on the quiet."

Her father took the phone and chatted with her for a few minutes, wisely staying out of affairs of the heart. Before he hung up, he gave the phone back to her mom.

"Want us to come out there?" she offered.

"Not right now," she said. "There's a big fundraiser that Patrick is throwing in March. Why don't you come for that? I'll have my assistant make your travel arrangements."

"I look forward to meeting your Michael," her mom said.

"His name is actually Miguel," she said quickly. "But everyone calls him Mike."

"He gets more and more interesting as the days go on," Anna said with a laugh. "I'll talk to you later. We love you and we're proud of you. Don't worry about anything more than that."

She hung up and sat in silence for a minute before realizing she needed to call Phyllis back. Dialing quickly, she spoke the second the publicist was on the phone so that she wouldn't change her mind. "Tomorrow is Valentine's Day," she said. "I just looked at the calendar and saw it now. Book us at some super fancy spot where we'll be seen. If we need to fly to Boston, we can, but I'd rather stay around here. Dermott is still a pest if you need to use him."

"Not giving him this access," Phyllis said firmly. "I'm going to get him to leave, he must be desperate for a scoop if he's still hanging around there. To his credit, he didn't accuse you of having an affair with that Austin creep like the other reporters did, and he even said it was out of character for you. I'll throw him a bone and get him back to the west coast."

"That's true," Natalie said. "Are you sure we shouldn't just use him for this?"

"No," Phyllis said. "I think he's overplayed his hand regarding you, and I'd like a more respected publication. I'll text you the details. Want me to get legal involved in this Austin situation as well?"

"Yes, please," she said with a sigh. "I need to fight back."

"Consider it done," Phyllis said. "For the record, I confirmed that it's the husband who brought the story to the paper. No one has corroborated it, including Brie."

"How did they get the picture of her crying?"

"He gave it to them," Phyllis said. "He sounds like a really great guy. Let's make sure he gets what he deserves."

***

After having spent the entire day preparing all of the details for their big date, Natalie wasn't surprised when a rack of dresses arrived at her apartment early the next morning. She had called in a favor with a designer in Hollywood, who had immediately gotten dresses on a plane to be delivered to her. All she had to do now was choose one, and the rest would be sent back. They were almost all red, with a few pink and black options.

Holly knocked and came in, carrying a cup of coffee. "Oh, my. What are we doing?"

"I had these sent to me for my date with Mike tonight," she said. "I need something that will get me attention and also show the world that I'm with my Valentine."

"Anything you wear will get you attention," Holly said. "Try some on."

An hour later, she had selected the dress. It was red, form fitting at the top, with a skirt that swirled around her as she walked. The simple straps looked like roses, delicate against her skin and wrapping around her bare back.

Holly had been fingering a dress on the rack every time she came out of the bedroom to show off an option, and Natalie pointed at it. "You try that one on," she demanded.

"Oh, no. These are yours," Holly said.

"They are mine to give away, too. Try it on."

Holly beamed at her as she pulled the dress off the rack and disappeared into the bedroom, coming out with an even bigger smile on her face. "I'll pay you back, I swear," she said.

"You will not," Natalie insisted. "It was made for you. Make sure Liam takes you somewhere amazing."

"I will," Holly said. She scurried back into the bedroom and came back out into her street clothes. "I feel like I should go get my hair done or something."

"You don't have to go anywhere," Natalie said, checking her watch. "The glam squad will be here in two hours. They can do both of us."

"Are you sure?" Holly stared at her. "I've never done anything like this before."

"Enjoy it," Nat said. "It will make it more fun for me to have company to get ready with."

It would also keep her mind off the worry that she was subjecting Mike to unfair treatment by the press and his former fans. When she had texted him earlier asking if her plan was alright with him, he had responded quickly telling her whatever she decided was fine with him. She just hoped that he didn't end up regretting his trust in her. There was no turning back once he was officially recognized as her love interest, and she just prayed that the criticisms she had received over the years wouldn't impact him in a negative way. It was hard enough to withstand the hate that was sent her way, she couldn't handle it if he were to receive the same just for being associated with her. But for tonight, she would trust in the advice she was given and enjoy the time with him.

Chapter 21

Mike waited patiently in line at the florist along with half the male residents of Windsor Peak, all of whom had waited until the last minute to pick up their orders. Some poor fools hadn't ordered ahead and were being directed to the grocery store, leaving with their heads hanging, knowing they had messed up. Jake was three people in front of Mike and caught sight of him as he turned to leave.

"Hey," Jake said. He was holding two bouquets, one large and the other smaller. "You have plans with Nat tonight?"

"I do," he said. "What's with the two sets of flowers?"

"Both are for Shea, don't go spreading any rumors. One from me and the other is from Charlie," Jake explained. "I almost had to buy two more, for the baby from both of us, because Dan was getting Calle flowers. But I talked myself off the ledge. Izzie is too little to know what Valentine's Day is."

"No girlfriend for Charlie?"

"If there is, he can buy his own flowers," Jake said. "He had practice tonight, so I offered to pick these up for him. I'll stick them in the garage so he can surprise Shea when he gets home. Seeing their relationship develop is almost as good as having my son back in my life."

"I can imagine," Mike said. Everyone in town knew how rocky the relationship between Jake and Charlie had been when Jake returned from Afghanistan after years of service. It was nice to see the extra effort they were both putting into their family life.

The florist indicated for Mike to step up to the counter, so he wished Jake well and moved up to collect his flowers. When he had called two weeks prior, he had encouraged the florist to go big, and she obviously took him at his word. The other men in line started mumbling under their breath, one jokingly calling out that he was making the rest of them look bad. He laughed and headed out, only to stumble upon Dermott at the exit.

"Are those for Natalie?" he asked, snapping a picture of Mike holding the flowers.

"You must be a very brave man," Mike said in a low voice. "I told you to go away."

"No, you told me to stay away from her. I'm not anywhere near her right now, just asking you some questions. Now that Natalie's affair with her friend's husband has come out, people are confused about your relationship with her. Is it just as a bodyguard? Is there another woman in your life? Or are you pining away for Natalie?" The reporter pressed on as Mike pushed past and walked toward his truck. "What's the real story between Natalie and Austin?"

Mike unlocked the truck and placed the bouquet carefully on the passenger seat before making his way around the truck, careful to keep his mouth shut. He knew the other man was recording him, and he couldn't blow up on him as much as he wanted to. Best to remain silent and let the night speak for itself.

"Hey, man," Dermott tried again. "Throw me a bone. I've been stuck up here in Vermont trying to get the scoop for a while, and now all these other reporters are going to show up and trump me. At least admire my persistence."

Mike slammed the truck door and started it, pulling out of the space quickly before he could start asking his own questions. Was there a town full of people trying to get a look at Natalie? He frowned as he dialed JJ's number, drumming his fingers on the steering wheel while it rang.

"It's Valentine's Day and my wife goes to work in an hour," JJ said when he answered. "This better be important."

"Are there more reporters in town than just the Dermott guy?"

"How would I know?" JJ asked, then sighed. "I'll have someone check over at the Inn and I'll text you, okay?"

"Thanks. Sorry to have disturbed you," Mike said, clicking end on the call. Nothing more could be done until he knew the full situation.

He pulled into his driveway and was immediately on guard to see a small sedan parked off to the side of his garage. He rarely got visitors, and this car didn't belong to anyone he knew, so he got out ready to throw them off the property. Instead, a small, well-dressed man emerged, peering at Mike over glasses.

"Are you Miguel?"

"Who's asking?" his voice was low, practically a growl, but if this was a reporter, he was going to be furious at the intrusion.

"My name is Mario," he said. "I'm a tailor from Burlington. I got a call this morning asking me to come dress you for an evening out. Your dimensions seemed off on paper, but I see they were accurate. I understand you have a reservation, so I'll be quick."

Mario pulled a few suit bags out of the back of his car and gestured toward the house. Mike unlocked the front door, and the tailor followed him inside. "There's a bedroom through there," he said, pointing. "If you need to hang things up in a closet. Otherwise, we can do this wherever."

"The kitchen is fine," Mario assured him, draping the bags over the back of an island chair. "I'll get these out of the bags if you want to disrobe."

Mike stifled a laugh but did as he was told. When he was down to boxers and a t-shirt, Mario held out a pair of black pants to him. "Who arranged for all of this?" Mike asked as he pulled the pants on.

"A woman named Phyllis," Mario replied. "She terrified me over the phone, so I have to make sure you look impeccable."

Mike tried to pull on the blue shirt he was handed, but it was too tight to get his arms in. Mario immediately pulled out a silver-grey shirt that went on smoothly. They went through three jackets before they found one that Mario was satisfied with. He pulled out several ties and draped them around Mike's shoulder before pulling three away and leaving him one that was shades of black, silver and red.

"You'll need black dress shoes," Mario ordered. "If you don't have any, I'll go get them from the car."

"I do," Mike said. He ran upstairs and grabbed the nicest pair he owned, then jogged back down to the kitchen. "Are these okay?"

"Perfect," Mario said. "Put them on so I can check the length of the pants."

An hour later, Mario disappeared with the discarded clothes after giving Mike specific orders about how to button the jacket and confirming that he knew how to wear a tie. The new suit and shirt were pressed and hanging in his bedroom closet, the shoes polished and ready by the door. Mike was a little surprised that Mario hadn't stayed to sign off on his bathing and shaving process but was glad to have the house to himself.

Natalie was full of surprises, and he had to execute a few of his own before they went out for the night. She had raised the bar, and his flowers suddenly felt insignificant compared to the care she was showing the night. He retreated to his office to make some calls, ready to even the playing field.

***

He felt surprisingly nervous as he drove to pick Natalie up. They had been nearly inseparable for weeks now, and had established an easy, caring relationship. Tonight felt like a turning point, where he was really expressing how deep his feelings for her ran, and had the hope that she felt the same way. He wasn't sure he was ready to express that he was in love with her yet, but it was close.

After parking in her driveway, he grabbed the flowers from the back seat and made sure his suit was buttoned as ordered before walking up the steps to her door. Seconds after he rang, it swung open, and she took his breath away. The red dress from New Year's Eve flashed through his eyes, but this was even better. It was both sweet, with flowers running along her shoulders, and unbelievably sexy.

"You are the most stunning woman alive," he said, mentally slapping himself for how un-smooth it came out. "I can't believe you're going out with me."

"Happy Valentine's Day," she said, smiling at him. "You look pretty amazing yourself. I like the suit."

"Oh, yes. Happy Valentine's Day," he said, mentally slapping himself in the head. "These are for you."

She took the flowers and smiled even more, burying her face in them for a smell. "Gorgeous," she said. "Thank you. Did you leave any flowers for the rest of the town?"

He laughed, stepping inside and closing the door behind him. "A few," he said. "They weren't too happy with me."

"I'm sure," she said. "Let me find a vase, and then we can get going."

He watched as she searched her small kitchen, then turned to him with a frown and empty hands. "I'll go check the main kitchen," he offered. "I'm sure there's something out there that will work."

"Do you have something at your house?" she asked before he could leave.

"I'm sure I do," he said.

"Let's just take them with us," she suggested. "I packed a little bag in anticipation of being invited there after dinner. The flowers will be okay until then."

His heart fluttered again at the recognition that they were on the same page for the night. He had made the plans earlier, expecting to have to convince her to come back with him, thinking she would want to get home to Midnight. "Where is Midnight?" he asked, realizing he hadn't seen the dog yet.

"With Holly and Liam, of course," she said with a laugh. "I think they share custody or at least would like to. Liam surprised Holly with a fancy, catered meal at home so they can enjoy some privacy. Holly and I spent the afternoon getting ready together. She looked gorgeous and I can't believe he didn't want to show her off, but I guess it is a sign of how much he's changed. Liam said Midnight was welcome to join them for the evening."

"Perfect," he said. Spotting the bag on the floor by the door, he picked it up and gestured to the door. "Ready?"

"I am," she said, then hesitated. "Are you? If you changed your mind about going this public, I understand."

"Trust me when I say that I will never be ashamed or nervous about being seen as your romantic partner," he assured her. "I'll be as public or private as you want, either way is fine. If this helps to end the speculation about Austin and Brie, let's do it. But if you're even a little unsure, or nervous about being out in public, then we can do like Liam and Holly, have a nice dinner at my house."

"No," she said. "I always feel safe with you, no matter where we are. And I feel like this is the easiest way to end the rumors. I just feel bad dragging you into it."

He stepped closer and put his hands on her shoulders, pulling her closer to him. "You don't have to drag me anywhere," he said. "I'm always going to be right by your side, as long as you'll have me. Nothing anyone says online or in the media will change my feelings for you, I promise."

"Sweetest man alive," she whispered, stretching up on her toes to kiss him. "Now let's get out of here before I ruin my makeup, which took an hour to have done."

"I think I'd take an hour of makeup over an hour with Mario," he said, helping her into her coat.

"Who's Mario?"

"The guy that Phyllis sent to my house," he explained. "He brought enough suits to dress the whole town, and he may have seen parts of me you haven't seen yet."

"We'll have to fix that, won't we?" she teased him with a wink over her shoulder as she walked to the truck.

They chatted about mundane things as he drove them to the restaurant, where Wyatt had agreed to give them a table easily in view of the expected press outside. Mike had been informed that Phyllis had made several phone calls to make sure photographers would be present to catch them getting out of the car, and likely through the large window as they ate. It would likely make him feel as though he was on stage while eating, but he was happy to show his feelings for Nat to the world.

When he parked, he noted several other cars that immediately shut off and had doors flung open. By the time he walked around to help Natalie from the truck, there were at least six photographers clustered around them, snapping pictures. Natalie smiled at them, then placed a hand on Mike's cheek as she was emerging from the car, turning his lips to meet hers. The crowd went crazy, asking questions over each other.

Natalie ignored the questions and linked her hand with his. "Thanks for coming out tonight," she said. "Miguel and I have a reservation to celebrate our first Valentine's Day together. I hope you'll all stay warm."

Mike felt a small thrill run through him at the sound of his full name coming off her lips. It was a small acknowledgment to the world that she knew him well, and was celebrating who he was, and he appreciated it. That one clip, if it made it online, would thrill his mom for weeks.

A staff member stepped out to hold the door open for them, conveniently leaving it open long enough for Natalie to slip out of her jacket and turn to the cameras and wave. Mike followed her lead, placing a hand on the small of her back while watching her do her thing.

Wyatt appeared, greeting Mike with a handshake and Natalie with a kiss on the cheek. "You guys sure you want the hot seat?" he asked, gesturing to the table in front of the window.

"Yes," Mike said, nodding. "We'll be eating on stage tonight."

"Just so you know, I did my best to make sure the other tables in the dining room were full of actual couples and not reporters," Wyatt told them quietly. "But I can't be certain of a few."

"Please don't worry, Wyatt. We need the exposure, so we're okay with whatever happens," Natalie assured him. Mike noticed the relieved look on Wyatt's face and realized the other man had been more stressed than he appeared.

Mike pulled out Natalie's chair and then settled in across the table from her, glancing outside quickly to see they were indeed on camera. "Let the show begin," he whispered to her. She smiled and took his hand, and he pushed thoughts of tabloids and social media to the back of his head. Tonight was about celebrating their feelings for each other, it was time to focus on that and the beautiful woman across from him.

Chapter 22

By the time she was halfway done with her first glass of wine, Natalie felt like she had relaxed enough to enjoy the evening. The pictures were taken, the subtle statement to the world done, and now she could just enjoy her evening. There was no point in worrying about how either of them, or they as a couple, would be perceived in public opinion. As her mom had reminded her again a few hours ago, all she could control was how she felt and what thoughts ran through her own head. With that in mind, she took in the man across from her.

Mike looked dashing in his new dark suit, cut just right to showcase the breadth of his chest and shoulders. Used to seeing him in jogging pants and hoodies, it was a good shock to the system to see him so done up. He had lost the slightly terrified look that he had when they pulled into the parking spot and photographers had rushed at them and was regaling her with the tale of Mario.

"Phyllis is a force," she said when he finished. "I'm sure he dropped everything when she called. Knowing her, it was a combination of fear and a large sum of money to get him to rush right to you."

"I was lucky that he had the right sizes," Mike said. "Shockingly, they aren't common. Mario assumed she must have called a few other tailors to find one that had the right stock. He said he keeps a few on hand in every possible size, so she got lucky."

"Well, she picked a good one," she said. "That suit is beautiful."

The waitress interrupted to take their order, looking star-struck and fumbling with her pen. Natalie smiled at her and tried to appear as unthreatening as possible. "The last time we were here, Wyatt chose our menu," she said. "Could you ask him to do that again? Unless you wanted something particular, Mike?"

He shook his head and closed the menu. "Whatever he makes is good for me," he agreed.

"I'll let him know," the waitress said, scurrying away.

"You scared her," Mike said teasingly.

"I didn't mean to," Nat said. "I smiled nicely and everything."

"People just aren't used to someone so beautiful also being nice," he said. "It would only be fair if you were to act like a diva, just to make the world more even."

"I'm sure I've had more than my share of diva moments," she said. "The last few months have really put what is important in perspective."

"I have a hard time seeing you acting poorly," he said. "You've never been like that here."

"Trust me, it's happened. One movie I was so frustrated with how I was being treated that I snapped on the costume designer. It wasn't her fault, she was doing what the director told her to do, but I made her cry. I felt terrible after," she admitted.

"What was the issue?"

"I spent half the movie virtually naked," she explained. "Which didn't fit with the story at all. I had to threaten to quit to get them to dress me appropriately. When I fell in love with acting, it wasn't just about attention, and I wasn't willing to sell just my body. I want to be respected for what I do."

"Did that happen often?"

"All the time. I have to fight to have any nudity exclusions added into my contracts," she said. "It's easier now that I'm well established. But when I first started, it was unheard of. I just couldn't imagine my dad sitting in a movie theater and I'm on screen topless."

"That would be awkward," he agreed with a laugh.

"And it's not why I wanted the job," she said. "I didn't do it for money or attention. Those are secondary perks or annoyances, depending on the day. I fell in love with the storytelling and getting to be someone else. Portraying a warrior fighting monsters on screen or being a heroine in Nazi Germany. Those are things I'll never do in real life, but I can do them on screen. And when directors look at me as more than a body, it means I get to push the limits on what I do."

"I get that, believe it or not," he said. "When I went to college on a football scholarship, the expectation was that I was there to do a job on the field. My education was secondary, and I didn't see it that way. Football was a way to get into an amazing school and get a degree in something that would hold value forever. I had to push past the stereotypes about dumb jocks, so I get what you're saying."

"Exactly," she said. "We're more than the stereotypes."

"That we are," he said. He held up his glass of wine to clink with hers, and she felt the connection between them deepening. No one had ever really listened to and understood her like he did, and for the first time, she was feeling grateful for what had brought them together. Without that incident, who knows if they would be sharing this meal together and have the promise of love on the horizon?

***

After they finished every bite of their meals and shared a rich chocolate dessert, Mike drove them slowly back to his house. She felt a thrilling sense of anticipation as she sat in the passenger seat, thinking of the rest of the night. The heavy feel of his hand in hers and the warmth of the leather beneath her created a heady sense of awareness, and she could tell from the tension in his shoulders that he felt the same way. Now that the show part of the evening was over, she was looking forward to spending the remainder of the holiday in a private setting.

He pulled into the garage, closing the door behind them to shut out any cameras that may have followed them. She didn't wait for him to open the door this time, instead climbing out quickly and circling to where he was retrieving the flowers from the backseat. She caught him as he closed the door, tugging on his belt to move him closer to her, where she could reach up and kiss him.

"This has been an amazing night," she whispered. "Thank you."

"You might want to prepare yourself," he cautioned her. "I have a few surprises for you."

He led her into the house, pausing in the mudroom to take her jacket and remove her heels. She had half his shirt buttons undone and her lips sealed to his when she heard the click of a door, and paused to look at him in confusion. "Is someone else here?"

"Come with me," he said, not answering her. He led her up the stairs to his bedroom, where she saw more flowers everywhere. Petals were strewn on the bed, and bouquets stood on every surface. The room was lit faintly by candles, which she was relieved to see looked battery operated.

"It's beautiful," she said in amazement. "You did all this for me?"

"One more thing," he said, pulling her into the bathroom. His massive tub was filled and steaming, with bubbles and rose petals floating at the top. A champagne bucket was placed next to the tub, two glasses dangling from it. He stepped closer to her and pulled the zipper down on her dress so slowly it almost caused her to rip the fabric with her own hands. "I wanted you to have the soak you've been dreaming of."

"It looks big enough for two," she said, stepping out of the dress and holding his gaze. "Even when one of them is you."

He laughed and began pulling off the suit, while still trying to keep his hands on her. "This is the best night of my life," he said.

"Mine too." His thoughtfulness was almost overwhelming, and the romance of the evening put any thoughts other than Mike out of her head. No one had ever gone to such lengths for her before, no matter how much they declared to love her. This man showed it in the simplest ways, and it meant the world to her. Settling into the hot water with his arms around her, a glass of champagne in her hand was a moment she would remember forever.

***

Mike was gone when she woke up, the window across from the bed showing snow falling heavily outside. She headed downstairs in the t-shirt of Mike's that she had slept in, which fell below her knees, and made herself a cup of coffee before snuggling on the couch with a blanket. She wasn't a good driver on a clear day, so there was no chance she was heading out in this storm to get home, she decided. Pulling out her phone to text Holly, to ask her to keep Midnight a little longer, she groaned when she saw the number of notifications on the screen.

Ignoring all the texts but the ones from her team, she chose Phyllis's to open first. It was a simple thumbs up emoji, which had her uttering a sigh of relief. If Phyllis was happy, then all must have gone well. A new message came in from her before she could embrace the feeling, with a link to a popular magazine. She clicked on it, seeing pictures of her and Mike on the top of the page, along with a headline asking the real Natalie to please show herself.

A quick scan of the article told her that Wyatt had been correct in assuming some of the people in the dining room had been reporters. Someone must have been close enough to hear most of their conversation, and detailed Natalie's thoughts on exposing herself on screen. She groaned, knowing her manager was going to have a fit about this. It was one thing to quietly negotiate it in a boardroom, another to have the world know that there was no chance they would see her naked in a movie.

The article went on to discuss her recent publicity regarding the shooting and stated that the fragility she had showed went against the tougher side she showed on the screen. It even speculated that the hard exterior she showed in public could be the real Natalie Cloud, and this softer version was an act for the press.

The author summarized that the relationship between herself and Mike was authentic, noting the heat that was evident between them. Someone had even gotten a picture of the bouquet of flowers in the back of his truck, and a picture of them pulling into his garage to end the evening. There was no mention of Brie or Austin, so the night had been a success, even if she had caused slightly more damage along the way.

She clicked over to Instagram, wanting to take a quick glance at the comments. Even though she knew rationally that no good could come of it, she had a sick urge to want to see what people were saying. Many of the comments were positive, complimenting her and Mike as a couple, but there were several asking what he could see in someone as selfish as her. One woman even tagged his profile and tell him she sent him her number in a message because she would be much better to him than Natalie ever could be. Fortunately, Mike had turned off commenting on his own page, which he rarely used, so he wouldn't get inundated with notifications.

She groaned and tossed her phone to the side at the same time she heard the front door open. Mike must have decided to come home early with the weather so bad, which made the day look that much brighter from her perspective. Instead of sitting here alone worrying about what was being said, they could do something to take her mind off it. Tossing the blanket off, she jumped up to meet him at the door, stopping short when she realized it was two strangers coming into the house.

An older couple were in the open door, wearing heavy coats and hats, pulling small suitcases off the porch as the snow swirled in around them. "Rosie, you need to go inside and get out of the way," the man said. "I can get the bags in myself."

"I over packed, and I don't want you to catch a cold trying to get my things," she argued. "Just let me grab one, Kevin."

The woman grabbed one small suitcase and stepped into the house, catching sight of Natalie as she did. Her face lit up, and she turned back to her husband. "Kev, look who's here."

"Oh, dear," he said. "We didn't mean to just show up and startle you. Mike gave us a key years ago, and we thought no one was home. Rosie, let's go back to the car."

"No, don't be silly," Nat said quickly. "Are you Mike's parents?"

"Oh, yes. I'm Rosalita, but you can call me Rosie. And this is Miguel's dad, Kevin. We are so sorry to intrude on you like this," Rosie said, pulling off her coat and boots before walking towards Natalie. Her voice was musical, with a faint accent hinting of her origins in Mexico. She was petite, with a slightly darker skin tone that Mike, but the same brown eyes. "Can I give you a hug? I feel like we know each other already."

Natalie let herself be engulfed in the other woman's arms, feeling as safe there as she did in her own mom's embrace. However, she quickly realized that she was wearing nothing other than their son's t-shirt and wanted to get dressed before his dad came in all the way. "I'm just going to run upstairs and get dressed," she whispered to Rosie, who nodded.

She raced up the stairs, kicking herself for not having her phone in her hand. Did Mike know they were here? Should she try to leave? Thoughts raced through her head as she pulled leggings and a sweater out of the bag she had packed and put them on. She kept Mike's heavy socks on her feet since they were so warm and brushed her teeth before heading back down the stairs. Mike's parents were in the kitchen, his mom behind the island and his dad sitting at it with a hot cup of coffee in front of him.

"Would you like some coffee, dear?" Rosie asked. "I made a whole pot."

"Sure," she said, smiling at her.

"My sweet Rosalita is going to make some of her world-famous cinnamon buns. You're in for a treat," Kevin said with a smile. "She makes them from scratch, and they are amazing."

Natalie settled in next to Kevin and sipped her coffee, watching as Rosie got to work. They chatted easily among themselves and asked her questions about herself without being intrusive, and didn't seem the slightest bit fazed at having found her in their son's home. She had to hide a smile with her coffee mug when she thought about how her own parents would react to walking into Mike in her house, half dressed. Her dad was retired military, and although he turned a blind eye to many things Natalie did out of love for her, this would have thrown him into a tailspin. He needed time to prepare, so being caught off guard with Mike in front of him wouldn't have gone well.

The warmth and charm that came from Rosie and Kevin reminded her of Ben and Stella. It was easy to relax in their presence and just enjoy the cooking demonstration happening right in front of her. Any instinct to run or hide was gone as she laughed with them, thinking that they were as perfect as Mike had made them out to be. She could easily see why Mike had such a romantic streak, and why he wanted what he had grown up with as an example. A life with him would be like this, full of love and laughter, and kindness that she was still growing used to.

Chapter 23

Everyone turned to Mike when he walked in the door, his father comically frozen with a cinnamon roll halfway to his face. His mother had the good sense to look slightly guilty before hiding it behind a big smile, waving at him.

"You're letting all the cold air in," she said. "Come on in, the rolls are just out of the oven."

"What are you doing here?" he asked, toeing off his boots. "You didn't even call. Stassi just texted me to warn me."

"She's a busybody, that sister of yours," his mother said. "We're grown adults, and if we want to visit our son, we should be able to without permission."

"Mom, it's a blizzard out there," he said, kissing her on the cheek. He went over to hug his dad, pausing after, unsure of how to act with Nat in front of his parents. He wanted to kiss her but felt awkward. Instead, he sat next to her and squeezed her hand under the counter.

"We have lived in New England our entire marriage, since your father convinced me to leave the sunshine of Mexico to be with him," his mom said with a sniff. "You think we can't drive in some snow? Besides, we left yesterday and stayed at the Inn last night. A little romantic getaway for us on Valentine's Day. We—"

"Nope. We don't need to hear any details," he said to his mom. Turning to Nat, he went on. "My mom has a tendency to over share."

"She also makes the best cinnamon rolls I've ever had," Nat said.

"I love her already," his mom said, beaming at Natalie.

"You might want to get one before I eat them all," his dad warned him. "Are you home for the day now?"

"Yes, the gym closed and everyone canceled. A lot of my clients overindulged last night with the food, wine and chocolate, and the snow was a good excuse to recover," he said. "I thought I was going to be able to spend a quiet afternoon with Natalie. Alone."

"I was thinking we could play some board games," his mom said, purposely missing his point. "You must still have them around from when we were all here this summer? Or we could play cards. Do you still have that one we all loved?"

"Elevens? Yes," he said. "Nat, you okay with this? We can pretend they aren't here and lock ourselves in my man cave for the day."

"Miguel, that's rude," his mom said, as Natalie laughed and shook her head.

"Cards sounds perfect," she said. "I should warn you all that I'm viciously competitive. Like an unhealthy level."

"Then you'll fit right in," Kevin said. He pushed his plate and mug back and stood. "I'm just going to unpack a little while Miguel eats, and then we can get started. Rosie, come help me."

"You don't need help," she said.

"Let me be a little more obvious," Kevin said. "Let's give the kids a minute alone."

"Oh, yes. Sorry. Of course you need help," Rosie said, grinning at Mike as she pulled off the apron she wore. "I'll be back. I want to get some soup going before we play games."

"I have cans of soup," he said. His mom turned and glared at him, so he put his hands up. "Okay, yes, yours is better."

When his parents disappeared behind the downstairs bedroom door, he leaned over and kissed Natalie thoroughly, the way he had wanted to earlier. "Hi."

"Hi yourself," she said. "Your parents are darling."

"They are, and then a few other things," he said. "Are you sure you're okay here with them? If they get to be too much, we can hide downstairs or we can go to your place."

"No, that would be rude. I'm enjoying getting to know them," she said. "They really are as in love with each other as you said. I thought you were exaggerating, but it's so obvious."

"Oh, we would have heard sordid details if I didn't cut her off," he said. "My mom has always been very open to talking about sex with us, as long as we were being careful and with someone we cared about. Even though none of us wanted to be part of the conversation, she persisted. Before I went to college, she sat me and half my football team down to lecture us on consent and not doing anything with a girl who had been drinking. It was mortifying."

"But smart," Nat said with a smile. "She might have saved one of you from doing something stupid."

"Very true," he said. "You're really okay with spending the day playing games? Anything from Phyllis that you need to deal with?"

"I will call her soon," she said. "I got a text with a thumbs up early this morning, and then a link to one article, but she didn't say much. I assume she's overall happy with the result, or I would be hearing more from her."

"Anything I can do?"

"There are several women on Instagram that would answer that question for you," she said with a laugh. "But no, I'm good. I'm happy that we put our relationship out there, and overall, the response seems good. It helps that you're so devastatingly handsome and also look like you could kill anyone who disagreed."

"The devastatingly handsome thing is the most important, right?" He leaned over and kissed her again, feeling her soften in his arms. "You sure you don't want to hide out from my parents?"

She laughed and pushed him away. "Yes. I couldn't be downstairs fooling around with you while your parents are up here."

"That doesn't bode well for my evening plans," he said. "I had been hoping to convince you to stay again."

"Well, they already caught me in nothing but your t-shirt this morning," she said. "Let's see how the day goes. If I stay, I'd like to try to get Midnight here. I miss her."

"I can have Jake bring her by," he offered. "He's out in the plow and will be over to do my driveway. He's up at Patrick's now, so he will be at Liam's soon enough."

"That would be perfect," she said. "Will you text Liam and tell him? I don't want to look at my phone if I don't have to."

"Unfortunately, my oven will be in use from now until my mom leaves," he warned her. "If you need another hiding spot, let me know. There's a safe in my office."

She laughed and nodded. "I'll keep you posted."

He fired off a text to Liam and Jake, asking that they get Midnight and her stuff over. Liam responded and asked if Nat needed Holly to throw some stuff in a bag for her, and Mike made the decision for her, agreeing. She didn't seem to be in a hurry to leave, so whatever he could do to make it easier for her to stay, he would do.

***

The storm blew out of town early that evening, and the town Facebook page encouraged anyone who wanted to go out to be careful. Although the plows had been out all day, the roads were still slick, and JJ wanted as many people to stay home as possible. He suggested walking, and everyone in Mike's house had laughed at that before agreeing to stay in for the night. They enjoyed a roasted chicken basted with rosemary that was his mother's specialty, along with a bottle of wine that he knew would help make his parents bedtime even earlier than usual.

Natalie insisted on doing the dishes with Kevin, leaving Mike alone with his mom on the couch, waiting for Wheel of Fortune to start. She lowered her voice and edged closer to him, a rare sign of subtlety from her. "I like her a lot," she said.

"Me too," he said. He glanced over to where Nat was laughing with his dad, acting nothing like the millionaire diva that she was accused of being in the press.

"She's not what I expected," Rosie continued. "You see all this stuff in the magazines, but it just isn't true. She's sweet and fun, and so smart. She beat the pants off of you, and you weren't letting her win. She fits right in with us, which makes me so happy. I have

239

to admit, though, originally, I wanted to make sure you weren't in over your head."

"That's the reason behind the unannounced drop in?"

"Partly," she said, nodding. "And I also miss you. I haven't seen you since Christmas."

"It's barely February," he pointed out. "And it's not like I come home every weekend. I do have a life here."

"I know, but you usually come once a month, or have us all here," she said. "It's not like you to be away from us for long."

"I honestly didn't even realize it. I'm sorry," he said. His family was incredibly important to him, and they had gone to extraordinary efforts to see him play football over the years. It wasn't easy or cheap for his parents to travel to see him play during his college years, but they did it and never made it seem like a chore. His siblings had to deal with just one parent at their events if they coincided with his games, and he knew they had every right to feel shortchanged, but they never complained.

"It's okay," his mom said, reaching over to pat his hand. "Falling in love takes the focus off everything else, doesn't it?"

"I've never felt this way before," he told her. "It's scary sometimes."

"Why?"

"She can't stay here forever," he said. "Her home is in California."

"No, her movies are made there," Rosie said. "She probably has a house there, and friends. But her home is with you. I can already tell that girl loves you and you'll figure out a way to make it work."

Before he could respond, his father and Nat came over to join them, carrying the remaining wine. He topped off Rosie's glass before settling in on the opposite couch from Mike. "Come sit here, my love," he said to his wife. "Let the kids sit together."

Rosie moved over to sit next to her husband, and Natalie took her spot with Mike. After ten minutes of competing to solve the puzzles first, Rosie yawned and nudged Kevin with her elbow. "I'm ready to call it a night," she said. "I have a chapter to finish of my book, and if I stay out here any longer, I won't be awake enough to read."

"Works for me," Kevin said, standing and then helping her from the couch. "I brought a new book along, thinking we would be spending the day reading by the fire. I didn't know I'd be losing card games to a movie star all day." He winked at Natalie as he said it, and she laughed.

"I can't help it that I'm good," Nat said. "I warned you all that I'm competitive."

"I can't believe anyone is more so than Mike," Rosie said. "We are so used to losing to him, it was nice to see him take a loss today."

"I'll get her next time," Mike promised. "Have a good night's sleep."

"You too," Rosie said. "Both of you. I'll see you in the morning for fresh waffles."

"Mom, I can't keep eating like this," he groaned. "But yes, I'm in."

"No early clients tomorrow?" Natalie asked as his parents closed the bedroom door.

"No," he said. "It's Saturday, so it's usually a little lighter. And I asked Ashley to take a few for me at the gym so I could be here. I didn't want to leave you to wake up alone with my parents."

"They really are amazing," she said.

"You got the stamp of approval from Mama Collins," he told her. "She likes you a lot."

"That's a relief," she said. "I thought we were getting along well, but it's nice to confirm it."

"You ready for bed?" he asked her.

"Jeopardy hasn't even started yet," she said with a laugh. "And Midnight needs to go out again."

"I'll take her out now," he said, waking the dog when he jumped to his feet. "We can do trivia upstairs."

"Why does that sound dirty?" she asked, laughing as he pulled on his coat.

"I don't know, but I'm happy to make it that way if you are," he called out before leaving through the patio door. He waited on the covered porch for the puppy to search out her spot and take care of business. Earlier, he had gone out to shovel a patch for her, but she had promptly run out of that area and rolled around in the deeper snow. The backyard was fully fenced, so Mike wasn't as worried about the dog getting out of the yard as he was that she would get lost and cold, so he watched as she made her way around. Once she came back to him, he brought her inside and tried to dry her with a towel he had left by the door, giving up as she wiggled away from him.

"Poor baby," Natalie crooned. "Are you cold?"

"Yes," he said.

"I was talking to the dog," she said. "But come on over and I'll warm you up too."

"Let's put her crate near the fireplace and then we can go upstairs," he suggested. "I can set the timer on this one to stay on for two hours, and I think a little skin to skin might be necessary to warm me up. Especially in front of the fire upstairs."

Natalie laughed and raced up the stairs in front of him. She paused a the landing, glancing back down towards the bedroom his parents were in. "Should I stay in a guest room?" she whispered to him.

"Absolutely not," he said, pulling her into his room. "I just told you I'm on the verge of frostbite, and you're the only one who can save me."

"Well, if it's a matter of life and death," she said, slowly unzipping his hoodie. "I owe you one."

Chapter 24

"How did things go with your publicity stunt on Valentine's Day?" Dr. Jones asked Natalie. Their regular Monday morning appointment had been something to look forward to for the first time since they had started, Natalie had realized.

"It went pretty well," she said. "We were featured in a lot of the tabloids and on social media, and then it died down pretty quickly. Mike is getting a lot of messages propositioning him, but he just thinks it's funny."

"No worries about trust there?"

"With me and Mike? Not at all," she said honestly. "He always makes me feel like the only woman for him."

"And is he the only man for you?"

"Yes. For now. Or maybe forever," Natalie stumbled over her words, frustrated with herself.

"I get the sense that he thinks of this as forever," Dr. Jones said. "Just based on what you've said."

"We've only been together for two months," Natalie said. "Not even. It's a little early to talk about that, don't you think?"

"It's never too early to make sure you're on the same page," Dr. Jones replied. "The earlier you have those important conversations, the better."

"But what if we aren't?"

"Then you need to deal with it," Dr. Jones said. "It's the fairest thing to both of you, to make sure both of your hearts are protected. Communication and honesty are the foundations of a healthy relationship."

"You told me friendship was," Natalie said, stubbornly crossing her arms. Realizing she looked like a child, she uncrossed them and then reached for a tissue to fiddle with.

"To start one, yes," Dr. Jones said. "And it's certainly important that the friendship remains once you're committed to each other. But other things matter too, like communication, passion, honesty, dedication to each other. It all factors in, and the better balance you have of everything, the better chance you'll make it."

"I don't want to lose him," she said. "What if I bring it up and we aren't on the same page?"

"And what if you are? Which scares you more?"

Natalie found herself unable to answer, and the uncertainty was worse than anything else. Her heart screamed at her that losing him would be the worst thing to happen, but her brain was yelling back that she would endure. She was used to putting on her armor to protect her heart over the years. If she needed to do so again, she could. She had softened since arriving in Windsor Peak, but that didn't mean that the inner toughness that had helped her navigate Hollywood wasn't still there. The last few months had shown her she could survive anything, even something as horrible to think about as losing Mike.

***

"Are you ready?" Holly's voice called out to her from the other side of the door, snapping Natalie back to reality. She went to open the door, unsure what her friend was talking about. Had they made plans for the evening that Nat had forgotten?

"For what?" she asked, moving aside so Holly could enter. Holly was dressed in workout clothes and sneakers, her hair pulled back into a ponytail, so they clearly weren't going out for drinks.

"Our self-defense class," Holly reminded her. "Remember? Ashley is going to do it right after the gym closes, so it will just be our group there."

"Oh, I totally forgot," Natalie said. "I have to change. Give me five minutes."

She quickly threw on a pair of yoga pants and a sports bra, followed by a tank top and a sweatshirt. Shoving her feet into sneakers, she found an elastic in her bathroom and swept her hair back. Satisfied, she went back to the living room, where Holly waited.

"Okay, I'm ready," she said. She put Midnight in her crate and made sure the door was locked before following Holly to the car.

"Are you good? I haven't seen you in days, and you seem a little off," Holly asked.

"Yes," she said, sighing. "I had an amazing weekend with Mike and his parents, and then therapy this morning threw me for a loop."

"You met Mike's parents?" Holly looked shocked. "How did that go?"

"They're amazing," she said. "Honestly. I was sad when they left yesterday to drive home. We had so much fun."

"That's great," Holly said. "I was a nervous wreck meeting Liam's parents for the first time. I can't imagine having them stay with us for an entire weekend. I would never have made it through. We both said it was better they were at the Inn, but once the youth center is finished and the whole house is his, they'll be staying with us for sure."

"I'm sure you'll be fine," Natalie assured her. "I've met them several times. They are both very nice."

"You aren't involved with their son," Holly said. "That changes things. But they were nice to me. I just felt like I needed to be on my best behavior."

"Liam is their son," Nat said, laughing. "They can't expect perfect behavior from anyone when he's around."

"He's different now, being away from the Hollywood life," Holly said. "He says he really likes it. Any chance you're thinking of sticking around too?"

"I don't know," Natalie said slowly. "Mike and I haven't gotten that far yet."

Holly raised an eyebrow and glanced over at her as she pulled into the parking lot at the gym. "Maybe you haven't, but I bet he has."

"What do you mean?"

"He's not going to be happy if you leave," Holly said. "I almost think he'd give up his life here to follow you, if I were being honest. He's crazy about you, and I think he's really hoping you'll stay."

"I just don't know yet," Natalie answered. "I never thought of this as a permanent move. I only came out for a few days originally, and when everything happened, I didn't want to be alone in California, feeling scared."

"And now?"

"Now I love having friends like you guys, and obviously Mike plays a big part in it," she admitted. "I've really grown to like being here, and the more I'm able to get out and be a part of the community, the more I like it."

"We sure like having you here," Holly said. "When I came for the holidays, I never expected to stay. This place is pretty magical. It's hard to even think about leaving."

They entered the gym to find Ashley waiting for them in the lobby. "You guys are the last to arrive, so I'm just going to lock the door," she told them. "Why don't you head into the room with everyone else?"

Shea, Kendra, Emma, and Zoe were in the room already, dressed in similar gear. The volume increased as Nat and Holly joined in catching up with their friends until Ashley came in with a no-nonsense look on her face.

"Are we ready to get started?" she asked. A man Natalie didn't recognize came into the room, and Ashley pointed at him. "This is Kirk. He is here to help me teach the class, and for you guys to beat the crap out of. Don't feel bad, he puts up with me and can take it."

Ashley went through some basic steps with them over the first hour, demonstrating simple moves to get them out of a difficult situation easily. She had them practice on Kirk, correcting them if she felt like they were holding back, or fixing their form. Once they all felt confident with those moves, she gave them a water break and then got them settled on the mat again. "I want to go through some more intense things now," she said. "Those kicks and punches will help you get out of most predicaments, but things like being grabbed from behind are different. A lot of what I need you to focus on is staying calm in the situation. I'm going to give you the skills to take care of yourself, but only you can come up with the mindset that you can do it."

Ashley seemed to be staring at Natalie, who nodded slightly. She knew that a big part of feeling safe again was in her head and feeling confident enough in her ability to protect herself. She watched carefully as Ashley demonstrated what to do if someone were to grab her from behind. Ashley easily put Kirk on the floor, causing the rest of them to laugh nervously.

"You made that look way too easy," Kendra called out.

"You can do it," Ashley assured them. "It's all in the body positioning and confidence."

One by one, they practiced, and everyone was able to get Kirk down by their third try. When Kirk grabbed Natalie from behind, she had to prevent herself from panicking. The instant his arms closed around her, she wanted to scream and forgot everything that Ashley had just showed her.

"You're okay," Kirk whispered. "Just think."

She took a deep breath and went through the steps in her mind, forcing her body through the motions. The first time she failed to get him on the ground, but by the third time she succeeded. She looked up at her friends and felt a huge smile spread across her face as they cheered for her.

"See? You can do anything," Ashley said, fist bumping her. "Believe in yourself."

They went through a few more scenarios until the women were all so exhausted they could barely raise a hand. Ashley laughed when they claimed exhaustion and told them all they were dismissed. They all thanked her and Kirk before piling out to the parking lot.

"I think we all deserve a drink," Kendra said. "Want to meet at the Palace? Or we can go into Plates if you would rather privacy, Nat."

She thought about it quickly while her friends waited patiently. The world was a lot less scary with these women in her corner, and she felt even more confident after the lessons from Ashley. She was a far way still from fully recovering from the trauma of being held at gunpoint, if she ever did, but she was ready to reenter the world. At least, the Windsor Peak world.

"Let's go to the Palace," she said.

They all piled into cars and drove the short distance, finding parking spaces along the main street. The bar was only half full, almost all locals that Natalie was familiar with, and all of the men in their lives were watching a hockey game while playing darts. The game ended when the women walked in, each man abandoning it in favor of a kiss.

"How are you here? You were on duty with the kids," Kendra asked Dan as he leaned in to kiss her.

"My dad was bored," Dan explained. "Said he could handle getting Calle to bed, and Declan was already sleeping."

"Charlie is on baby duty at our house," Jake said. "He's a pro."

"You guys are brutal," Shea said. "One night out for us, and you can't handle staying home alone."

"We miss our wives," Dan said. "And it was Mike's idea. Blame him."

"Liam started it," Mike said. He leaned down and kissed Natalie. "But I was all in, if it meant I got to spend some time with you."

The crowd around them groaned, JJ muttering something about Mike being a suck up, but Natalie smiled at him. "I'm glad you're here."

"How was your class? Think you could beat me up now?" Mike asked, putting his arm around her.

"Want me to demonstrate?" She grabbed his wrist and looked up at him.

"No, thanks," he said quickly. "I'll take your word for it, I promise. Don't hurt me."

She laughed, and instead of twisting his wrist, kissed the back of it. "Never."

"I had Liam pick me up and bring Midnight with him," Mike said. "I know that was presumptuous, but I really don't think I can sleep alone. The boogie monster might attack me, and I wouldn't have you there to defend me."

"No, that's perfect," she said. "I was going to suggest we pick her up, so you saved us some time. Your bed is far superior to mine. And I wouldn't want to leave you defenseless, now that I'm actually trained like a superhero."

They enjoyed a drink and some appetizers with their friends, helping to encourage Patrick and Jake to take the stage for an impromptu show. The brothers were both talented singers and guitar players, and it was a treat for the small crowd that was still there to listen to them play. Before she knew it, the bar was closing up for the night and she was walking to the car, hand in hand with Mike.

"Want me to drive?" he asked, and she nodded. She loved that he didn't demand. He always asked her opinion on anything, even something as simple as who should drive home.

"I think I'm going to be sore tomorrow," she admitted as they entered his house.

"Really? You work out a lot," he said. He went to where Midnight's crate was and let her out, holding up a finger to let Nat know he would be right back before disappearing into the backyard with the dog.

She went into the kitchen and grabbed two bottles of water from the refrigerator before setting the coffee maker up for him to use in the morning. He would return the favor before he left, a simple way they showed kindness to each other. It wasn't something she would have ever thought of before Mike, but his way of looking out for her made her want to do the same for him.

"She's all set," Mike said, bringing Midnight back inside. "Took care of business and got a good run in, so she should sleep well."

"Thanks," she said. "I got us waters, anything else you need?"

"No," he said. "I have ibuprofen upstairs if you really think you'll be sore, though. Or do you want to take a hot bath before bed?"

"No, I'm too tired for that," she said. They climbed the stairs together, and she yawned loudly when she entered the bedroom. "I guess that's pretty obvious."

"I'll give you a quick massage," he offered. "That should help move things around and get you right to sleep."

"Last time you gave me a massage, I didn't get to sleep for hours," she said teasingly.

"I didn't have to get up five hours later, and you weren't so tired," he said.

"You don't have to do that," she said. "You're right, you have to get up early."

They brushed their teeth side by side, and she swapped out her workout clothes for his t-shirt that she always wore to sleep as he stripped down to his boxers. She climbed into the bed before him, giving her a chance to admire him for a moment.

"You're staring," he said as he climbed in next to her, reaching over to pull her closer.

"You made me less tired for a second there. I had some ideas," she said, before yawning again. "But I'll save them for tomorrow."

"Good plan," he said, kissing her on the head as he switched out the light. His breathing got slower within a few minutes, and his arm across her grew heavier. "I love you."

Her eyes snapped open, wanting desperately to roll over and see if he was awake. A soft snore answered her question, making her certain he was talking in his sleep. She considered how the words had made her feel before smiling and whispering them back to him.

Chapter 25

For the next week, Mike found himself at the youth center each night, building sets for the play that the students were putting on. Natalie was there from the time school got out, if not earlier, working with them on everything from stage direction to costumes. Liam and Patrick had also been roped into the production, helping the kids learn lines and dance moves. Seeing Natalie surrounded by young kids all clamoring for her attention was giving him thoughts about the future, and by Friday night he was ready to burst.

When the last student had been picked up, he laid down his hammer and turned to her. "Are you ready to get out of here? I'm starving," he said.

"Liam said he could order pizza," she responded. "Do you want to eat here?"

"I grabbed some meals at Palace Plates earlier," he said. "I was hoping for a quiet night together. I feel like we've barely had a chance to talk all week. By the time we end for the night, we're both so exhausted we fall right to sleep."

"Anything on your mind?" she asked, looking nervous suddenly.

"No, you?" His senses were going into overdrive, and the lack of time with her plus his chaotic schedule all week had him on edge.

"No," she said. "That works for me. Can you get Midnight in the car, and I'll be right there?"

He clipped a leash to the dog and walked her quickly before putting her in the backseat of his truck. He had learned the hard way that when a puppy had to go, it didn't matter where they were. He didn't want that to happen in his truck, that was for sure. Natalie joined them a minute later, climbing in next to him and waving to Holly and Liam as they entered the house.

"You sure everything is okay?" he asked again, the uncertainty eating away at him.

"I'm positive," she said. "Relax."

"The play is coming along," he said as he drove.

"It really is. Seeing their hard work pay off is amazing," she said. "I've never been on this side of things, and especially with kids who are getting over their shyness to be a part of it. It's remarkable. And some of them have real talent."

"Don't go putting ideas in their heads," he warned her.

"Why? They can dream. I know I did as a kid, and it paid off. I'm sure you did the same, about football, and it came true for you."

"I just don't want you to feel badly if they are disappointed later," he pointed out. "Or what if they come to you in a few weeks, thinking you're going to help them be discovered?"

She crossed her arms, and he recognized the stubborn light in her eyes. "Then I'll help them."

"All of them? Or are you going to break it to the ones who aren't good enough?"

"Why are you in such a bad mood?"

"Why are you changing the subject?" he shot back at her, then immediately regretted it. Winning an argument wasn't important right now, and he needed to calm down. "I'm sorry. I shouldn't have said anything. If you want to encourage them, go ahead."

"That doesn't sound sincere," she said in a sulky voice.

"Let's eat and then maybe we'll both feel better," he suggested. They went into his kitchen in silence, where he pulled the trays out of the refrigerator. Zoe packaged them up and sold them as ready to heat meals, allowing for no work on his part. He stuck them in the oven and set a timer, turning to see Natalie uncorking a bottle of wine. She silently poured two glasses and handed him one before taking a seat at the island.

"What's really going on?" she asked, sounding calmer than she had in the car.

"I didn't get to see you this week, not really," he admitted. "I'm clearly not handling it well."

"I was here with you every night," she said. "And we were both working at the youth center."

"But not together, not really," he insisted. "We were physically in the same place, but busy with different things. And surrounded by people all the time. I just didn't get a chance to talk to you."

"Let's talk now," she suggested. "What has you so on edge?"

"I love you," he blurted out. "It's been on my mind for days, weeks even, and it's getting harder and harder to keep it to myself. But I feel like I'm going to freak you out by saying it."

She smiled at him. "You said it in your sleep a few nights ago."

"I did?" When she nodded, he slapped himself in the forehead. "I'm such an idiot."

"You are not," she said gently. "And I happen to love you back."

"You do?"

She nodded, and he crossed the kitchen in two steps to swoop her off the chair and into his arms. She wrapped her arms around his neck and met his lips with as much enthusiasm as he felt, and suddenly, his hunger for food was replaced. He carried her over to the oven to turn it off, then returned his attention to her. He intended to show her exactly how much he loved her, and burning down his house would be too much of a distraction.

***

When they finally made it to his bed hours later, he toyed with her hair as she lay across his chest. "What does this mean for our future?" he dared to ask her.

"I don't know," she said softly. "I just know that I love you, and I've never felt like this about anyone before."

"I feel the same," he admitted. "It's almost overwhelming, how deeply I feel. Could you stay here? Move in with me? Spend our lives together?"

Painful seconds ticked by while he waited for her to answer. "I don't know," she said finally. "There's a lot that goes into that. It's not as simple as you're making it seem."

"It kind of is," he said. "I love you; you love me. We want to be together."

"It's also only been two months," she said gently. "I can't make promises that I don't know I can keep. You just told me not to do it to the kids, why would you ask me to do it to you?"

"I would promise you forever right now," he said stubbornly. "I know you're it for me."

"I need us to have some normal-life time together," she said.

"What does that mean?"

"I mean, we've been trauma bonded for so long—"

"Don't give me that," he said, feeling annoyed. "Did your therapist say that? I was in love with you long before we got held at gunpoint."

"You were in love with the idea of me," she said. "Not me. I just need to make sure this is real before I make any life-changing decisions."

"And if I tell you that I know it's real for me?"

She didn't answer for a long minute, making him second guess pushing too hard. "I feel that way too," she said. "Let's just agree to love each other and give it some time. Don't you think we need to see what every day, normal life looks like together before we move forward? What if you hate living with me?"

"I would never," he said. "And I do feel like we have been living our lives, and we fit together."

"But this isn't normal for me," she said, the gentleness in her eyes taking the sting from the words. "I don't live in Windsor Peak. I have a job that is really demanding and time consuming, and it's far away from here. You need to see what that part of my life is like before you decide that you want to be a part of it. This can't be all about me making changes and adapting to your life. There are going to be times where I have to be gone for months, and we need to figure that out too."

"Will you move in here with me at least?"

He felt her nod against his chest and then heard her laugh softly. "I'm pretty sure I already did."

She fell asleep within minutes, and he was left staring at the ceiling. Why didn't she want to talk about the future? Did she love him less than he loved her? Or was the pull of her life in Hollywood greater than her feelings for him?

***

He slipped out of bed early the next morning, needing to see some clients who he had missed the week before. Glancing back at where Natalie slept peacefully before he left the room, he vowed to find a way to make her want to stay. As he went through the workouts, he found it hard to focus on the people he was working with, but instead, his thoughts constantly drifted back to Natalie.

As he left the gym mid-morning to drive to a private client's house, he realized he had an extra half hour, so he took a detour. Something had been bothering him for a few weeks now, and he finally had the time to do something about it. When he parked his car and knocked on the door, he could see lights through the glass. It swung open, revealing Stella smiling up at him. She looked tired, and his worry kicked into overdrive.

"Mike, what a nice surprise," she said. "Come on in."

"Hey, Stella," he said. He glanced around the small cottage where she lived with Ben, which was behind the big house that Dan and Kendra lived in. Stella had lived in this cottage alone for years, helping Ben to raise his boys after he was widowed. When they admitted their relationship to his sons a few years ago and got married, everyone had been thrilled for them. They had opted to move into the small cottage, allowing Dan's growing family the bigger space, shortly after the younger couple had married. "Is Ben home?"

"No, he went into town," she said. "Is there something I can help you with?"

"Actually, you're the reason I'm here," he said. He sat at the kitchen table where she indicated, and she sat across from him after he refused the offer of a drink or food. "I wanted to check on you."

Her face paled slightly, and he could tell she was holding back on him when she spoke. "Why would you need to do that?"

"You signed yourself and Ben up for workouts," he reminded her. "You told me how much it meant to you, that you both get fit and stay healthy. But ever since the first session, you haven't been there. I know you saw your doctor to get clearance to do the exercise, and I suspect something is happening."

Her eyes dropped to her hands, which were working her wedding ring in a circle on her finger. A long silence filled the room, and Mike sat back in his chair, more than certain his instincts were right. When she spoke again, her voice was quieter, with an edge that suggested he not push the matter. "I'm just fine, Mike," she said. "I appreciate your concern. I've had some second thoughts about exercising at my age, and didn't want to discourage Ben. He's enjoying it so much. Thank you for that."

"Stella, if there is anything I can do—"

She cut him off with a nod and a push back on her chair. "Thank you. I really need to get moving. I have a meeting down at the church in a half hour."

He let her hustle him out of the house, hearing the lock click into place as he stood on the porch, as if she could lock out the questions he had brought as well as his body. Glancing over at the house, he saw smoke coming from the chimney and lights on, which indicated Dan and Kendra were home. Across a field, the same sight was visible at Jake and Shea's house. He debated talking to either of them about his suspicions, but knew how deep their love for Stella ran, and how upsetting it would be. And what if he was wrong? He couldn't live with himself if he disrupted everyone and was off base.

Walking slowly to his truck, he decided his best course of action was to keep his mouth shut and his ears open. If something changed or he became more confident in his thoughts, he would talk to his friends. Stella had been their only mother figure for most of their lives, and none of the Burrows boys were in any way equipped to face the thought of losing her. Worst of all would be Ben, who was finally able to show his love for her publicly, after all the years of hiding it.

No, he was not going to be the bearer of bad news he wasn't even confident about. Maybe she really had just changed her mind about working out, and that was fine. The last thing he would want to do is shame someone into exercising or bringing attention to a lack of interest. She had every right to skip the gym if she so chose, and he would leave it at that.

He finished with his last client earlier than expected, and rather than driving straight home, he took a detour. Something else had been on his mind for days, and this one he was sure he could take care of on his own. He drove the short distance to Stowe, parking outside a custom jeweler. JJ had mentioned the shop where he had gotten Zoe's ring made, and Mike realized that he had driven past a million times without noticing. At least until the last time he drove through with Natalie, when the shop sign had caught his eye and started his imagination running.

A soft bell chimed when he entered, happy to find the store empty. A man emerged from a back room and smiled at him, asking how he could help. Mike walked slowly through the cases, asking questions as he went. When he reached the rings, he stopped, staring at them.

"Is there something in particular you're looking for? We also make custom pieces," the man offered.

"I think I might need to go that route," he said. "Can you show me some ideas?"

The man's eyes lit up and he picked up an iPad off the case, gesturing to a small table near the front window. They both sat and the jeweler started scrolling through pictures, taking notes on things that Mike liked and disliked.

"Could you give me ten minutes to make some sketches?" the jeweler finally asked, looking satisfied with the information he had.

"Sure," Mike agreed. "I'll just look around some more."

A woman came out to assist him, and by the time the designs were ready to be looked at, he had chosen and paid for a necklace and matching earrings to bring home to Natalie. Taking his seat at the table, he looked at what the man had designed and grinned at him. "That's exactly what I'm looking for," he said. "You got it perfect."

"Excellent," he said. "Let me get you a price."

He was back minutes later with a figure written on a piece of paper, which Mike responded to by pulling his wallet out and handing him a credit card. "How soon can this be ready?"

"A week," the jeweler promised. "Perhaps a little less. I'll give it top priority."

He left the store, feeling like he had taken a step in the right direction for not only his future, but Natalie's. Maybe she wasn't ready to make a decision, but it was past time. As he had told her in New York, when you're afraid of something, the best thing you can do is look it in the face and conquer it. Putting it off only made it worse, and the devil on his shoulder was telling him that the longer he waited, the less chance he would have the nerve to ask.

Chapter 26

"There, that should fit now," Natalie said, helping a young student into a hemmed dress. The little girl was playing a princess in the play, which combined royals, superheroes, dinosaurs and rock stars in a hysterical fashion that only children could pull off. The girl twirled around, admiring herself in the mirror, before hugging Natalie and running back to show her friends.

"Are you a seamstress now?" The voice coming from behind her caused her spine to stiffen, and she turned in shock to find Brie standing in Liam's barn turned youth center.

"What are you doing here?"

"I came to talk to you," Brie said. "I wanted to come a few weeks ago, but I got held up."

"I imagine trying to ruin my life caused some wrinkles for you," Natalie said stiffly. She moved to walk past her old friend when Brie put a hand on her arm to stop her.

"Please. Let me explain," Brie said. "I didn't know he was going to do that."

"Likely story," Natalie responded. "You put me in that position to begin with."

"Not on purpose! I didn't know, he just wanted to meet you and Mike so badly. I had no idea he was in so much trouble at work, or that we had no money. I swear," she said. Tears were running down Brie's cheeks, and Natalie had to toughen her heart against them.

"And you're here now, why? To get more information that you can sell to the tabloids?"

"No," Brie said. "Not at all. I came to apologize."

"You could have sent a message saying that," Natalie pointed out.

"I tried, but you must have blocked me," Brie said. "Which I don't blame you for at all."

Natalie realized her phone number had changed after the story came out linking her to Austin, and clearly Brie wouldn't have had the new one. She kept that information to herself, not trusting the other woman enough to share. "Regardless," she said. "I don't think we have anything to talk about. This is why my circle is small."

"I want to be a part of it," Brie said, sounding whiny. "I was telling you the truth when I said that I've missed you for years. And I told Austin that I wanted a divorce. I was so upset at what he did."

"At what he did to me, or to you?" Natalie stared at her, seeing the truth in her eyes. "You weren't mad that he threw me to the wolves, you're upset that you look bad in the situation. He's broke and his image is tarnished, which hurts you as well. All you ever cared about was how you looked to everyone around you, making sure people looked up to you. But you married someone who played you for a fool, and you want me to save you now."

"That's not—"

"Did you come here looking for money?" Natalie cut her off and saw the answer in Brie's reaction. "How much? What do you need to walk away and leave me alone forever?"

"Excuse me," Liam's voice interrupted, and Natalie realized she was nearly screaming. "Hi. I'm Liam, and this is my home. I think I know who you are, and I'd like to walk you out." He pointed at the door, his steely gaze on Brie as she fumbled with her bag.

"I just wanted—"

"Now." Liam's voice cut Brie off, and she hung her head, walking to the door. He followed close behind, slamming the door shut, making the students nearby jump.

Natalie was horrified to realize that so many of the kids had overheard her yelling and struggled to figure out what to do or say. Patrick saved the day, stepping into the crowd and bringing the attention to himself. "And that," he said. "Is how you effectively work a dramatic scene. Didn't Miss Natalie do good?"

The students all grinned at her and started clapping, believing him that she had been doing a performance for their benefit. She managed a weak smile and waited until Patrick had directed them to the stage before she sank back into a chair, the sobs taking over her body.

"Nat," Patrick said. He was kneeling in front of her, a concerned look on his face. "You're okay. She's gone."

"I know," she said, gasping for a breath. "Thank you. And you, too." She reached over and squeezed Liam's hand as he came to her side.

"We're always here for you," Liam said. "I made sure she left. You are not giving her a dime."

"Absolutely not," Patrick said. "I don't know what their game is, but you've been through this before. You can't believe every sob story, or you'll be broke."

"I thought she was my friend," Natalie said softly. "When she came back the first time, I thought she was sincere. Even now, I don't know what to believe."

"Your friends are right here," Liam said, gesturing between himself and Patrick. "And everyone here in town. These are your people. Not her."

"What if she was telling the truth?"

"She must have her own tribe that she can turn to," Patrick said. "She hurt you years ago and did it again this time. When someone shows you their true colors, you have to believe them."

"He's right," Liam said.

"Do you want me to call Mike?" Patrick asked gently.

"No, that's okay. I'll get it together and finish out the rehearsal," she said. "They don't have much time before the big performance."

"What do we think all our Hollywood friends will think of this?" Liam asked, lightening the mood. "We timed it perfectly, so they can see the play and attend the fundraiser. I think I'll be getting directing opportunities thrown at me after this."

Natalie laughed, wiping away the last of her tears. "They'll have a full house, that's for sure. My parents are coming as well, the town is going to be overflowing that weekend."

"Are you sure you're okay with my parents staying in your apartment?" Liam asked. Natalie had offered the space to him when he mentioned the Inn was booked solid on the weekend of the fundraiser, and he had been frantically trying to furnish a bedroom in the main house for them. Her belongings had slowly and steadily all made their way to Mike's house, and she hadn't even been in the apartment in days.

"Absolutely," she said, nodding. "I'm never there, and Mike wants to have my parents and his whole family at his house. It will be interesting, to say the least."

"You should get some cameras in there," Liam joked. "It would make for a great reality show. Or documentary."

"I'll pass," she said. "My life is crazy enough without inviting more chaos."

***

As Natalie was driving home, her phone rang, showing Kendra's name on the screen. Although they texted regularly, it was rare for her friend to call, especially during the dinner rush at the restaurant. "Your friend is here," Kendra said when Natalie answered. "She's making quite a scene, crying at the bar. Even Desmond has no idea what to do with her."

Natalie sighed and changed the direction she was going to turn so that she would go through town. "I'll stop there now, thanks," she said.

She parked and walked slowly into the restaurant, dreading the confrontation. Why Brie couldn't have just left town was beyond her, and now she had to deal with her once and for all. Even though Patrick and Liam told her not to, the easiest way to get rid of her was likely going to be offering financial help to get her through the divorce.

When she entered the Palace, Brie was sitting smack in the middle of the bar, empty seats on either side of her. The ends of the bar were crowded with locals and tourists, all eyeing her with disdain. She had a cocktail glass in front of her and a stack of balled up paper napkins. Desmond shot Natalie a look of sympathy as she made her way to one of the empty seats next to Brie, and he slid a glass of wine in front of Natalie as she sat. She smiled at him gratefully before turning to the other woman.

"What is this really all about?"

"I thought we were friends," Brie said, hiccupping. "And you let them treat me like that."

"I thought we were friends, and you let your husband plant a lie about me in the tabloids," she pointed out. "All Liam and Patrick did was ask you to leave a place you hadn't been invited to. They didn't publicly humiliate you."

"Maybe I should sleep my way to success like you did," Brie practically snarled at her. "Then I'd have men to do my bidding for me."

"Okay, that's enough," Natalie said, pushing the chair back. "I came to see if we could resolve this, and you're insulting me. You should leave. Making a scene here isn't helping you, and I'm not going to be treated like this. You were horrible to me in high school and I forgave you constantly, and nothing has changed."

"Me, horrible to you?" Brie stood up, her voice rising. "You were snobby and pretentious and looked down on everyone."

"No, I wasn't," Natalie said. "I was shy and hid in your shadow. And anything good that happened to me, you stole it away. Like you did Nick, when you slept with him when he was drunk enough to think it was me. That was because I had dared to get the lead role in the school play, and because I was happy to have my first boyfriend. You didn't even like him, you just did it to punish me. You broke my heart, and when I went to Hollywood, I swore it wouldn't happen again."

"He was an easy mark," Brie snarled. "Anyone who would follow you around like that needed a reality check. You weren't going to stay with him, all you cared about was going to California and seducing a casting director to get a job."

"How long have you been making that claim?" Natalie asked. "Because I hear it all the time, and I never knew where it started. It sure wasn't reality. I worked my butt off to get the jobs I got. Yet some anonymous source was always quoted in stories, making those claims. You must have been dying of jealousy this whole time, thinking of how to get back at me. Did you think I would try and sleep with your husband? Then you could use that against me?"

"Do you know how much we would have gotten if we had something like that on tape?" Brie blurted out, then seemed to realize what she said.

"You did know what he was going to do, and you were a part of it. This was probably the reason behind your first visit, to try and get close to me and set me up," Nat said. "You really would have done that to me? Why?"

"Because everything comes easy to you," Brie screeched. "You were prettier than me, smarter than me, everyone liked you more. I spent all those years making sure that you would do what I said, that you would be loyal to me, and then you just left without a word."

"You slept with my boyfriend a week before prom," Natalie reminded her. "Two weeks before graduation. Of course, I left without talking to you again."

"I did you a favor," Brie said. "Everything in your life that you have is because of that. You wouldn't have had the confidence to go to Hollywood if that didn't happen, and you know it. And I had to sit and watch as you became more and more famous, and richer than I'll ever be. How is that fair?"

"I worked hard for it," Nat said. "I didn't expect anything to just happen for me. I would have gotten where I am because I wanted it. I made it happen, not you."

"But I made you who you are! Don't you see that? I was the one who taught you how to use your looks, and your sex appeal, to get what you want. You owe me," Brie said, slapping a hand on the bar.

"I owe you nothing," Natalie said. "You need to leave this restaurant, and this town, and never contact me again."

Nat turned to leave and was shocked when the entire bar broke into applause. Locals started calling out to Brie to leave, and Desmond approached with a grin on his face. He placed a hand over Natalie's, holding her in place as he looked at Brie. "Drinks are on the house," he said to her. "If you leave now."

Brie gasped and looked around, shocked that the room seemed to be against her. Natalie stood her ground as Brie grabbed her purse and jacket and ran out of the bar with one last nasty glare back.

"Sit," Desmond said. "Finish your wine."

Natalie sank back into the chair, and before she knew it, Kendra and Zoe were on either side of her. "You did amazing," Kendra said. "I'm sorry that she hurt you so badly."

"It was a long time ago," she said. "I didn't even realize all of that would come out."

"It wasn't so long ago that she tried to do it again," Zoe pointed out. "She would have ruined your life this time if you had let her. That woman is evil."

"I should probably warn Mike, in case she tries to go see him," Natalie said.

"I texted him," Zoe said. "And JJ, who will make sure she leaves tonight."

"Has she been drinking here for a long time? I don't want her to get hurt," Natalie said.

"It was just seltzer and some cranberry juice," Desmond said with a wink. "I had a sense that she didn't need anything stronger than that."

"Smart boy," Kendra said with a grin. "That's why I wanted you working here."

"That and my charm with the ladies," he said, with a nod toward a group of young women at the end of the bar. "I should get back to them."

"I should get home," Natalie said. "Mike must be worried."

"Want me to pack up some dinner for you?" Zoe offered.

"That would be amazing," she said. "I don't want him to be hungry and mad, that is a bad combination."

Both women laughed and nodded. "They're all that way," Kendra said. "I should get back to it, I wanted to finish the receipts so I can get home. Call me if you need anything."

Natalie posed for a few selfies with tourists who approached her shyly and spoke to some locals while waiting for the food. Once Desmond delivered the bag, she left cash on the bar for him and waved to her new friends as she left. She had sent Phyllis an update on the incident, expecting it to make its way to social media, and wanted to be with Mike when it did. He would find a way to make it all seem better, and Phyllis would figure out how to deal with the situation. All she had to do was keep her head up and focus on the positives in her life, and the top of that list was waiting for her to bring him dinner.

Chapter 27

Mike was trying desperately to ignore the stories that were circulating about Natalie following her confrontation with Brie. The video had surfaced, taken by someone in the restaurant with a front row seat, and been analyzed to death by every magazine, talk show host and online critic there was. Natalie's co-stars had all risen to her defense, telling stories about how hard working she was and dedicated to her career. They all stated that the rumors about her sexual prowess were wildly exaggerated, if not outright false, and no one in Hollywood came forward to claim otherwise.

The only exception was Austin and Brie, who were determined to extend their fifteen minutes of fame. They booked interviews with any outlet that would take them, from the looks of it, and claimed that Natalie had, in fact, slept with Austin. Brie cried at his side as he told the story of Natalie seducing him to get back at his wife back for an imagined slight years before. Although Mike knew every word they said was a lie, it made his blood boil.

"I don't know how you guys do this," he griped to Patrick and Liam mid-workout session. "Let them talk about you when you know it's all lies."

"It usually goes away if you ignore it," Patrick said. "It's like a fire. If it doesn't have oxygen, it dies."

"But they keep giving them more attention," Mike said. "If I have to see their faces one more time, I'm going to lose it."

"Have you talked to Phyllis?" Liam asked, pausing his treadmill to hear.

"Every day. Sometimes more than once," he said. "Natalie seems to have an open line with her."

"She'll handle it," Liam said confidently. "She's the best in the business."

"There must be more that I can do," Mike said.

"Do exactly what Phyllis says, and nothing more," Patrick said. "If you make any move outside what she tells you to do, you'll regret it."

Mike sighed, knowing that his friends were right. Phyllis had been the ultimate coach through all of this and was supporting Natalie in just the right combination of kindness and firmness. While Mike felt useless in the process, letting those best equipped to handle it run the show was the best decision. For the moment, anyway.

As he drove down Patrick's driveway, his sister called. He debated answering it, sure it would be another onslaught of information about what was being said but couldn't bring himself to ignore her. "Hey, Stassi."

"Mike, have you been online?" Her voice was hurried and immediately put a knot in his stomach.

"No, I'm just leaving Patrick's. What's happening now?"

"Two things. The first is that someone put out that you own the gym," she said. "I don't think it's a big deal at all, but I knew you would freak out."

"Of course they did," he said, increasing his grip on the steering wheel. "What are they saying?"

"That you're a secret millionaire who's been lying to his friends and clients for years," she said. "But it's ridiculous, because everyone knows you played in the NFL. Obviously, you have money. Oh, and there are pictures of your house to back up the story."

"Thanks for letting me know," he said. "It's really not a big deal, I just wanted to keep it private. People will look at me differently if they know I'm the boss, you know?"

"I thought they knew?"

"Ashley does, because she's the manager," he said. "And a few other people, but most of them just think I'm there as a trainer. What's the second thing?"

"That cheerleader that you dated the year you got hurt is talking," she said. "Nothing terrible, but she says you broke her heart."

"I went on like two dates with her," he said. "She dumped me as soon as I found out I needed knee surgery and was done for the season."

"Mike, you've always been the best big brother in the world," Stassi said. "I look up to you for so many reasons, not just because you're taller. I want to make sure that you're okay."

"I am," he said.

"Really okay," she persisted. "Remember when you first went to Alabama, and you were so homesick? You called me every night, and we got through it together. I'm here for you, no matter what."

"I know, Stass. And I love you for it," he said. "I promise you that I'm fine. I'm in love, and I'm happy. Nat is amazing, and you're going to be best friends as soon as you meet."

"You've just always had a soft spot for the underdog," she said gently. "Your entire career was protecting people, and now you still try every day to keep the people around you safe. Someone needs to look out for you."

"And I appreciate it, I really do," he said. "I know you're there for me, and my friends here are as well."

"The movie stars you couldn't be bothered to fix me up with," she said with a sniff.

"Hey, I ask you to come visit all the time," he said with a laugh. "Not my fault you're too busy. How are things there?"

"We're holding down the fort here," she said. "I'm going to stay at home for a few nights to make sure no one bothers mom and dad. Mom got a call from that Phyllis lady, she told us what to do. Basically, don't talk to anyone about anything."

"Sounds about right," he said. "Thanks for keeping an eye on things there."

"Mike, can I ask you something?"

"Anything," he responded.

"Is she worth it?"

"Stass, she's more than worth it," he said. "She's the woman of my dreams. My entire future is hinged on her."

"What if it didn't work out? Would you be alright?"

Her question hung in the air for a minute. He thought about the ring that he had stashed in his safe alongside his Super Bowl rings, and the dreams he had of his future. Then he thought about what it would be like to see Natalie walk away from him, and he knew it would rip his heart out. "I'd have to be," he finally said. "But I won't let it happen."

"Just look out for you, okay? Make sure you're being honest with yourself and with her about what you need," she said. "I have to run. Dad is trying to make popcorn on the stove and I'm pretty sure he's going to burn the house down. Love you."

He turned the truck around and drove back to Patrick's, where he caught Liam just about to walk out the front door. "Can you go back inside? I need to talk to you and Patrick," he said.

"Sure," Liam said. "Everything okay?"

"I hope so," he said.

Patrick was in the kitchen and looked surprised to see them come back into the house but gestured to the couches. "What's up?"

"I just talked to my sister," Mike said, pacing in front of the fireplace as his two friends watched. "She asked me if I would be able to handle losing Nat and it has me spiraling a little."

"Did you and Nat have a fight or something?" Liam looked confused, and looked at Patrick, who shrugged.

"No," he said. "A bunch of stuff came out about me in the press today, I guess. Nothing major, it will all be forgotten tomorrow. But it made me realize that there will always be forces trying to break us apart, you know? And I need to figure out how to fight back."

"You really can't," Patrick said gently. "Our lives are pretty public, at least the parts that we show. You and Nat made your relationship part of the story, and it's hard to back away from that."

"You think we made a mistake?"

"No," Patrick said. "You did what was necessary and right for you guys in the moment. But people have always come for her, and she's seen in a certain way. It's not right or fair, but that's how it is. Liam and I, we can be in love and people think it's sweet. When Natalie does the same, people assume she's in it for the wrong reasons. She's using you to get back at the married boyfriend who won't leave his wife, for example."

"Or because you own the gym she works out at," Liam said with a smirk. "That was a surprise, but I don't know why you had to keep it a secret. Especially from us."

"I know, you guys are way richer than I will ever be," he said. "It's dumb. I can't explain it, but I just felt like my money stuff should be kept private."

"Nothing will be private as long as you're with Natalie," Liam said. "That's a fact of life. If you want to be with her, that is part of the package. They will examine every aspect of you, your family, your business. Nothing is off the table. You either embrace and ignore, or you let her go."

"I'm not letting her go," he said. "And I thought I had no issue with people digging in my past. But people lying about me, and attacking her with lies, that's too much."

"It's why we let the professionals handle it," Patrick said. "You have to be able to ignore it."

"How do Emma and Holly handle this?"

"You would have to ask them," Patrick said with a shrug. "The press really hasn't gone after Emma. They heard her story, and it got a lot of sympathy, and she's so sweet that they really leave her be."

"Same with Holly," Liam said. "Once they figured out that I was in a serious relationship, the press went crazy. Just like it did when Patrick went public with Emma. But Holly has never met someone who wasn't her friend, so they just take a few shots at my playboy days but leave her alone."

"It's not like I'm a scumbag," Mike said. "You guys are making it seem like I'm getting more heat because I'm not as sweet as the girls."

"That's not it at all," Patrick said. "It's because of how they've painted Nat for years. That's why she pretended to date me for a long time, it took the heat off her. Liam here slept his way around the world, and they see it as charming. Natalie just acts like a sex kitten, and she's seen as a tramp. It's a total double standard, but that's the reality."

"I bought a ring," Mike heard himself say. "A few weeks ago."

"Wow." Liam turned to look at Patrick, then back at Mike. "Are you going to ask her to marry you? That's going to really make things hot for the two of us, for the record."

"I want to," Mike admitted. "But I also worry that it's too soon and it could freak her out. And I haven't even met her parents yet. You guys are like her brothers. Would you give me your blessing?"

"Absolutely," Patrick said. "Once you fully come to terms with living the public life. You need to have an honest conversation with her about what the future looks like, where you'll live, whether you both want kids. All of that. You've been honeymooning together, not officially living together, and it's all going really fast. It might not be a bad idea to slow down and see what happens."

"We've got a movie to film soon," Liam said. "Maybe that time apart will help you both figure it out. And honestly…"

"What?" Mike demanded.

"I think you need to make sure that she's moved past the trauma," Liam said. "She's been different the last few months. In a good way, lately, but not herself. Natalie can be tough, and calculating I suppose you would say. She knows how to get what she wants, no matter what. She keeps everything and everyone at arm's length, only showing what she wants us to see. This version of her is new for us too, seeing her relaxed and not camera ready every minute. I hope this is a permanent change, because it's good for her to be open to people around her. Seeing her with the girls is new, I don't think she had many girlfriends before, and I love seeing it. But what if in six months she's bored here, and wants to get back to her regular life? Or what if one day you wake up and realize that you guys were bonded by an event, and once that has worn off, you feel like strangers? What if you want different things?"

"Don't say that," Mike said, feeling his hackles rise. "I love her, and it has nothing to do with what happened."

"I know you feel that way," Liam said. "But does she?"

Mike stared at Patrick and Liam, who had quickly become two of his best friends, and had no words. The question rocked him more than he cared to admit, and a little voice inside told him that was what he had been afraid of this whole time. Was he rushing things because he was worried that she would wake up one day, be healed, and be done with him?

He walked to the door without saying a word, ignoring their voices and asking him to stay. Liam called out an apology just as the door closed quietly behind him, and he jogged to his truck. As he drove away from Patrick's house, his phone rang, showing

Natalie's name on the screen. He ignored it and drove, no destination in his mind. He needed to escape his thoughts and had no idea how to do that.

***

Hours later, he pulled into his driveway and noted the lights on inside that indicated Natalie was there. She usually was when his day ended, and he had been taking it for granted. He had asked her to live with him, but he had meant permanently, and his friends had him questioning whether she had the same idea. Did she just think of his house as a crashing pad, like what she had at Liam's? A place to recover until her real world called her home?

He parked in the garage and closed the door behind him, walking slowly into the house. Even after hours of driving aimlessly, he wasn't prepared to see Natalie curled up with a book on his couch. She had a mug of tea on the coffee table, snug under a blanket with the fire going and Midnight sleeping on her lap. It looked like she was exactly where she belonged, and he second guessed himself even questioning it. Would it be better to leave it alone, enjoy it while it lasted?

"Hey, you," she said. "How was your day?"

"It was okay," he said. He pulled off his sweatshirt and dropped it on a stool at the island, along with the backpack he had forgotten to leave in the mudroom.

"I was debating dinner," she said. "I picked up some things from Plates, so we could heat them up. Or if you would rather, we could order in."

"I'm not hungry right now," he said.

"You? Not hungry? What's wrong?"

283

"Can't I just be not hungry?" he heard himself snap and saw the hurt look on her face. "I'm going to shower. I'll be back down."

After spending too long standing under the rainfall debating his options, he pulled on a pair of sweatpants an a t-shirt and went back to face the fire. Losing his temper meant he had to tell her what was running through his mind, and it was the only thing that made sense. If he kept all these questions in his mind, he would officially go crazy.

Natalie was sitting up, knees tucked close to her chest and her arms wrapped around them. She looked like she was trying to shield herself from whatever was coming, and he felt even worse about himself. "I'm sorry I snapped at you," he said.

"Will you please tell me what's going on?"

Chapter 28

Natalie watched the emotions flit across Mike's face, settling into quiet resignation as he took the chair opposite her. His conscious choice not to sit next to her stung, and she had to fight back tears. Obviously, she had become too comfortable here in his home, or he had grown tired of her being too much work. She resigned herself to the idea of leaving with grace even before he started speaking and was mentally packing when he finally started.

"I love you." The words were so different from what she had been expecting, it caught her off guard.

"I love you too," she whispered. There was obviously a big but coming, and she steeled herself against it.

"I mean, I love you in a forever kind of way," he said. "The kind where I want to marry you and have babies and sit in our rocking chairs in fifty years while our grandkids play on the lawn. That kind of love."

Now she was thoroughly confused. No one had ever started a breakup talk like this before, and she had no idea what to say. She searched his face for a clue, and got nothing, so she simply nodded.

"When I asked you to move in here, I meant for good. Not for a few months while you continue therapy, but forever. And now I'm realizing that we never had a conversation about that," he said. "I was just living in my own happy world, thinking we were on the same page. But now I'm having second thoughts."

"About loving me?"

"No." His head snapped up, and he met her eyes for the first time. "I'll never question that. But I look at how we started, and I have to wonder if we would have gotten to this place if we had just been Patrick's friends. If you had just come here for the week to get away from a stalker in California, would we have fallen in love?"

"I can't answer that," she said honestly. "I don't think anyone can. You could barely talk to me when I first got here."

"Beyond that," he said, waving a hand. "That day of the shooting, we had been having fun. We went horseback riding, and we were actually talking for the first time. Did you feel anything for me then? Before your life got flipped upside down?"

"Mike, you're asking me impossible questions," she said. "Yes, I was having a great day, and I was thrilled that you finally talked to me. I was having fun flirting with you, seeing you blush. I can't tell you if I would have fallen for you because everything did change hours later."

He stood up and paced in front of her, making her stomach churn. Something had obviously brought this on, but she didn't know what to say or do to assure him of her feelings.

"Do you plan to go back to California?" he asked, throwing her with the change of subject.

"I have a contract," she said. "We film in Georgia in a few months, and I'll have to go to Los Angeles as well. And I do have a house there, responsibilities I can't ignore forever."

"What happens when that time comes? Do you leave here and not look back?"

"Absolutely not," she said. "I had put off talking about the movie filming, because it feels like it's still far away. But I had hoped that you would come with me."

"And just wait around while you work?" he stared at her, looking shocked by the suggestion.

"Well, you train Patrick and Liam. And me, when I decide to workout," she said, trying to lighten the mood. "I know Emma will be there, and she tries to do a lot of charity work while Patrick is busy. Holly will go too, but she'll take a nursing assignment there, I'm sure."

"I should hang out with the girls?"

"Don't say it like that," she said, annoyed on her friend's behalf that he would minimize it. "I just meant that there are ways you could find fulfilment while I'm working. Or if you don't want to come, you don't have to. I can come back on my days off."

"And then what? We have a long-distance relationship forever? With you in California, and me sitting here, hoping you'll pop in for a day?"

"You aren't being fair at all," she said. "We've been together for a few months. I didn't know I had to give up my career so you would feel secure. I honestly hadn't thought about how it would work, because I figured you and I would talk about it and find the solution together."

"Are you thinking of living here between movies?" he asked her, and she hesitated, making him hang his head.

"I'm not saying no! But I also really hadn't thought about it," she said, pleading with him to listen. "I've been so caught up in what happened, and then the press stuff, that I only think day to day. And every day, I'm happy here, with you."

"I can't go day by day," he said. "I need to know what's going to happen. I'm all in, Nat. And I can't spend every day wondering if you're with me because I'm convenient. Because you feel safe."

"That's not it at all," she said. Daring to stand, she moved to stand in front of him, putting her arms around his waist. When he didn't move, she rested her cheek against his chest. "This is my favorite place to be. And yes, I feel safe with you, but that's not all. You make me smile. You're considerate and do things that you know will make me happy. I love taking care of you in little ways, and I'm learning what those things are. You make me feel like I'm important, but not because of what I do for work, because of who I am. I want to tell you every funny thing I see, or ask your opinion, before anyone else. You matter to me more than anything else, you have to believe that."

"People keep asking me if we're trauma bonded," he said. "And I don't know. Is that the thing that holds us together?"

"No," she said. "We are so much more than that. You've helped me see that was just a thing that happened to me, to us. It was a moment. It doesn't define us."

"What do we do?" he asked, his voice a ragged whisper.

"Believe in me. Believe in us," she begged him. "Don't give up on me. We have things to figure out, but we can do it together. It's only been a few months. We have our whole lives to figure it out."

"I just want to know that we'll be together. I know I sound ridiculous, but please just tell me that," he said.

"We will," she said. She stretched up to kiss him to solidify her promise. "I'm here. And I'm yours."

"Let's get married," he said. The words shocked her, and she pulled back and stared up at him.

"You know I can't do that, right? Not now. Not yet."

"But you just said—"

She cut him off by putting her hand on his chest. "I know. And I meant that. But getting married isn't proving anything, and we can't just jump into that."

"JJ and Zoe did," he said.

She bit her tongue to point out how childish he sounded and sighed. "You know that's different."

"Why?"

"First of all, they had been friends for a long time," she said. "Secondly, we both have a lot of assets that we need to protect."

He took a step back from her, looking shocked. "You think I'm trying to marry you for your money?"

"No. But we both should be protected," she said. "This is your home. You have a business. You have plenty in the bank. Neither of us are in this for what the other person has, and the easiest thing is just to let the lawyers make sure our assets are secure."

"Dan could fix that tomorrow," he said. "You're just making excuses."

"Mike, this is too fast," she said. "You have to see that. You haven't even met my parents yet, and I haven't met your siblings.

Can't we just enjoy where we are and know that is the end goal for both of us?"

"You don't think it would be good for your image to be married?" He looked as though he regretted the words as soon as they came out of his mouth, but he said nothing more.

"Because I'm such a tramp? Spending the night with-or living with-a man I'm not married to? Even though you're doing the exact same thing, and you aren't worried about your image?" She crossed her arms and stared at him, not surprised when he hung his head. "I think I'm going to head out for a bit. We both need some time to calm down before we really say something we would regret."

She turned on her heel and hurried to the mudroom, where she stuck her feet into boots and grabbed a jacket. Running to her car, she tried to hold in the sobs and lost the battle, making it hard to see as she drove down the long driveway. She put the car in park at the end, where she knew she was out of sight of the house, and let herself cry. How had things gone so terribly wrong so quickly?

***

Emma answered the door when Nat knocked, and she virtually fell into her friend's arms. She hadn't known where else to go, other than to get on a plane and get out of Windsor Peak. But doing so would have confirmed the end of her relationship with Mike, and she didn't want that. She just wanted someone to help her understand what had gone wrong and how to fix it.

"What's wrong?" Emma asked, pulling her further inside so she could close the door. "Are you hurt?"

"Not physically, no." She wiped at her tears with the sleeve of her coat and then let out a half sob, half laugh. "I'm a mess."

"Should I call Patrick home? He's over at Jake's watching a game," Emma said.

"No, it's okay. This is more girl stuff than anything," she said.

"Let me alert the girl power signal," Emma said, pulling out her phone. "And open a bottle of wine, and we can get to the bottom of this."

Within a half hour, the room was full of the women that Natalie had come to think of as her best friends. They had all dropped everything to come when they heard she was upset, and all wanted to help her. It brought a fresh wave of tears, this time of gratitude, because this was still new to her.

"Tell us what happened," Holly asked gently.

They were all sitting in the living room, wine in hand, ready to solve her problems. Natalie took a fortifying sip and then started to explain the conversation with Mike. "It came out of nowhere," she said after telling them the details. "I am so confused. I do love him, and I want to be with him. But I can't marry him to prove that."

"And you shouldn't have to," Kendra said. "You could carry on as you are forever, if you wanted to. There's no rule that says you have to get married."

"But the press already portrays me as such a hussy," Natalie said. "This isn't helping that."

"According to the tabloids," Shea said. "You were with Patrick for a number of years, which we all know is false. Then you had a few dates, which we knew was to send a signal that Patrick was free to date Emma. And now you're with Mike. That's not a lot of men, and only one of them is real."

Natalie nodded. "But remember, the press also thought I had an affair with Austin. And every time I even look at someone, it gets blown up. If I meet someone for the first time on a red carpet, there is immediately a rumor about us circulating. Sitting next to someone at a party means that we're lovers. When I do a love scene in a movie, everyone assumes I'm also sleeping with them in real life."

"That's because you're good at what you do," Zoe said. "You convince everyone that it's real."

"I have been so careful for years," Natalie said. "I have to dress one way to have the image Hollywood wants, but then I get slammed for it. Fans want me to be sexy and desirable, but then they find it insulting. If I dress down, I get ridiculed. I'm supposed to be tough, but then I'm trying to hard. I just want to be happy."

"It sounds to me," Kendra said. "Like there are two different issues going on, and you're getting them mixed up in your head. The first issue is the perception of the press, or fans, of you. And the second is your feelings for Mike."

"True," Nat said. "And also, the fact that he thinks I only care about him because I'm trauma bonded to him. How do I fix that?"

"Time and repetition," Shea said. "Just like teaching. You keep showing the same thing over and over, even if you get frustrated. When it clicks one day, then it was worth it."

"Maybe he could go to therapy with you?" Emma suggested. "You guys could work that out in one session, I bet."

"The press is a different story," Holly said. "From what Liam has said, there isn't much they'll say if it's not sensational. But what if you found a female reporter who you trusted, and let her share your story?"

"Definitely female," Emma said in agreement. "Not that Dermott guy. He's a pest."

"I can ask Phyllis to look into that," she said. "Or at least, consider it. That's a good idea, if anyone would even pay attention."

"The double standards are worth pointing out," Kendra said. "If no one will listen now, the message is still there. Little girls like Calle will see you standing up for yourself and realize they should be judged by more than what's on the outside. You have power, don't ever forget that."

"What do I do about Mike?"

"You love him, right?" Shea asked gently.

"Very much," Natalie said, choking down more tears. "I feel secure in knowing he loves me, and it kills me that he doesn't feel the same way about my feelings for him."

"There must be something you can do to show him, without having to get married," Zoe said. "And I say that as someone who did need to get married to let myself admit I was in love. But if you aren't ready, then you wait. And we'll think of a different solution."

Natalie listened as her friends tossed ideas around, each getting more ridiculous than the one before. Her nerves were settling, and she was overwhelmed with gratitude for the kindness and friendship these women had shown her. They had taught her that sisterhood was real, and the strength of women coming together was unmatched. They would have her back no matter what, and she would return the favor without question. She knew she would be okay, no matter what happened with Mike, because of the people in this room. She had come to Windsor Peak to escape, but she realized that in doing so, she really had found her place.

Chapter 29

His mood had gotten progressively worse as the day went on, and Mike knew his clients were taking the brunt of it. Pushing himself to his limits while encouraging them to do the same hour after hour had worn him out, and he was sore in places he hadn't thought about for years. It was what he deserved for pushing Natalie so hard the night before. What had he been thinking?

Insecurity was new to him, and it wasn't a feeling he enjoyed. His entire life he had succeeded at things, and most had come easy to him. He had never been in a relationship like this, where he felt off balance, and he had no idea what to do. His mother told him he was a fool, when he called her earlier for advice, and his dad told him to apologize. His friends had checked in, alerted to the crisis by their wives and girlfriends, and he had declined their offer of help. It was his problem to fix, and he had no idea how to do it, but flowers seemed like a good start.

The florist finished wrapping the huge bouquet she had put together for him, and with a pitying look, suggested that he swing into the bakery for some treats to go along with them. He walked across the street, relieved to see that Piper was alone in the store through the window. She smiled at him as he entered and then frowned.

"What did you do wrong?" she asked.

"Why do you assume that?" he challenged her.

"You have the biggest bouquet I've ever seen, and you must be here for chocolate to go with it," she said. "That equals a screw up."

"Yeah, you might be right," he said with a sigh. "I need a box of those truffle cookies that you make, please."

"On it," she said. She pulled a box and some parchment paper out and started filling it before speaking again. "Want to talk about it?"

"No, thanks. I'm an idiot."

"Usually true," she said. "But love makes us do crazy things."

"It should be easier than this," he said, unable to help himself.

"No, it shouldn't." She shot him an incredulous look over the counter. "It should be hard, and worth fighting for. Think about what they say in marriage vows. You have to be willing to battle through the bad stuff, no matter what."

"I am, but shouldn't I also feel secure every day?"

"What's making you feel insecure?" she asked.

"Have you seen her? I'm dating one of the most famous, desirable women on the planet," he said. "I am not anywhere near her equal."

"That's your opinion, and I'm a little shocked to hear you say that," she said. "You're obviously handsome and insanely in shape, but more importantly, you're a good guy. You're nice to everyone around you, patient even when frustrated, and fun to be with. From my perspective, you're more than even with her. You know what my grandmother used to tell me?"

"What?"

"Fall in love with someone who loves you more than you love them," she said. "But I think that's horrible. Because no one wants to be the one who is loved less, you know? You need to just trust in your heart, and love as much as you can, and hope that it comes back to you. That's all we can do."

"You're a wise woman, Piper." He accepted the box of cookies and passed her his credit card. "Thank you for this."

"If you can't do, teach, right?" She winked at him and laughed. "Taking relationship advice from me should probably come with a warning label, but I hope I helped a little."

"You did," he said. "I'll see you later."

He drove home slowly, only to realize when he got there that Nat would be at Liam's, for play rehearsal. The kids were in the final days before they took the stage, and the energy was high when he arrived. Students who were participating were racing around in their costumes, while others were feeding off the energy and bouncing off the walls. The noise level was off the charts, and Mike considered turning around and waiting, but then his eyes met Natalie's.

Even from across the room, the zip that he felt when she was around went from his brain to his toes. Every part of him was desperate to fix things, and he couldn't believe that he had been dumb enough to push her so hard. Why would he risk losing her? He mentally slapped himself as he made his way through the crowded room.

"Hi," she said softly when he approached.

"I'm sorry."

She blinked at him, then offered a small smile. "Me too."

"You have nothing to be sorry for," he insisted. "I messed up. I feel like such a fool, because I'm just insecure and a mess."

"You have no reason to feel insecure," she said. "I'm honest about my feelings, I promise. I just don't want to rush anything. I need to get back to my normal life so we can make sure we're still feeling the same way."

"I have to admit, a big part of me wants to beg you not to say that," he said. "The idea of you going back to California and forgetting about me is too much to bear."

"Is there any part of you that could consider coming?"

"Mr. Mike, are those cookies?" A precocious little boy named Robbie asked as he pointed at the box Mike held.

"They are," he said, never losing eye contact with Nat. "I got them for Miss Natalie."

"My mom says that we should always share," Robbie retorted, making both adults laugh.

"You're right," he said. "Why don't we take these into the kitchen and see about splitting them up. I'll get Miss Natalie another treat."

"Did you do something wrong?" At Mike's inquisitive looks, Robbie continued. "My dad brings flowers home when he's in trouble."

"A little bit, yes," he admitted. "But also, I just wanted to give her something pretty."

The little boy nodded sagely. "Girls like that."

He followed Robbie after Natalie gave him a little head nod, indicating they would talk later, and he should distribute the cookies. At least, that's how he chose to interpret the moment.

***

Hours later, they pulled into the driveway at the same time. A small part of him was relieved that she had come back, he had almost been expecting her to return to Liam's. Their parents upcoming visit might have something to do with that, but all that mattered was they were under the same roof tonight. He would take the time to make things right, no matter what. Thoughts of the ring that was safely stored in the safe flashed into his head, but he immediately dismissed them. She had already made it clear that wasn't the solution, and begging wasn't a good look.

He had stopped for a pizza and salad on the way home, but he opened her car door for her before retrieving them from the backseat. She looked tired, and he hated that he was a part of her stress now. Following her into the house, he placed the food on the island and then gathered her into his arms.

"I'm really sorry," he said. "I probably shouldn't have tried to say that in the middle of the ruckus the kids were creating, but I couldn't wait any longer."

"You don't have to be sorry," she said. "Believe it or not, I understand the feelings of insecurity."

"You? The most beautiful woman in the world?"

She laughed and pushed him back. "I also understand the feelings of hunger, and if you don't feed me very quickly, I'm going to fall over."

"As you wish," he said, winking at her. He grabbed plates and forks from the cabinets and plated some pizza and salad for her. He retreated back to the kitchen before getting his own food, grabbing a bottle of wine and pouring two glasses. She accepted hers with a smile.

"I'm already feeling better," she said. "Thank you."

"It looked a little crazy there with the kids," he said.

"They were off the wall," she said with a laugh. "Everyone had changes they wanted to make, or suddenly didn't like the part they were playing. It was all I could do not to scream. But we finally got to run through the whole thing, and it was adorable."

"When do your parents arrive?"

"Thursday," she said. "What about yours?"

"Same. It's going to be interesting."

"They'll get along great," she predicted. "I think it will be fun to have them all here."

He raised an eyebrow at her. "Those words might come back to haunt you."

She laughed, then wiped her mouth and turned to him with a serious expression on her face. "I want you to know that I'm serious about my feelings for you," she said. "I have no intention of anything changing in the future, but I also need to feel secure in your feelings about me. And until I'm back to my normal life, I don't think I can feel that way."

"What makes you think I'd feel differently about you?" he challenged her.

"I don't think I like the person that I was before all this happened," she said. "I was selfish and constantly putting on a show. I never would have left the house dressed like this."

He took in the leggings and sweater she was wearing, which he had gotten used to seeing her in. "I think you look great."

"For Vermont," she said. "But in California, I have to dress the part. I can't go out with my hair in a ponytail and no makeup on, because they'll take pictures and rip me apart. I need to always look like a movie star, and act like one."

"But if you don't like it, why keep doing it?"

"It's my job," she said. "And I do love acting. I love being able to put on a character and be braver than I am, or smarter, or the ugly duckling. I can go back and relive moments in history that I wasn't a part of, and feel like I was. And I make people happy when I do a good job, which is important to me."

"First of all, you could never be an ugly duckling," he said. "Secondly, I don't want you to stop acting if you love it. But why feel the need to put on a show outside of the stage?"

"What if this, right now, is part of the act?"

"What do you mean?" he was shocked and couldn't hide it from his face.

"I worry that I've lost the difference between who I really am versus what I pretend to be," she said. "What if I find out I was playing a part to get through the trauma?"

"Do you think that's what you're doing?"

"I don't know," she said, sighing. "I don't think so. But it's possible. And I could go back to being selfish and cold, and you'd be stuck with me. I can't do that to you."

"But you asked me to come with you to California," he said.

"I did," she said, nodding. "And maybe it would work. Or it could be a flaming disaster. I know right now, I don't want to live without you, wherever I am. And I don't think that will change, but you might find you don't want to be with me anymore."

"That's not possible," he insisted.

"You're being stubborn," she chastised him. "Anything is possible."

"Where does that leave us now?" he asked, panic rising quickly.

"Enjoy where we are? Don't rush into something that would make us have bad feelings about each other?" she suggested. "I don't want anything to change. I just want to be here, with you, and see what happens."

"That's hard for me to accept," he admitted. "I know it can't all be on my terms, but this feels like it's all on yours. I have to wait and see if you decide to move back, or if you change in some drastic way. It makes me feel a little like a passing toy, keeping you entertained while you're here."

"What could I say that would make it less so? My parents are coming here to meet you and your parents," she pointed out. "I'm living here. I told you I love you. What else can I do?"

"I don't know," he said. The weight of the words sat heavy on his chest, but they were all he could say. He had a sense that his time with her was going to end suddenly, and it would crush him. Maybe it was better to keep the rest of his thoughts to himself, at least for the time being. They seemed to be going in circles with no destination, and he was afraid that if he kept pushing, he would push her right out of the door.

Chapter 30

"Why do you feel the need to go back?" Dr. Jones asked, her notebook propped on her knee as she sat across from Natalie. Nat had just finished explaining the turmoil between herself and Mike and was hoping to find a path forward with her counselor.

"That's where my job is," Nat responded.

"No," Dr. Jones said. "You already told me that you go to Atlanta next to shoot the next movie. At most, you'll be needed in California for a few weeks. Lots of people travel for work and are away from home for a long period. Why can't you be like that?"

"Do you know how hard it was for me to be seen as a serious actress in Hollywood?"

"No."

"For years, I only got called for auditions of things that required nudity, or graphic sex scenes," Nat explained. "I took one small role in an indie film because they didn't want me to do any of that, they wanted me to just act. It was the best six weeks, and that movie blew up my career. Suddenly, people wanted to pay attention to me for more than just my face or my body, and I ended up with this role that would define my career. I get to show young girls that women can be as tough as men, and I don't have to do any love scenes to diminish it."

"Then why would you need to parade around in Hollywood in skimpy dresses? If the image you want to put out to young fans is that you can do anything a man can do, prove it. Live your life the way you want to, not the way executives or the press demands you do," Dr. Jones said. "We haven't known each other long, but I've seen you flourish in the last few weeks. Are you enjoying working with the youth center on their play?"

Nat nodded. "It's the most fun I've had in a long time."

"Do you see how beneficial you are to this community? They value you as Natalie, not a face on a movie poster or a hero on the screen. They like you because you show up for their kids, and you offer smiles to them when you pass in the streets," Dr. Jones said. "You've become a part of this community, and I think it suits you. But know what else I think?"

"I'm afraid to say yes," Natalie admitted.

"I think you're afraid," Dr. Jones said. "But this isn't about the shooting. This is about showing your real self to those you care about. You're scared they'll reject you. For years, you've kept your personality locked down. It started when you were growing up, moving all the time with the military, and feeling like you needed to change your personality to fit in at new schools. Then you finally become close to a friend, and she betrayed you, teaching you the wrong lesson. You thought you had to stay distant from people to protect yourself, and that's what you've done for years. Maybe you've shown your real self to the people you are close to, like Liam and Patrick. But for the most part, you've been closed off for a long, long time."

"I had to protect myself," Nat said, hating that she sounded petulant.

"From whom? Because you were already putting out conflicting versions of yourself," the therapist said gently. "Behind the scenes, you were fighting to not be seen as a sex symbol. In front of the press, you were oozing sensuality. It sounds to me like you kept yourself so locked down, it's uncomfortable to be in your own skin now."

"If I was just myself out there, they would rip me apart."

"And it would hurt more if they were critical of your true self?"

"Of course! Don't you think that's the worst thing that could happen?"

"No," Dr. Jones said, shaking her head slowly. "I don't. I think not living your life fully and completely is the worst thing I can imagine. You only get one chance here, Natalie. You need to live the life you want to look back on and feel satisfied with."

***

The therapists' words rattled around in her brain as she cruised through town, unsure of her destination. When she spotted Emma, she waved and pulled into a parking spot, running to catch up with her friend.

"Hey," Emma said. "What are you up to? I was supposed to meet Patrick for lunch and he just bailed."

"Is everything okay?"

"He just said he needed to go talk to his dad," Emma said with a shrug. "It's unlike him to be so close lipped about what's happening, so I didn't push hard. He'll tell me when he's ready. Do you have time to grab something to eat with me?"

"I hope everything is alright," Nat said. "I'd love to have lunch."

"We were going to the Palace, but if you'd rather the bakery, we could go there," Emma offered. "It's a little quieter in there."

"No, the Palace is fine," Natalie said. "I'm less scared now. Being out every day with the kids and being in town more has helped me so much."

"And therapy is going well?" Emma asked as she pulled the door open to the restaurant.

"I just came from there," Nat said. "I feel like we're moved from talking about the trauma to figuring out my relationship issues."

"You and Mike are still having trouble?" Emma frowned as they sat at a table in the corner, slightly away from the other customers. "I thought you had worked it out?"

"I don't know if it's trouble," Natalie said. "But we still have different ideas of where we should be I guess."

"What do you mean?"

"He wants a commitment, and I'm not sure of what I'll be doing tomorrow, never mind a year from now."

"But you could agree to be exclusive, right?" Emma frowned, studying her as she asked.

"Oh, we're past that point," Nat said with a laugh. "I moved in with him."

"Is that official?"

"Yes?" Natalie heard the question in her own voice and wasn't surprised when Emma jumped on it.

"Permanent as in while you're here," Emma asked. "Or this is your home now?"

"I guess I didn't really clarify that," Natalie said slowly. "That's what I'm struggling with too. If I go back to Hollywood, I'll fall back

306

into the same rhythm. Parties, being seen, meetings, constant pressure."

"I see that with Patrick when we go to California," Emma said. "He changes a little."

"That's what I keep trying to tell Mike," Natalie said. "I don't know if he would like the me that lives there."

"Of course he would," Emma said, dismissing the idea with a wave of her hand. "You two are so compatible, and the way you look at each other tells me it's forever. When I go out with Patrick, he's tenser. He sleeps less. We spend a lot of time with people I know he doesn't like very much, but he has to be nice. It takes a lot out of him. But I love him for letting me see those weak moments and allowing me to support him through it."

"You don't get annoyed that he's different than he is here?"

"No," Emma said definitively. "Once we get behind closed doors, he's the Patrick that I know here. And I know that he's looking forward to getting back here as much as I am. I think what you need to ask yourself is which Natalie do you want to be? The one who has really flourished here, or the one who lives there? Because I feel like you've really found out who you are since you got here."

"You don't think it's the trauma talking?"

"Is that what you're afraid of?" Emma looked shocked. "No. I don't. I started getting to know you before that, remember? I know you as the friend who offered to charter a helicopter to help my sister run away in Vegas if needed. The one who helped raise a ton of money for the horse rescue. The one who hugged me on a red carpet to send the signal that I was welcome there. You've always been thoughtful and kind, and that's the same person sitting here now. You were just more reserved, and I feel like since coming here, you've really blossomed and become confident in your ability to be a good friend and be appreciated for who you are."

Natalie smiled at her friend, grateful for her words. "Thank you, that means a lot. I honestly have never felt so mixed up in my life."

"Well, you had a focus before," Emma said. "You're goal oriented. You wanted to be a movie star, and you're one of the biggest in the world. Everything I've seen you set your mind to; you've accomplished. What is your goal with this relationship?"

Natalie sipped her iced tea and considered the question. She had been so caught up in the feelings, and her worries about the future, she hadn't really thought of it that way. "I think it's to marry him and have his babies," she said with a quiet laugh. "He's the most amazing man I've ever met. And this is the first time I've ever felt like I was going to catch on fire when I was with someone, you know?"

"I do," Emma said, nodding. "It's like that for me with Patrick too."

"Mike wanted to get married," Natalie admitted. "And I was tempted to throw caution to the wind and run to town hall."

"Really?" Emma's eyes bugged as she stared at her. "Wait until I tell Patrick."

Natalie laughed. "I probably just got him into trouble. Are you guys talking about it?"

"Yes," Emma said with a nod. "He hasn't asked officially. But we talk about it, and both know that's where we're headed."

"And you know where you'll live?"

"Here," Emma said. "I'll travel with him as much as possible, which will get harder when we have kids. But he's worth whatever hard stuff comes up later in life. We'll figure it out as it comes."

"I wish I could be in that same place with Mike," Natalie admitted. "I feel like we're just struggling to communicate."

"All you can do is be honest about your feelings, and make sure to listen to what he's saying. Both the words and in actions," Emma said. She paused as their waitress delivered the salads they had ordered, smiling her thanks before turning back to Nat. "Trust in what you have."

"That's good advice. I'm going to try," Natalie said. "Are you ready for the fundraiser this weekend?"

"It's a circus," Emma said with a laugh. "Patrick has so many people flying in, we took up all the open rooms at the Inn, plus we have people staying with us. A handful will stay in Stowe and just come over for the gala, which helps. I'm at the point where I might have to start asking people for their spare bedrooms."

"We have both sets of parents and Mike's siblings coming," Natalie said. "We're full. But if you need help with anything else, just let me know."

"Thanks," Emma said. "I think it's under control. Patrick hired a party planner to take care of most of it, which is a relief. Just the transition from youth center to ball room requires more manpower than I have."

"It's nice of you and Patrick to organize all of this."

"It's the least we can do," Emma said. "Seeing the good that Rex has done for Jake really pushed Patrick to want to do more. The service dogs make it possible for our veterans to live as normal a life as possible, and we want to make sure we can help a lot of them. Jake already has helped other friends get in touch with the organization to start the process, and he loves that he can actually point people to something that really helps."

They finished their lunch and hugged goodbye on the sidewalk, leaving just enough time for Natalie to beat the school buses to the youth center. The final dress rehearsal was the next day, making this the last day to get the kids to focus and learn their parts.

The afternoon flew by, with adjustments made to costumes and frequent reminders of lines, but the kids seemed more settled than the previous rehearsal. She reminded them as they gathered their backpacks that they had one final day left, and they needed to arrive the next afternoon ready to work. The play would go on Friday night, whether they were prepared or not.

As they all departed, she realized with a pang that the end of her time with the students was approaching. She had enjoyed the last few weeks and appreciated their enthusiasm for every aspect of putting the play on. It brought her back to her early days, when she had fallen in love with acting, and she was happy to have helped create this show. It could be her only stamp on this little town which had made such a huge impact in her life.

"Look at you, the little acting coach." A deep voice from the shadows behind the stage had her jump, but she relaxed when her frequent co-star Zane stepped out. "I didn't mean to scare you."

"I'm a little jumpy these days," she said. "I didn't know you were coming in today."

"Liam picked me up an hour ago," he said. He walked over and gave her a bone-crushing hug. "I didn't want to come in and disrupt things, it looked like you were barely holding it together."

"It's a lot like herding cats," she admitted. "Patrick and Liam were supposed to be helping but both seem to find an urgent task each afternoon."

"Sounds about right," he said. "I plan to be very busy tomorrow afternoon, so don't get any ideas."

"Busy with what?" She put her hands on her hips and challenged him.

"I heard great things about this trainer the guys work out with," he said, a teasing lilt in his voice. "Thought I should check him out."

She slipped her arm around his waist and squeezed. "I'm glad you're here."

"Me too," he said.

Her phone chimed with an incoming text, and she groaned when she saw Phyllis's name on the screen. She read it quickly and rolled her eyes before sticking her phone in her pocket.

"What is it?" Zane asked.

"My publicist," she explained. "She wants to set up an interview for me with a reporter from Vanity Fair. She thinks it might put an end to this gossip about Austin and change the public perception of me."

"How do you figure?"

"The press is determined to paint me as a tramp," she explained. "They constantly run with stories and pictures making it seem like I'm sleeping with Mike, Patrick, Liam - probably you now, too."

"I think that rumor went around a while ago," he said. "I think it helped my street cred."

"Exactly! It helps your image and hurts mine," she fumed. "If I did want to sleep with half of Hollywood, why should it matter? You do, and everyone loves you."

"Hey now. Why am I taking shots?"

"Zane, you know it's true," she said. "You live your life in a way I never could, but people act like I do. I'm tired of it."

"The interview is the solution?"

"Maybe. If she can get the right reporter, which she thinks she has," she said. Before thinking it through any further, she pulled her phone out and texted a response. "I'm going to do it. I'm sick of hiding."

"I'm not sure what I walked in to," Zane said with a big grin. "But I love it. Feisty Nat, I'm here for it."

Chapter 31

Their parents arrived early on Thursday morning, and Mike was glad he had taken the day off. His siblings weren't driving over until Saturday, which made the introductions between the two sets of families a little easier. Natalie had insisted on going to pick her parents up at the airport alone, since his parents were due to arrive early. He had told her his parents had keys and would be fine, but she insisted on going alone. A part of him was happy to see that she felt confident and independent enough to take the trip alone, even though he missed her as he prepared the house.

Rosalita arrived in a blaze of energy, asking him a million questions about Nat's parents that he didn't have the answer to. "Mom, can you sit and relax for a few minutes? You're making me dizzy."

Kevin, who was lounging on the couch, laughed. "She's been like this for days, son. She'll settle in once she meets the in-laws."

Rosie's eyes lit up and she turned on Mike. "Do you think that's a possibility? I liked her so much when we were here last, and I love how happy you look around her."

"She makes me happy," he said. "I hope one day we'll be able to make it permanent. But she needs more time, and I have to respect that."

"By a few months in, we were married," she persisted. "When you know, you know."

"I do know," he said. "But I'm respecting her feelings."

"Did you ask her?"

"We had a conversation about it," he admitted. "But no, I didn't propose yet. I will when the time is right."

"Does that mean you already got a ring?" His mom was ruthless, nothing would sneak by her.

"Yes," he said. "But she can't know that. It would freak her out."

"Can we see it?" Rosie clapped her hands and bounced on her feet. "Please?"

He sighed and went into his office, retrieving the small box from the safe. Just holding it felt heavy with anticipation yet made his steps lighter with the knowledge that this was his future. He just needed to trust in what he and Nat were building and not freak out.

"Here it is," he said, showing his parents the ring.

"Oh, Miguel," his mom sighed. "It's stunning."

"The jeweler did a really good job," he said. "JJ had gone to the same guy to get the perfect ring for Zoe, and he was right. The guy knows what he's doing."

"I would guess you had some part of that," his dad said.

"I tried my best," Mike replied. "I just hope that she likes it when I do ask."

"Why are you waiting?" his mom asked, pushing for answers he didn't have.

"She's not ready yet," he said. "This can sit in my safe for the next ten years, as long as I know that it will happen one day."

"You're happy?" Rosie asked, tears brimming in her eyes.

"I'm so happy, mama. She makes me feel things I never thought was possible," he said. "She's everything I could ever dream of in a wife."

"Oh, my baby," she cried, rushing over to hug him. They both tensed up when the sound of the garage door opening filled the room.

"I need to put this back in the safe," he said, rushing from the room. He had just relocked it when the door opened, revealing Natalie, followed by a well-dressed couple.

"Hi," she said, smiling at him. "Mike, these are my parents, Marilyn and Bruce. Mom and dad, this is Mike. And his parents, Rosalita and Kevin."

"Call me Rosie," his mom said, pushing past him to embrace Natalie and then her mom.

"It's nice to meet you," Mike said, reaching out to shake Bruce's hand.

Marilyn hugged him and smiled at Natalie. "You're right, he is a giant."

Natalie laughed, the sound seeming to light up the room. She looked relaxed and happy, and it warmed his heart even more. "I had to warn them," she said. "Seeing you for the first time can be off putting."

"Is that how you felt when you first saw me?" he asked, drawing her closer to him.

"The first time I saw you was on FaceTime," she replied. "And even then, seeing you compared to Patrick, it was shocking. Seeing you in person was even better."

"Oh, lovebirds," Rosie said with a sigh, placing her hand over her heart. "This makes me so happy. Marilyn, come with me. Do you want some tea?"

The two moms disappeared, the dads following behind. Mike lingered with Natalie for an extra moment, taking the time to kiss her. "Are you sure we're ready for this?"

"We better be," she said. "No getting rid of them now, every hotel within a thirty-mile radius is full."

They all enjoyed a lunch that Mike had picked up at Windsor Palace, and then Rosie and Frank had disappeared to their room to unpack, which Mike knew meant they needed a nap. Natalie pulled him into the kitchen while her parents finished their coffees at the table.

"I have to go do an interview," she said. "I'm sorry the timing on this is so bad. Phyllis flew in last night with the reporter and a photographer, and I'm meeting them at the Inn."

"Do you want me to come with you?" He was shocked that she had set this up and hadn't said a word to him.

"No, it's okay. My mom is going to come, and Phyllis will be there. This is something that I need to do," she said. "This is a good thing, I promise. Trust me."

"Always," he promised. "If you need me, I'm just a phone call away."

"You'll be okay with my dad and your parents?" She shot a glance over to where her parents were in quiet conversation. "I hate to leave you to entertain the three of them."

"I'll be fine," he said. "Don't forget, I have the power of Rosie on my side. Or maybe I can take our dads to the golf simulator, since my mom mentioned wanting to catch up with Stella. I'll see what we can work out."

"I'll go straight to the dress rehearsal after the interview," Nat said. "Should I meet you guys back here, or do you want to go to dinner?"

"I'll text you once we make plans," he said. "I know Kendra has karaoke night planned at the Palace, since there is a big crowd in town. That might be fun?"

"Sounds good," she said. "I'll touch base with you later."

She kissed him before gathering her mom and heading out the door. The house seemed unnaturally quiet with just him and Bruce in the room, but he grabbed a bottle of water and went to sit at the table. They studied each other for a long moment before Bruce spoke.

"I remember watching you play, you were impressive," he said. You won a few Super Bowl rings if I'm not mistaken."

"Thank you," he said. "Yes, I have three. Would you like to see them?"

Bruce looked shocked. "You keep them here? Yes, I'd love to."

"I have a safe," he answered. "I figured they are as safe here as the bank, and people like to see them. Give me a minute."

He returned to his office, pulling the Super Bowl rings out in their heavy boxes. Seeing the engagement ring, he paused before stuffing it in his pocket. Returning to the living room, where Bruce had settled on the couch, he explained what each game the rings were from as he handed them to him. The other man studied them carefully, without removing them from the box.

"You can take them out," Mike said. "I don't mind."

"Are you sure?"

"Of course. Try them on, if you want."

Bruce looked thrilled as he carefully held the rings one at a time, sliding them onto a finger and laughing at how big it was. "I feel small," he said. "But this is a once in a lifetime opportunity, thank you. My friends will be jealous."

As he accepted the last ring back from Bruce, he swallowed down his nerves and looked at Natalie's father. They didn't know each other well, barely at all, other than a few FaceTime's over the last few months. But the older man seemed kind, and he had to take advantage of the moments he had. "I wanted to talk to you privately," he said. "I am crazy in love with Natalie and would like nothing more than to marry her. We aren't there yet, she's made it clear she needs more time, but I wanted to ask your blessing face to face. If I wait, I'm afraid the opportunity will come up and I won't have had this chance."

"I appreciate how much you have supported her over the last few months," Bruce said. "Being far away from her when she's struggling has been hard for both Marilyn and myself. The only thing that kept us away from here was knowing she had you, and trusting Patrick's word that she was alright."

"She wasn't for a long time," Mike admitted. "We had to drag her out of the house regularly, the first few weeks it was only to therapy. The more she did that, the better she got. The first time we got her out to a restaurant was a big deal. I was glad to be there for her, though. I love her. I have since the day of the shooting, if I am being honest."

"You realized your feelings about her when someone was shot?" Bruce looked confused, and Mike didn't blame him.

"No," Mike corrected himself. "Before that. We spent the morning together, working out and had gone for a horseback ride. It was the first time I saw her relaxed, and we talked about things that I never would have thought we would have in common. Books and music, sports teams, and just basic life philosophy. We got along so well, and I wasn't intimidated by her after that. I realized she was a real person, not just a poster on the wall, and I enjoyed being around her. I wanted to know more, get to know her even better. When we walked into the house, all I was thinking about was asking her on a date. It took me a full minute to realize what was happening when we got inside."

"As you know, I served in the military for many years," Bruce said. "I found myself in many dangerous situations, but the scariest thing that has ever happened to me was finding out that she had a gun pointed at her. I thought I would always be able to protect her, and in that one instant, I could have lost her. I don't know if I would have survived it. Marilyn and I both feel that we owe you for saving her."

"We saved each other," Mike said. "I had no idea that she was hitting the panic switch on the alarm at the time. I'm so grateful that she was able to stay calm enough for that. I was focused on talking sense into him, thinking I could convince him to leave her alone. At the same time, also trying to figure out how to get close enough to fight him for the gun, or how to shove her back out of the door. I would have died for her that day, and I'll protect her every day for the rest of our lives, if she'll let me."

"It sounds like you'll protect each other," Bruce said. "To answer your question, of course you have my blessing. I know I speak for Marilyn as well. If Natalie agrees to marry you, we will fully support it and welcome you into our family."

"Thank you," Mike said. "I really appreciate that. I know it will mean a lot to Nat, she loves you both so much. Now to just get her to agree."

"I can tell you from experience that she's stubborn," Bruce said with a laugh. "And she has pride in her independence and what she has accomplished on her own over the last ten years. Even now, facing the mess that Brie created for her, she held her head up and faced it head on. As long as you always treat her as your equal, and respect her voice in your relationship, you'll have a long, happy life together."

"That's good advice, thank you," Mike said. "I may try to take care of her more than I should, when I should trust that she is capable of doing things herself. As much as I like being there for her, seeing her shine is just as thrilling. She is more than my equal, she's my other half."

***

Mike herded the parents out to the car after they had a self-described happy hour at his house. His mom and Marilyn were fast friends already, and had made arrangements to meet Ben and Stella at the restaurant. They had declared that the "kids" should have fun while the older folks enjoyed a nice dinner, and based on the bottle of wine they had polished off in record time, something told him their table might be more fun.

When they entered the restaurant, Desmond was behind the bar, and he pointed out two tables that were set up directly in front of the karaoke stage. One was for six people, the other twelve, with Stella and Ben at the smaller table. Jake, Shea, Dan and Kendra were settled at the larger table, and he spotted JJ and Zoe coming in from the kitchen. That left just Natalie, Patrick, Emma, Liam and Holly to enter, which would cause quite a scene in the crowded restaurant. He greeted his friends and then went to say hello to Ben and Stella.

After hugging Stella, he studied her face. "Are you doing alright?"

"I'm just fine," she said, patting his hand. "Stop worrying about me."

"Why is he worried about you?" Ben demanded. He missed nothing when it came to his family, Mike realized.

"Because I didn't quite click with the workouts," Stella said smoothly. "I might try again soon, but for now I'm pleased to see you taking it so seriously."

"I'd have more fun if you were with me," Ben said. "You never told me why you had a change of heart."

"Let's talk about it later, darling," Stella said. "I want to enjoy the evening with our friends. Mike, I see Natalie coming in with Patrick and Liam. Oh, and Zane is here too."

JJ stood and grabbed another chair from near the kitchen, and the rest of the group settled in at the table. Mike only had eyes for Natalie, who had walked in flanked by two of her famous friends.

"Are you okay?" he asked her, leaning in to whisper in her ear.

"Yes," she said, nodding. "I'm always okay when you're with me."

"How was the interview? Is Phyllis still here?"

"No, she went right back to the airport with the reporter," she replied. "It went really well. I have a lot of respect for the reporter, and I think she'll do a great job."

"I'm happy for you," he said. "Especially if you think this will help you reclaim who you are."

She leaned over and kissed him and then put her head on his shoulder. "I'm getting there. And I have great news."

"What is it?"

"Dermott is gone," she said. "Phyllis set up a meeting with him and agreed to an exclusive interview with one of her up and coming actors. She promised him quality time, as long as he left Windsor Peak and forgot about me once and for all."

"That's amazing," he said. "You think we're done with him for good?"

"Yes," she said, nodding. "Phyllis is a force in Hollywood. If he went back on his word, he would regret it. And probably find it hard to work there any longer."

JJ leaned across the table to speak to them. "I couldn't help but overhear you talking about Dermott," he said. "I wanted to let you know that I spoke to the police in California a few weeks ago, and they assured me that he wasn't a suspect in the stalking. But they called me back today to let me know that they arrested someone last night for trespassing on another celebrity's property, and they think it's the same guy. He hasn't admitted to anything yet, but according to the detective, the style was the same as what happened at your house."

Natalie smiled at JJ and then Mike, looking relieved. "Thank you, JJ. I can't believe that's over too. Things are really looking up."

Mike returned the smile, trying to ignore the sudden worry that there was nothing keeping her from returning to California now. The original fear that had brought her to Vermont was now gone, and she was recovering from the shooting. He could only hold her hand and say a silent prayer that he really was a part of her brightening future.

The night passed in a blur, with their table taking up the majority of time on stage. Jake and Patrick were professional level singers, and when they left the stage people clamored for more. When Mike caught Natalie yawning behind her hand and looked over to see the two mom's doing the same, he excused himself from the table.

Desmond looked up from the two women he was flirting with when he approached the bar. "Hey, man. What's up?"

"Can you settle up our tables for me? I need to get Nat and our moms home for the night," he said.

"You want both checks?"

"Yes, please." He passed over a credit card and waited for Desmond to return with the slips, which he added generous tips to and passed back. "Thanks. I'll see you this weekend, I'm sure."

"You know it," Dee said with a grin. "Kendra is closing down early so we can all go to the event on Saturday, and Friday we are opening after the performance. A lot of the staff has kids that are in the play, so we all want to go show our support."

He returned to the table and collected Natalie, and both sets of parents, saying a quick goodnight to their friends. The group all decided to leave at the same time, causing a ruckus as the tourists tried to get a last-minute selfie with the four celebrities at the table. Mike saw the look in Natalie's eyes and made a quick decision, turning their smaller group to duck into the kitchen. The staff didn't blink an eye as they all ran through and out the back door, allowing her to avoid the worst of the crowd. It was a sign of what was to come over the weekend, as even more fans arrived for the play and fundraiser. But together, they would get through it.

Chapter 32

An Instagram post Thursday night featuring her cuddled up with Mike in the bar, followed by a preview from Vanity Fair about the upcoming article, had Natalie's phone blowing up on Friday. Suddenly, everyone who was anyone in Hollywood wanted to make sure they were on the right side of the story, and to make sure they weren't exposed for bad behavior. Phyllis was thrilled, texting her that things had gone perfectly, and the reporter had been ecstatic about the insight that Natalie had offered. She ignored all of the messages, focusing her attention on the play that evening.

The kids were all excited and nervous, filling the space with energy that reminded Nat why she had started acting to begin with. It wasn't for fame, or to be seen as the most beautiful. It was for this feeling, the thrill of being on stage, which would never get old. She made a mental note to ask her manager to look into Broadway opportunities for her as she organized the performers, or maybe to find a chance to direct. Her world felt more open suddenly, but she needed to talk to Mike about all of it first. As much as she wanted to chase the opportunities to be seen as more than a pretty face, she couldn't envision doing anything if he wasn't at her side.

The students received a standing ovation that went on for several minutes, and Natalie soaked in the joy they exuded. Their beaming smiles as they sought out their parents and loved ones in the crowd warmed her from the inside out. It got even better when they stripped off their costumes and ran out to receive hugs and flowers, and Natalie posed for pictures for a full hour before the last cast member left.

Mike was patiently waiting in his front-row seat, assisting with pictures when needed and sitting to let her speak privately with the parents who wanted to thank her. His support was always evident, and it added to her feelings of confidence.

"Thank you," she said, sitting on his lap when the last family left. "I'm so glad you're here."

"Nowhere I'd rather be," he said.

"This could get old," she warned him.

"What could?"

"Being on the sidelines, waiting for me," she said. "Red carpets, parties, all of it. I'll have to talk to people and do things, and you'll be stuck waiting for me."

"I'll happily wait for you anywhere and anytime," he said. He pulled her closer and kissed her. "It's my biggest honor. Seeing you do your thing, that was as good as winning my first Super Bowl."

"What?"

"I mean it," he said. "Seeing how you came alive up there, watching them. I could feel how much you loved it, and I have never been so proud. Having you as my teammate in life is going to make it exciting and I am ready for it."

"Did you see all the posts about us this morning?" she asked, still not sure he knew the full scope of what life with her would be like. Being in the spotlight constantly could be draining, and his role had always been a little out of it. As a football player, he had fame but not the huge fanfare that some other positions found. Being with her would be constant eyes on him, and she needed to be sure he understood.

"I did," he said. "The picture of you for Vanity Fair surprised me. I expected you to be fully glammed out."

"The reporter expected it at first too," she admitted. "When I told them I wanted to do it in my Windsor Peak clothes, they liked the idea. It's different than what they usually do, and it goes with the message I want to send."

"What's that?"

"I'm more than my looks," she said simply. "I should be looked at the same way my male costars are. I shouldn't feel like I need to wear skimpy clothes, or allow people into my bedroom, to maintain my status in Hollywood."

"You are much more," he said. "You're smart and caring and giving. The world should see that."

"That was an important lesson I've learned these last few months," she said. "Allowing people to see that side of me wasn't easy, but it's necessary. I shared more with the reporter than I ever thought I would."

"And you feel good about it?" His beautiful eyes were on hers, showing nothing but love for her.

"I do."

"Good," he said. "Does this mean we can wear jeans and flannels to the event tomorrow night?"

She laughed, standing up and offering him a hand. "No such luck," she said. "I want to see you in a tux."

"She just loves me for my body," he said with a teasing lilt in his voice, making her laugh.

***

Rosie prepared an enormous breakfast for everyone, which they lingered over for almost two hours. When they realized how much time had passed, the men headed to the golf simulator, while the women went to Liam's to prepare for the evening. Event staff was handling all the preparation for the dinner and dancing that would take place, so Natalie had arranged for hair stylists, manicurists and makeup artists to pamper her and her friends. After the stress of the week, it was some much-needed pampering, which she thoroughly enjoyed.

Her mom was next to her as they had pedicures done and glanced down at Natalie's hands. "You should have your fingernails done, too."

"I plan to," Nat responded. "But that was a weird thing to say."

"Hmmm." Her mom refused to meet her eyes and busied herself with her phone.

"Want to explain?"

"Not really, no."

"Mom."

"Yes, dear?" Marilyn studied the screen without looking up.

"What's going on?"

Marilyn sighed and looked at her. "You can't say anything."

"Now I'm really curious."

"Mike talked to your father and asked for his blessing," she said.

"His blessing for our relationship?"

"Yes, and then some," Marilyn said with a grin. "We both really like him."

"You're saying he talked to dad about proposing?"

"Maybe," her mom said hesitantly. "But you can't let on that I said anything."

"We had talked about it last week," Natalie said. "I think we need more time."

"I don't think he plans to do it now," Marilyn assured her. "But it's good to be prepared.

Natalie thought about her mom's words as her feet were massaged. While she didn't think she was ready to get engaged or married, she owed it to Mike to make sure he was comfortable with where they were. His efforts to speak to her father, and to be a good host for her parents all weekend, said a lot about his intentions. She needed to do the same, and tonight was the perfect opportunity.

***

The men arrived a half hour before the dinner event was to take place. They had all agreed to prepare for the gala at Patrick's house, since the women were all together. Mike had been careful to include both of their fathers, knowing they would enjoy spending the time with Ben. When they arrived on a party bus, a legion of handsome men in suits, the energy changed in the house. The women, who had been enjoying champagne together in their gowns, perked up as their partner came into the room.

Natalie was eager to see Mike after having spent the day apart. He was the last to enter, having held the door open for everyone else. When their eyes met across the room, she felt as if the air was crackling between them. He looked amazing in a tuxedo, even better than she could have imagined. The fabric looked molded to his broad shoulders and then hugged his waist. He looked like the perfect combination of GQ and her best friend, and she couldn't stop herself from crossing the room quickly to kiss him.

"You look amazing," he said. "I'm going to be the most envied man in the room tonight."

"Right back at you," she said. "I'll be fighting off women to get a dance."

"Yours is the only name on my list," he promised. "Other than my mom, that is."

"And I know Stella will want a dance with all her boys, and you're certainly one of them now," she said. "I can handle that."

The entire group walked to the event space together, marveling at the transformation. During the day, it was a large space broken into smaller rooms, allowing the kids to focus on different activities after school. The portable walls had been removed, reverting it to the open ballroom it had been when Liam had purchased the property. The dance floor had been put back in place in front of the stage, which held a full band. Catering staff lingered along the walls, and two bars were set up. A long table in the back of the wall held silent auction items, and more were ready for a live auction later in the evening.

"This is amazing," Mike said. "You guys did good."

Patrick and Liam high-fived each other, while Emma and Holly beamed at their sides. Their group found their reserved tables before signaling to the event manager that they could open the doors to the guests. Soon, the room was full of neighbors and high-powered guests who had flown in from all over the country.

The mix of locals, who Nat had grown familiar with, and Hollywood elite was jarring and yet reassuring for her. Her two worlds had come together, and both were surviving. She felt no need to put on an act for the other celebrities or producers, instead allowing them to see her smile and have fun with her friends.

When the band started to play, Mike appeared in front of her, offering his hand. She accepted and allowed him to lead her to the dance floor, where he pulled her close. She let herself enjoy the moment before pulling back to gaze up at him.

"I just realized something," she said.

"What's that?"

"Looking around here, seeing our neighbors mixing with the people I would socialize with in California, I realized," she said. "I can be both."

"Both what?" He asked, looking puzzled.

"I can be a small-town girl who lives with her boyfriend and volunteers to help the local school," she said. "And a movie star who attends big events. I can be a sex symbol and also be vulnerable. I can go work in the big city but be a country girl at heart."

"Are you saying you'll stay?" he looked hopeful, and she smiled at him.

"Yes," she said. "I want to be where you are. And I like who I am here. I have been questioning if you would like the person I am if I go back, but why do I need to go back to that person? I need something positive to come out of what happened to make it something I can live with. And I don't know if I ever would have been brave enough to take risks if I hadn't been forced to."

"Risks like loving me?"

"That's the easiest thing I've ever done," she said. "You make me feel safe and respected. You listen to me, laugh with me, and ask my opinion on things. I look in your eyes, and I see my value. And I know that it's so much deeper than what I look like, or what I do for work."

"Those are on the list," he said with a smile. "But I love your heart. I love the woman who spent weeks helping kids be brave enough to stand on a stage in front of everyone and put on a show. Who would rather be cuddled on the couch with her puppy, watching reality TV, than putting on a fancy dress and going to a party. Who was calm and smart enough to save our lives in a crisis."

"We saved each other," she said. "And you've helped me to discover who I am, and who I want to be. Seeing myself through your eyes, being loved by you, has helped me realize all that I can be. I want to be someone that you're proud of, and that this little town is proud to call one of their own. Spending time with people who are actual friends and care about me, and helping the kids with the play, it's all made me feel like I belong here. With you."

"I love you so much," he said. He kissed her, and she lost herself in the moment. Realizing where they were, she laughed and pulled back.

"I love you too," she said.

"If I asked you right now—"

She put a finger over his lips. "Not now. Soon, but not now. Right now, I promise I'm yours. Where you are, I am. You're my world."

"I'm going to do it soon," he warned her. "Prepare yourself."

"I can't wait," she said. "You make me so happy and make me feel secure. No matter what, as long as you love me and we're together, I'll be okay."

"Same," he said, smiling down at her. "But fair warning, I did buy a ring already. It only seems fair that you know that, since everyone else does."

"Word travels fast in this town," she said. "And my mom kind of spilled the beans."

"I had to have it ready," he said. "I know that you're my other half, and having the ring just seemed right. I didn't want the right moment to come and have to put an elastic band on your finger. Or one of my Super Bowl rings."

"I'm sure your former teammates appreciate you not doing that," she said with a laugh. "It might make them look bad for not doing the same."

"You're my favorite teammate of all," he assured her. "I'm sure they would understand."

"Even if it means being on the bench when I'm working?"

"I'll carry the water bottles if it means I get to be on your sideline," he assured her. "And I know you would do the same for me. I never thought movie star Natalie Cloud would be setting up my coffee maker for me or making sure I have clean socks for the morning."

"Part of that is that I steal yours regularly," she said, laughing. "They're just so warm."

"But you do it for me," he said. "You take care of me, and I will always do the same for you. Wherever you go, I'll be right there with you. Even if it's not Windsor Peak, if you decide you want to live in California or anywhere else, I'll go. I'd follow you anywhere."

She was in the arms of the man she loved, surrounded by their friends and family. Two months ago, she couldn't leave her bedroom, and now she was finally feeling secure. And it was all because of the people in this room and the man who loved her so completely. She smiled up at him again, taking the chance to kiss him softly. "No following," she said. "We'll make the decisions together. But this is exactly where I want to be, in this little town, with you. You're home to me, always and forever."

Acknowledgments

Every time I finish a book, I look up and realize how much time has passed. My house is usually a mess, laundry is piled up, and I have a million unanswered text messages and emails. I spend so much time in Windsor Peak, I worry that I've missed key moments in life, but I'm so lucky to have an incredible support system that makes sure I don't miss anything important.

My parents, Arlene and Jim Giddings, who I dedicated this book to, are always there to help. They listen when I need to talk out ideas, even if they have no idea what plot points I'm trying to figure out. They show up at every event, and tell all of their friends about my books. Putting them out into the world is so scary, but they make it less so. I'm so glad they are a part of this, and couldn't be luckier to have them as two of my biggest fans.

Jeff and Danielle, who encouraged me to start before anyone else knew that I was going to try to write, and continue to offer encouragement. Plus, they have three of my favorite humans who double as my cheerleaders, Timmy, Tessa and Emmy. The kids going into bookstores and telling people that their aunt wrote these books will never get old! I love that they are all reading and writing more, and finding the joy that books bring. Plus, the girls let me braid their hair and go for pedicures with me, which my boys would never do! Now if you three could please stop growing up, I would really appreciate it!

Brendan and Taylor, I love you both and am excited for this next chapter for you both. Seeing you both in love, and knowing how happy you are, makes my heart smile. Conor, I am so proud of you and how well you are doing in college. Keep up the hard work, I can't believe it's almost over! You'll do amazing things in the world, and I'm so proud of you.

My friends, who I can't list out because I would forget someone and be mad at myself forever – but you know who you are. Whether you come to events, ease my nerves pre-launch, yelling at me in a rink to "go home and write", drag me away from the computer to socialize, laugh with me in the stands of a sporting event, text me to check in – thank you. I am so lucky to have you all in my life, and I hope I give back as much as I receive.

My husband is not a reader, and will never read my books, but shows his support in so many ways. I couldn't do this without him being behind me, and I'm grateful that he is every step of the way. Camden and Calum, you make me proud every day. Cam excels in everything he attempts and is thriving in high school. He thinks he's leaving me in two years to go to college, but we might need to have more conversations about that. Calum has been writing stories of his own in school, and sharing them with his teacher, who shared them with me. And then he won a Young Writers Award, which made me so happy. What's better than knowing you're inspiring your children to chase their dreams? (As long as the dreams are within a 60-mile radius, Cam). I love seeing who you both are becoming as men and will always love you.

And to my readers, which is still weird to say – thank you. You're making my dreams come true, and hearing from you or seeing someone share one of my books always makes my day. I am flattered and thankful that you choose to read these books, and I hope to continue bringing you stories you'll love for a long time!

Up Next

Yes, I am staying in Windsor Peak until you all get sick of reading them! Next up is a pair that you know and love, and I can not wait to bring you their story. They've been telling it to me for a long, long time now, and I'm hoping it keeps flowing this fast so I won't make you all wait long!

In the meantime, be sure to follow me on social media @deniselathamwrites and visit my website to sign up for my newsletter. Then you'll be in the know before the books hit the shelves! www.deniselatham.com

Please continue sharing the books with your friends and family, and leave reviews where you purchased the book. I can't tell you how much it helps, and how much I appreciate it!